3 x 3

The Singular Scribblings of an Uneasy Mind

by

Neal Neamand

A Red Boots Book

ISBN 979-8-3303-4296-9

3x3: The Singular Scribblings of an Uneasy Mind
Copyright © 2024 by Neal Neamand

ISBN: 979-8-3303-4296-9 (Paperback)
ISBN: 979-8-3302-3309-0 (Hardback)
ISBN: 979-8-3302-8219-7 (Ebook)

All Rights Reserved. No part of this publication may be reproduced, distributed, or transmitted in any form or by any means, including photocopying, recording, or otherelectronicor mechanical methods,without thepriorwritten permission of the publisher, except in the case brief quotations embodied reviews and other noncommercial uses permitted by copyright law.

The views expressed in this book are solely those of the author and do not necessarily reflect the views of the publisher, and the publisher hereby disclaims any responsibility for them.

Paper Wrights, LLC
www.paperwrights.co

Dedicated to readers everywhere

Sketches by Haika Powell
Cover Photo by Judy Bullard

Contents

Some Thoughts by Way of Introduction 1

I: *Sad Day in the Morning*

    Old Mr. Springer 4

    Black as Crows 22

    The Green, Green Grass of Home 32

II: *Boys and Girls, Men and Women*

    Secret Smelteries of Backwoods Pennsylvania 58

    Strawberry Sun, Raspberry Moon 76

    The Girls of Summer 91

III: *What Did You Expect?*

    A Very Grey Day 123

    Mud for the Dreamer's Temple 132

    Wide Open 163

Some Thoughts by Way of Introduction

For much of my adult life, words on paper have accumulated around me like snow drifts in winter. Printed pages, and sheets of paper with scribblings that filled every millimeter of space; slips, bits, and scraps of paper with notes and ideas. Some of that paper has been transformed into the stories in this book. Other stacks of paper await conversion to other stories.

When I first thought of writing, my focus was on the novel. I imagined that I would simply sit down and begin writing and when I was done, I would have a novel. I soon had to admit, however, that I had little practical knowledge of how that could happen. Eventually, I thought about short stories, hoping that in following that path, I would learn enough to write a novel.

So I began reading short stories in profusion. I'd guess that I have read thousands of stories – and I include here comic books that I read as a child, after all, comics are only stories that rely on drawings instead of words. I pondered the genre; what constitutes a short story? How does one construct a story? I couldn't answer those questions, so I turned to the on thing that might provide answers: I began writing stories.

Over the years, I've gathered a cache of rejection slips – one cannot consider oneself to be a writer without accumulating a substantial pile of these demoralizing slips of paper – trying to get my work into print. In this day and age, however, finding your way into print is not an easy proposition. Only one of the stories in this collection was ever accepted for publication, and that was quite some time ago. The editor of a small literary magazine somewhere in the mid-west accepted one of my stories. She wrote that she didn't think it all that good of a story but it made her laugh when I wrote it and I still get a chuckle from it. In any event, that was the good news; the bad news was that she had a back log of stories and it would be more than a year before my story would appear. The news got worse; the magazine folded long before my story was scheduled to appear. My fleeting chance at the brass the brass ring.

As for the rest of the stories, most were not even eligible for consideration. All suffred from maladies that only editors could enumerate and, as is the tradition among editors, they weren't talking. The stories I've assembled for this collection were crafted to express my own feelings and opinions. I use the word crafted not to suggest a level of quality of the stories, but because that is how I felt when I wrote them; that I was crafting the work. I leave it to the reader to decide whether the stories deserve such accolades.

And so, enough words about the stories. Herewith, I present my work in the hopes that readers will find in them some scraps of value and enjoyment.

I

Sad Day in the Morning

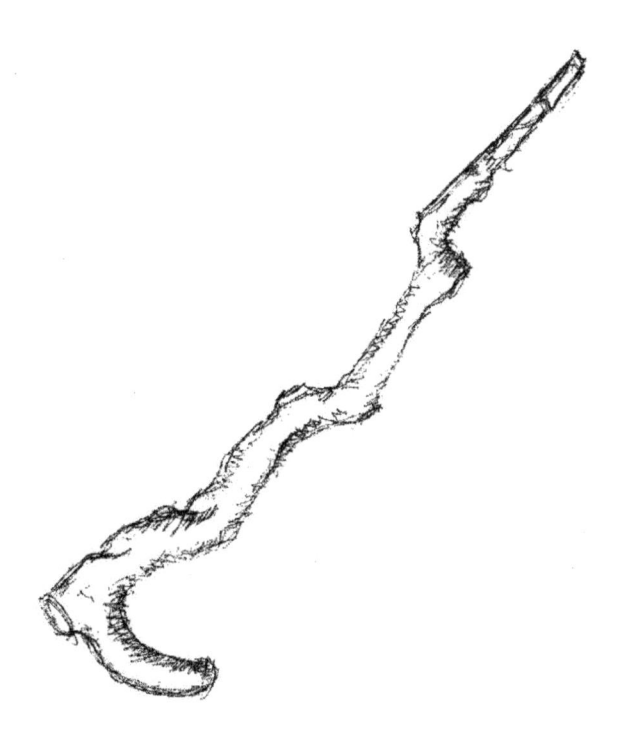

Old Mr. Springer

Kate came slowly up out of the glen, past the spring, on her way home. She looked neither right nor left, eyes downcast, her steps heavy on the woodland path. Coming out into the meadow, she glanced up to realize she was approaching old man Springer's cottage. She'd never liked the old man with his nasty eyes, his tangle of unkempt hair, his dirty, smelly clothing. Never a kind word, a generous look or gesture. When he did notice any of the village children, it was only to yell at them.

She'd never known him to single her out, however, until of late. Now, whenever he saw her, he stared with those wet, froggy eyes. She could feel him glaring at her, feel those watery eyes sliding like slugs over her body. She didn't understand his sudden interest in her, what she could have done to have earned his attention. She knew, though, that it must have something to do with the change. It had brought her the unwanted attention not only of old man Springer and her classmates - especially the boys - but, it seemed, everyone in the village.

She had begun to feel as though God had singled her out for punishment, apparently having found in her some sin of which she was wholly unaware. The death of her mother in the dim grey depths of the winter had been punishment enough. But then, as the daffodils and crocuses began to poke their heads from the moist March soil, the change had come upon her. Before the leaves had blossomed forth on the trees, her body had betrayed her.

Kate began to hurry, wanting to get past Springer's as fast as she could. She imagined that even now his eyes were focused on her, and the thought made her cringe. She ran along the path that skirted the end of the village and brought her quickly home. Careening into the dooryard, she saw her father, not yet left for the woodlot, emerge from the cottage. He looked at his daughter, and she saw the sadness on his face.

"Katie child, could you take care of the chickens before you leave for school? I'm late and Remey will be waiting for me." Kate nodded and went off across the yard as he gathered his tools and his lunch in a wooden pail. He straightened up to watch his daughter.

Every time Mic Merkold looked at her these days, he was purely amazed. She was barely 13 years old, and had always been a strikingly pale little girl, awkward and gawky, a nice- looking little girl, but certainly not a beauty. The girl's mother had not been a beauty either, and Mic admitted freely that he was hardly a man to turn a woman's head. Nor had there been any beauties on either side of the family, least not in Mic's memory.

Kate had stopped being a skinny, gawky little girl a few months ago. Mic wasn't sure when it happened; he only remembered that one day she'd been just Kate and the next time he looked, she'd suddenly been a woman. All trace - physically at least - of the little-girl-Kate was gone and in her place was this blond beauty with a voluptuous body.

Mic noticed that Kate had become excessively quiet since the changes had come on her. She stopped playing with her friends and seemed to spend most of her time moping around the house or else walking in the woods alone. At first her change in conduct confused him; he didn't know what to make of it. He thought, perhaps, she was still mourning her mother. Until the day he'd seen Kate being mercilessly teased by some of the boys in her class. Then he'd understood; Kate's new womanly body was a trial for her. She was still a little girl in a woman's body. But that couldn't last for long; it was just a phase that she'd soon outgrow.

Mic had noticed too how the men in the village stared at Kate. There was nothing subtle or surreptitious in their stares. They gazed at Kate with looks of open lust; they gawked. Their attentions visibly upset the girl and Mic tried to shield her as best he could. Of course, he'd known that the young men would act that way; that was to be expected. What he hadn't expected was the same reaction from the older men. It was as if Kate had set free some pervasive aphrodisiac that had affected all the men of the village.

As he'd observed this phenomenon, Mic had grown angry at the men. Even some of his closest friends, he'd noticed, had begun to leer at Kate. Just a few days ago he'd seen his workmate and hunting companion,

Remey Stelson, stare at Kate in open lust, licking his lips and rubbing his crotch much to the delight of the other men who stood watching. Mic had confronted him and had there not been others to intervene, the two might have ended up in a fistfight. He couldn't fight the whole village, however, so he sought to keep Kate away from their lewd stares as much as possible.

It was at a time like this, Mic realized, that a girl needed the guidance of her mother. But Kate's mother was gone. Deep in his own grief, Mic had tried as best he could to be both father and mother to Kate.

Mic shook his head and called to Kate as he picked up the bucket and his axe. Kate turned and waved at her father as he headed out toward the street on his way to whatever woodlot he was working that day. Kate finished up with the chores, quickly checked for egg, and likewise headed into the street, on her way to school.

Tilda Benay stood in the doorway of the one room school looking out over her charges. In the schoolyard, most of the children played a game of tag they called "yon-a-hay" because, she supposed, of the nonsense words they chanted as they ran from one side of the yard to the other. Here and there a few small groups of children stood and talked or played quietly, ignoring their boisterous classmates.

Out in the street, Tilda saw someone coming along the schoolyard fence and she recognized Kate. The girl came through the gate and up the walk, shoulders hunched, eyes downcast.

"G'd mornin', Kate," said Tilda.

"Mornin'," answered Kate without looking up. "Cow ran off this mornin' is why I'm late. She looked up uncertainly at Tilda, her eyes troubled.

"That's fine, Kate," said Tilda. "You just go on in. I'll be callin' the class in jus' a moment." Tilda watched the girl go into the school. She walks like an old woman with the weight of the world on her shoulders, she thought. She felt sorry for Kate, losing her mother so suddenly, still grieving, and then this confusing blossoming into womanhood. It's bad enough when it happens over the course of a year or so, but when it happens rapidly, in just a few months, it can be very difficult for a young girl. She wanted very much to do something to help Kate, to take her in her arms and comfort her, but she realized there was little she could do. Nature had given the girl a tremendous gift, but it would take a bit of adjusting. Time, she thought, would have to be Kate's doctor. Tilda gazed vacantly out across the schoolyard and thought of her own transition to womanhood.

The attention that so troubled the girl came, of course, from the men of the village. Her growing up was so fast, the changes so drastic, her beauty so breathtaking that the men simply could not keep from staring. When she was around, nothing got done. The men acted like little boys, desperate for attention. Or, perhaps, more appropriately, thought Tilda, they were like male dogs, their tongues hanging out, their eyes glazed over, their obsession evident in the distended fronts of their pants. Tilda had to chuckle to herself at the thought of the men so obviously under the influence of this young girl.

The men weren't alone, however, in noticing Kate's changes. The women also noticed, for all too often a creature so suddenly and sensuously transformed can spell trouble for wives and sweethearts. In the heady perfume of her blossoming, Kate could have plucked the men like wild strawberries in a June-drenched meadow. They'd all seen this before; a young girl suddenly matured and aware of the power her body granted her over the men. The women worried because they knew that the whims of a young girl high on hormones and lust knew no rules, no bounds, no limitations. Yes, reflected Tilda, we've all seen this before and some of us have even lived it.

They worried without reason as it turned out. Kate's metamorphosis had come to her early. She had become a woman in body, but in mind and spirit she remained a child with no inkling of the power which a body such as hers granted. She had no idea why the men stared, and the boys leered. Certainly, like all the village children, she'd seen animals engaged in the sex act, but somehow it seemed never to have occurred to her that such an act could have any bearing on her life. She had no interest in boys - let alone men. So, she remained shy and childlike and saw her newly voluptuous body as a source of pain and embarrassment.

Everywhere she went, eyes followed her, licking hungrily, trying to possess her image. In the presence of men, she had become self-conscious and confused. At first, she was embarrassed and flushed a deep red, but later she withdrew into herself, like a child with a disfiguring wound, seeking to hide her body. She took to wearing baggy clothing to disguise the swelling breasts and flaring hips. She avoided as much as possible those places where she might have to encounter groups of men or boys.

After a while, the men gradually began to gain control of their lusts and fantasies; they stopped staring so obviously. They still looked, only no longer so blatantly. Even the most exotic sight grows commonplace after a while and Kate's voluptuousness became finally just Kate. Not to say they stopped looking; the men continued to stare at Kate, only they did so surreptitiously, as Tilda realized when she'd one day caught her husband avidly gazing across the street at the passing Kate. There was something about the girl, Tilda realized; she seemed to have a narcotic effect on the men. Even after the sight of her had become commonplace, men still could not help but stare. The younger men did so unabashedly while most of the older men seemed to have resolved that they would not look at her. But when they encountered her in the street, when they spied her across the churchyard, their resolves failed them, and their eyes eagerly sought out the girl's body just as they had in the beginning.

There was only one set of old eyes that could not or would not dissemble and those eyes were in the grizzled head of old Mr. Springer. When old Mr. Springer encountered Kate, he stopped abruptly and leaned crookedly on his stick, staring as though he'd slipped into a trance. In the beginning, no one had noticed anything special in old man Springer's attentions. He was just another of the village men who found Kate grown too beautiful to ignore. It was only later, when the others stopped staring so overtly that people began to notice Springer. The women, more attuned to subtleties, more attentive perhaps, noticed it first. They remarked to each other and then, later, to their husbands, how the old man's rheumy eyes were drawn to the girl, the way he licked his thin, crooked, old man's lips at the sight of her.

They thought the old man's conduct reprehensible, the women did. The men were a little less judgmental, likely having to struggle with the same feelings as Springer, although most found his attentions extreme. Still, no one in the village thought much of it because the old man seemed so infirm, hobbling about with a stick to support him, weak with age. They were country folk, mused Tilda, they'd seen this all before and, she knew, they'd see it all again. Yes, they gossiped and clucked, but that was the nature of people.

Tilda roused herself from her thoughts, picked up her brass bell from the doorsill, and began ringing it loudly. "Children, children," she called, "time to get back to class."

Several days later, Mic went to Keller's woodlot to fall several tall trees for the sawmill. Remey was already there, sharpening his axe. They set to work and downed one tree and trimmed it out by lunchtime when Kate came with a lunch pail for her father. She spread the contents of the pail onto a log as Mic and Remey put their axes aside and joined her.

As Kate prepared to leave, Remey grasped her wrist, attempting to pull her to him. Slipping through his encircling arm, she pulled away. For a heartbeat she stood looking at him, shrinking back like a frightened forest creature; then she ran from the woodlot.

Remey shrugged and turned toward Mic. Mic's face was a mask of rage, a rage he was trying desperately to control. Attempting to make it seem like an innocent gesture, Remey smiled and shrugged his shoulders again.

"Keep your hands off her," said Mic through clenched teeth, his voice grating and raw.

"I didn't mean nothin' by it," said Remey, "It was just being frien'ly. Wha's the harm?" Mic stepped threateningly closer to Remey, into his space, thrusting his body aggressively forward, fists clenched.

"You meant it alright. I seen you watchin' the girl these past weeks, the way you act when you're with the other men an' Kate's around." The smile, uncertain at best, slipped from Remey's face and he tried to step back.

"Ah, you're crazy," he said to Mic, lamely seeking to defend himself.

"You mess with my Kate, and you'll see how crazy I can be," Mic answered. Slowly, he stepped back, away from Remey and as he did so a spark of anger burst into Remey's eyes. Sullenly they settled onto the log and ate the lunch that Kate had brought, tasting nothing but the anger that percolated through them.

In silence, the anger temporarily suppressed, they finished their lunch, picked up their axes and turned to the giant oak they needed to fell. They shouldn't have been working in that frame of mind, but they kept right at it, putting their anger into the swinging axes. The axes sliced and chopped through the thick trunk until the tree began to groan and list. Mic stepped back to let Remey finish the cut. Instead of falling clean and clear, the giant tree kicked back, the trunk whipping away from the stump and slamming into Mic as it fell.

It all happened so fast, there was no time to react. Remey ran for help immediately. He found Rollo Sanger in his barnyard and as they hurried down to the road, they encountered Dutz Avery. The three ran to the woodlot, but there was nothing they could do. All three knew as soon as they laid eyes on him that Mic was dead. They got the body out from under the tree trunk and carried it back to the Merkold cottage.

Dutz, one of the selectmen, went to the school and fetched Kate. She didn't cry. The life seemed to go out of her, her eyes went dull and vacant, and the strength flowed out of her as she slumped into a chair. Like a somnambulist, she moved through the coming days. Even at the funeral she shed no tears.

There was talk in the village as the story went around. Some thought that Remey'd managed the cut like that on purpose. Others cast no blame on Remey but thought the two were fools to be working while they were angry at one another. Most agreed though that the anger must have clouded Mic's mind and made him careless to be caught by the tree as he'd been.

After the funeral, Dutz arranged for the Reverend Hagode and his wife to take Kate in. So far as anyone knew, the girl had no living relatives, so the select men sent word to the provincial seat regarding the death of Mic Merkold and the situation of Kate. Word came back that a counselor was being sent to arrange for Kate's future and they anxiously awaited the arrival of this august person. Dutz took it upon himself to meet the stage. As fate would have it, the counselor arrived in the village late one afternoon when the village street was empty save for Dutz. He watched as a fastidious little man dressed in black stepped cautiously down into the dusty street. The man stood there next to the stage, his black hat in one hand, his leather case in the other, and looked suspiciously about. He was a short, slender man with thinning, sandy hair and generous sideburns. He had the look of a paper-pusher, decided Dutz, and stepped up to him.

"Counselor?"

The man peered myopically at Dutz and pulled a pair of small, round glasses from his inside coat pocket. Settling them on his nose, he gave Dutz a proper looking over.

"Yes," he said, "I am the counselor. Jeremiah Prethy, at your service."

Dutz introduced himself, picked up Mr. Prethy's carpetbag and led the man across the street to the Golden Sheaf. The inn keeper's wife, Mrs. Sauther, bowed and scrapped before the little man, registered him and presented him with a key to his room.

"I'd be pleased to assist you any way I can," said Dutz to the counselor, "take you out to Kate's an' such." The counselor clutched his leather case to his chest.

"Thank you, yes, thank you, Mr. Avery, was it? Should I need your assistance, I shall summon you. I'm sure this good woman will be able to assist me in reaching you. But, at the moment, I'd like to retire to my room."

Dutz nodded and tipped his hat to Mrs. Sauther and left. Mr. Prethy likewise nodded to the woman and headed up the stairs to his room where he freshened up and brushed the dust of travel from his clothes. He returned to the empty common room for a light repast, where he frustrated Mrs. Sauther's efforts to extract some small information from him. He ate alone before any of the regulars had come to the inn, a great disappointment to all who'd hoped to gain some advance notice as to what he meant to do on Kate's behalf.

Back in his room, Mr. Prethy opened his leather case and extracted from it a great sheaf of dry and dusty, but nevertheless very official looking papers. When the Commissioner had put the matter of the girl on his desk, Mr. Prethy had been stricken with a severe case of anxiety. Searching out the paper trail, finding the proper documents, had not been the problem. He glowed with an inner satisfaction at the ease and precision with which he'd resolved the matter of the orphaned girl. It had taken him barely a single morning to follow the trail, find the pertinent papers and come to a just resolution of the case. What had provoked the anxieties was rather the Commissioner's instruction that he travel into the country to personally settle the case. Now that he was here, although he was still nervous, he found it far less intimidating than he'd expected.

In his investigation, he saw this child Kate, the orphaned waif, alone in the wide world, a frail and wan child. He saw the grandfather figure, a man of gentle and generous ways who was about to become the child's protector, to guide her as friend and guardian on her journey to adulthood. Gaining control of his anxieties, a warmth grew within him, a pride in the humanitarian nature of his wisdom.

Early in the morning, the counselor came to the common room to take his breakfast. Having slept well, he was a little more talkative than he'd been the evening before, but still, he revealed precious little to the innkeeper or his wife. He sat quietly at breakfast, the morning sun shining in the window warming his back. He marveled not only at the quantity of the food placed before him, but at the quality as well. The fried eggs, the smoked ham, the thick cream and butter, fresh baked bread, the apples and pears all tasted somehow more vital than they did in the city. He ate slowly, savoring every mouthful. Lingering over a final cup of tea, the innkeeper placed a small glass of liqueur before him. It was the way of these country folk to finish their morning repasts with a sip of spiced honey liqueur.

Rising from the table, he returned to his room for his leather case and walked out into the village street. He'd already inquired as to where he might find Kate and since the village was not very large, he proceeded without incident to the little timber cottage off the West Road.

His progress was marked by eyes all along the street. Everyone in the village knew why he was there, of course, and everyone who was not away working watched the counselor on his unhurried journey to Kate's cottage. Women standing in doorways, men about their business, children playing in front of houses; all stopped to watch the counselor make his way down the street.

He took his time, basking in the importance that his mission had bestowed upon him. People were watching him, he knew, although he had no idea how many sets of eyes marked his progress. He rather enjoyed the feeling, the celebrity of it all. Also, to his surprise, he found that he enjoyed being out in the air and the sunshine, for ordinarily he was buried in the stuffy Hall of Records, closed off from the outside world.

Mr. Prethy strolled out the West Road to the end of the village. He breathed deep the fresh country air, feeling invigorated in the morning sunshine. He puffed up his chest at the thought of the good news he was about to bestow upon this tragic young girl.

As he approached the cottage, he found in the door-yard, a woman with her back to him feeding the chickens. A neighbor lady, he thought, looking about for the girl. Finding no others present, he approached the woman, clearing his throat to catch her attention.

Startled, she spun about to face him. He saw immediately that she was a young woman, a very young woman, full bodied and sensuous as only these country girls could be.

"I'm looking for Kate Merkold," he said.

"I'm Kate," said the girl, eyes downcast, in a voice so quiet that Mr. Prethy was sure he'd misheard.

"Kate Merkold," he said, certain that the young woman would then lead him to the child. Not a man to ogle women, Mr. Prethy found he was having a hard time keeping his eyes from dipping to the young woman's bosom.

"Yes," replied the girl, "I am Kate Merkold." Her voice was so soft, and she spoke so hesitantly that the counselor had to ask her a third time before he understood that the wan orphan child he sought was in fact this voluptuous but timid creature who stood before him. He introduced himself to the girl who had, of course, surmised who he was.

Mr. Prethy suggested they retire to the cottage so that he could show her the documents he'd brought and make her acquainted with the solution he'd worked out to her predicament.

When the counselor left the cottage some twenty minutes later, he was in a far less positive frame of mind than he had been upon his arrival. The disparity between the girl and the image he'd had of her was disconcerting enough, but as he'd talked and explained, she'd begun to cry and there didn't seem to be anything he could do to console her or to stem the flood of tears. He couldn't understand what made the girl so distraught and finally put it down to the so recent loss of her father.

Making his way back to the inn, contemplating the situation, Mr. Prethy stepped splat into a cowpie and for the first time he noticed that the street of the village seemed to be filled with animals - and their attendant smells. There were no sidewalks; that fact hadn't impressed itself upon his consciousness earlier, but the cowpie had brought it crudely to his attention. Still, the sunshine and the air - if somewhat malodorous - felt good to his body.

Back at the inn, Mr. Prethy ate a generous lunch, lost in his own thoughts. All about him, villagers ate and drank and cast inquisitive glances in his direction, but he offered no one the opportunity to initiate a conversation. Upon finishing his meal with the customary honey liqueur, Mr. Prethy arose and went to the innkeeper to inquire as to the whereabouts of the Springer abode. As he left the inn with his leather case under his arm, he was totally unaware of the turmoil that he left behind. Innkeeper Sauther had run directly into the common room and announced where the counselor was headed. He couldn't have caused more of a commotion if he'd tossed a wasp's nest into the room as everyone dashed to the windows to watch the counselor's progress.

Mr. Prethy, his confidence again bolstered by his noon meal, made his way down the village street. This time, however, he was growing unpleasantly aware of the realities of country life, and feeling nowhere so invigorated as he had on his first venture into the village air. Still, there was much that he could enjoy.

Only when he came to the woods did he find himself growing anxious. Out of sight of the buildings of the village, alone amongst the trees with creatures of all manner chirping and whistling and darting all about, he began to feel insecure. As he approached the cottage, he left the copse behind and walked along a field bordered by a fence. In the meadow a herd of cows grazed and, in their sociable way, came ambling over to the fence every bit as curious as the villagers who had watched from their windows and doorways. He'd never been that close to so large an animal before - aside from horses, of course - and he moved hastily to the far side of the path, hurrying along to the Springer cottage.

Knocking sharply on Mr. Springer's door, he glanced back nervously at the cows who continued to stare amiably. Inside, he could hear a shuffling and a moment later the door opened. Mr. Springer stood in the doorway squinting out at the counselor. He looked the fussy little man up and down, thinking that an undertaker or a preacher had somehow in error found his way to the cottage door.

"Who are ye?" he asked gruffly. "Whad'ja want?" The counselor stared back at this old man, the grey stubble thick on his face, and thin on his head. He peered at the rheumy eyes that looked him up and down, the suspicion so obvious that even the counselor recognized it.

"I've come to see Mr. Springer," he said, thinking that this apparition before him was only a menial.

"Well, ye found 'im," snapped the old man. Such a nasty old thing for Mr. Springer to have around, thought the counselor, still not realizing that his fantasy was a vagrant with no basis in fact. The old man just stood there, blocking the door, instead of bringing him in to meet Mr. Springer.

"Wha'je want?" grunted the old drudge. The counselor watched the cadaverous lips form the words, seeing the gaps and the stained and broken teeth in the dark hole of the man's mouth.

"I want to see Mr. Springer," said the counselor, growing impatient at the man's unpleasant nature.

"I sed je found 'im. Now wha'je want?" Slowly the truth of the situation began to dawn on the counselor. His mouth fell open and his eyes grew wide. There was no noble grandfather; this creature before his eyes was Mr. Springer. Still the counselor couldn't quite get his fantasy out of his mind, he couldn't understand why nothing seemed to be fitting together. First the girl and now this.

"Why . . . why . . . I've come . . . ." He fumbled to say something coherent as the old man stared nastily at him. He tried again. "I've come to settle a little legal matter with you . . . ah, Mr. Springer. That's . . . you. Yes?" The counselor had begun to perspire and was forced to pull his handkerchief from his pocket and mop his brow.

"Legal matter," said the old man, the words almost a snarl.

"Legal, yes. A matter . . . well it concerns you directly, you see. It's about the Merkold girl - Kate."

"Kate," said the old man suspiciously. The hostility fading uncertainly from his rheumy eyes, he seemed to draw back. "What about Kate?"

"Well, you see," began the counselor, it seems that you are the only relative the girl has.

And that means . . ."

"Relative? She ain't no relative ta me," interrupted the old man. The counselor still couldn't shake the idea that the real Mr. Springer would momentarily appear in the doorway and send this odious old creature away.

"If you're really Mr. Springer, Mr. Martin Springer, then I'm afraid that you are the girl's only living relative." The old man squinted at him.

"Of course I'm Martin Springer," he snapped, "Who the blazes je think I am?" His demeanor had grown less threatening, and he stood as though he feared the counselor would assault him.

"If we could go in and sit down, I could show you the official documents that prove what I am saying," said the counselor, holding up his leather case for the old man to see.

Inside, at the table that was one of the few pieces of furniture in the room, the counselor opened his case and drew out the same large sheaf of very important-looking papers he had shown Kate. He placed them on the table with much trepidation, its surface stained and defaced by crumbs and food stains. It felt greasy, as did the chair upon which the counselor hesitantly settled his meticulously groomed self.

As he showed the papers to the old man and explained what they meant, he noticed the ragged and slovenly attire of the man. All, he observed, in keeping with the condition of the cottage.

By the time Mr. Prethy had finished, old man Springer's habitually sour mood had improved to as near genial as was possible. He'd even gone so far as to offer the counselor a mug of stale beer. He could afford to be generous, for the man's diddling with his great stack of old paper had brought a windfall. The cottage, the personal properties, the animals - all that had belonged to Mic Merkold now belonged to him - Martin Springer. And that included the girl, Kate.

The counselor stared at the rancid old man. The hostility that had marked him had been replaced by a hunger that showed clearly in his twisted old face. Mr. Prethy, putting away his documents in his leather case, declined the stale beer and with great relief took his leave of old Martin Springer. The exhilaration with which he'd started this day had fled, and in its place, a sickly feeling had lodged in his body and soul. He had only to present his decision to the selectmen, have them sign and countersign the appropriate documents so that they could carry out the resolution in regard to Kate, and then he could leave for the city. The country village no longer held any appeal for Mr. Prethy and he longed only to get back to his Hall of Records where he could settle into his old routine amidst his beloved record books and documents. Banishing from his mind any further disturbing thoughts of the girl and old man Springer, he thought with longing of the dust and the stale air. Hurrying through his duties he managed to make the late afternoon stage.

Mr. Prethy gathered his leather case and carpet bag from his room and descended to the lobby of the inn where he settled up just as the stage was being readied for departure. He was anxious, in a hurry to be on the stage, and Mrs. Sauther, noting his agitation, called for one of the boys loitering around the inn's door. Kroger Edwards stuck his head in the door.

"Kroger, would you help this gentleman with his bag?" said Mrs. Sauther.

The boy took Mr. Prethy's bag and headed out to the stage, the counselor following close behind. The bag was stowed in the boot and Mr. Prethy climbed aboard, settling with a sigh into the leather seat.

Kroger watched the little man mop his brow and arrange his leather case on his lap. He knew, of course, that this was the man who'd come to settle things for Kate. He'd heard the rumors and wanted to say something about what this somber man had done to Kate, but he held his tongue. He stepped back and watched the stage pull away.

Kroger Edwards was a year older than Kate. He sat behind her in the schoolroom and when the changes came to her, he'd tormented her mercilessly. It wasn't that he disliked her; in fact, he liked her just fine. If anyone had confronted him and demanded of him why he was always after Kate, he would have been at a loss to explain it. It was just the way things were. He couldn't explain his conduct. When he was with his school-mates he had no choice; he had to tease her, try to brush against her, touch her breasts. But when he encountered her alone as he did several evenings a week when they both came to the meadow to bring home the family cows, he was almost shy with her. It hadn't always been like that. Before, they'd bantered and teased like brother and sister. Now, however, he was in awe of her body, confused by the demands that the sight of her awakened in his own body.

After the death of her father, the teasing stopped, even if the attention did not. Even the least sensitive of the boys had the sense to let her alone. Kroger felt very sorry for her and several times in the meadow, he tried to say something that he hoped might console her. But his words came out all jumbled and he was sure that she did not understand what he was trying to say. In her grief and her confusion, she withdrew further and after the counselor ruled that she must go to live with old Mr. Springer, she rarely spoke.

It was in the beginning of September that Kroger was at the meadow to fetch home the family cow. The cow was being balky that evening and he'd gone into the brush to find a stick with which to urge his point of view upon her. When he came back out to the meadow, he found Williams Edel attaching a lead around the neck of a big brown cow. They nodded and, each with a cow, set out for the end of the meadow.

"Kroger, you seen Kate around? Don't she come for the cow no more?" asked Williams Edel on this hot evening. Williams had been one of Kate's chief tormentors.

"She don't come no more," Kroger replied as he followed behind the family cow, gently tapping the big animal with his stick to keep her moving.

"Ehh?"

"Old man Springer sold the cow to Abrams Pattin. Ain't seen Kate since." Williams came up behind Kroger, leading his cow as they headed out of the meadow toward the road.

"My old man was wonderin' this mornin'. Said he ain't seen Kate in a week, ten days. Said Tilda Benay was askin'." They walked on in silence into the road, a cow ahead and a cow behind. "Don' suppose Springer went off somewheres with'er?"

"Nah, I seen Springer yesterday afternoon over at Kaufman's buyin' salt 'n' flour. Mean as ever. I feel sorry for her havin' to go off to live with that old pond scum."

"'N' Kate weren't with 'im?" asked Williams.

"Nah," replied Kroger. "The Rev'rend was there though, asked Springer about Kate, how she was 'n' all, 'n' he says 'Fine'. Just that one word, real sharp and snappy." Williams looked at Kroger, his eyes questioning.

"'N' then what?" he asked.

"Nuthin'. Springer quick paid for his stuff 'n' out the door." "Di'n't the Rev'rend say nuthin' more?"

"Not a word. It just got real quiet 'n' the only sound was Springer's coins hitting the counter-top".

The two boys lapsed into silence as the sky turned orange and gold with the setting sun.

They took their leave of one another, conducting their bovine charges to the barns behind their homes.

The next morning Kroger was asked several times by adults in the village whether he'd seen Kate. By midmorning, folks were beginning to gather in little clumps and the talk was all of Kate. No one had seen her in at least ten days and the selectmen were coming around to figuring that they ought to go on down to Springer's and make sure the girl was alright.

Kroger was sitting on the well-wall with Williams Edel and Franek Settel when, just before noon, chief selectman Trentor stepped into the street and looked around at the groups of people standing in the hot sun.

"'Ppears nobody's seen Kate in ten, mebee eleven days," he said loudly addressing everyone he could see. "Ed and Harry 'n' me, we figure we ought to go on down to Springer's and see the girl's all right." He didn't say anything more, turned to the other selectmen, and headed toward the end of the village. Kroger thought that what Trentor hadn't said was just as clear as what he had. He slid off the wall and started after the selectmen, as did nearly all the men and boys in the street.

It didn't take but a few minutes to walk down to the end of the village, down along Freyson's meadow and up the lane to Springer's place. The cows, curiosity evident in their big, soft eyes, came to the fence to watch. The men and boys, selectmen in the lead, walked up to the dilapidated cottage and gathered around the door. Trentor stepped forward and knocked loudly.

"Springer," he called, "open up. We need to have a word with you." Silence settled over the gathering in the noonday heat. Back in the woods, cicadas whirr, and forest birds called to one another, but nothing was heard to move in the cottage. "You in there, Springer? Come on now, open up the door," said Trentor, almost shouting now.

For a moment more, all was still and then the door opened slowly, and old man Springer was standing in the doorway. He was wiping his hands on a greasy rag as he stared out at the company in his dooryard. He squinted, his rheumy eyes blinking in the bright sunlight, looking first at the selectmen and then letting his spiteful gaze glide across the others gathered there. From within the scent of roasted meat wafted out into the dooryard.

"Wa'dje want?" he said.

"We came ta see Kate," Trentor replied, trying to peer around Springer into the dim interior of the home.

"Ain't here," sneered Springer.

"Well, 'en, where is she?" asked Trentor.

"Ain't here," Springer repeated. He looked at the men confronting him, and his insolence seemed to waver. "She's out . . . ah . . . pickin' berries. She's in the wood pickin' berries." It sounded, Kroger thought, as though Springer was trying to convince himself. He sniffed at the scent on the air.

"You better step aside," said Trentor. "We're gonna come in and have a look around."

"Ye can't do that, ye got no right," sneered Springer, but the men had already begun to crowd in through the door pushing the old man brusquely back into the room. Some of the men went through into the other room, some looked about the main room. All viewed the old man's abode with distaste, though all breathed in the aroma of the meat. Kroger slipped through the door and likewise stared around the room, his gaze coming to rest on the greasy, littered table in the center of the room. And in the center of which on a blue platter was a large ham, the juicy, pink flesh causing Kroger's mouth to water as soon as his eyes took it in. It had been a very long time since he'd had ham and he dearly wanted to step up to that table and carve off a thick slice for himself. But the men were all gathering in the center of the room. Springer stood sullenly by the table as if to defend his ham from the covetous eyes of the others. Trentor stood before Springer and stared hard at the grizzled old man, the grease evident in the stubble on his chin.

"Where's the girl?" he asked, but Springer said nothing, his eyes beginning to dart hither and yon like those of a cornered wild animal. "All her belongings appear to be here. Where is she?"

"Tol ya," Springer snarled. "Pickin' berries in the woods."

"Ain't no berries this time of year," said Trentor. Springer was silent, his darting eyes returning to the ham on the table. Trentor looked at the ham just as Kroger looked at the ham. Kroger looked around the room and realized that all the eyes in the room were directed to that prime flesh. Just at that moment a sound burst from old man Springer.

"Burp."

Martin Springer had been hungry for a very long time, but finally he was satisfied.

Black as Crows

When Henry Mafly stepped out into the chill February morning, the first thing he heard was the great, raucous caterwauling of the crows. There must be a million of them, he thought. He could see them darkening the branches of the trees down near the end of the street. They hated him; he knew it, knew in his heart that they hated him with a vengeance. And the truth of the matter was that he hated them every bit as much as they hated him.

The only thing he hated more than those fucking crows was Charlene. He didn't think of her as a person, a woman, or even as his ex-wife; he thought of her as a thing, an evil, scheming, conniving thing, as black in her heart as those fucking crows. Just thinking about her brought acid churning into his stomach and nasty darts of pain to his head. He had ulcers, he knew it, and migraines; he couldn't sleep, and he couldn't eat, and the only thing he could think about was that bitch and her traitorous ways.

All his friends, everyone who knew what had happened, said the same thing: it will pass, it just takes time; time. He wanted revenge.

Thoughts of Charlene jerked and jolted through his consciousness all day long, whether he was at work or - as today - had the day off. A series of endless loops played and replayed in his mind until he could think of nothing else. She seduced and stole away his best friend and the pain of that alone would have been enough to drive him mad. But there was the joint account she'd cleaned out, the most valuable and useful of their possessions she'd stripped out of the house while he was at work. And the lies she'd told to their neighbors and acquaintances, how he'd cheated on her, abused her, humiliated her. When in fact it had been she who humiliated him, connived, lied, cheated, and stripped him of his dignity. Oh, he could kill her, he could just kill her.

She must have been planning it for a long time, because she emptied the account and stripped the house on the same day. That day she'd moved to an apartment in the Willowood section of town. He'd been there, he'd seen it - the building anyway; a nice older building. She had an apartment on the fourth floor with a balcony that over-looked the alleyway.

He'd learned this from Frankie down at the Mobil station on Second and Mercer. She'd been in there that same day, flirting with him, and she'd told him about her new apartment. And Frankie had told Henry. He could still hear Frankie tell it.

"Whyn't ya come over an' see me some time," she says, chewin' her gum with her eyes big as half dollars," Frankie said. "With that breathy voice, ya know what I mean?" Henry knew exactly what he meant, and the knowing pierced his heart like a dagger.

So, he'd driven directly from the Mobil station over to 4723 Brennermont Road and seen for himself. He'd even tried the front door of the apartment building, but it was locked. So, he'd gone to the building next door and found the front door open. Like a spy or maybe a terrorist he'd made his way up four flights of stairs to the roof, surprised to find that that door, too, was unlocked. When he stepped out onto the roof there were sawhorses, scraps of wood, rolls of tar paper, and several planks lying about.

He walked over to the edge of the roof and looked at the building across the way. There, just opposite and a little below was the balcony to Charlene's apartment. The alleyway between the buildings was narrow, not more than ten or eleven feet, he guessed. As he looked at the windows and the balcony, a nervous energy flickered through him.

Henry turned back to the planks and eyeballed them. They were narrow, but long enough, he was sure, to bridge the gap. For a moment he thought about dragging them over and trying to slide them onto the balcony railing, but the sound of men talking loudly in the alley-way stopped him. He peered over the roof and saw several workmen heading for the side door of the building. A few minutes later, as he left the building, he passed them in the downstairs hallway.

In the building, and especially when he'd passed the men in the hall, he'd been so nervous that his knees nearly gave out. But once he was outside, back in his car, a feeling of superiority washed over him, as though he'd somehow pulled one over on Charlene. He felt like some feral creature that had pissed in his enemy's lair.

She'd shit if she knew I'd been here, he thought as he started the car.

That had been three days ago, and the pain and anger had grown like wounds that aren't allowed to heal. And to accent his roiling despair was the constant commotion of the crows. Ever since it all began the crows had been hounding him. They'd be back anytime now, he knew. It was as if she'd bewitched them and sent them to harass and mock him, as if they worked for her. After what had happened, he wouldn't put anything past Charlene.

All morning, he skulked from room to room. Charlene controlled his mind, and he could concentrate on nothing but her. He turned on the TV and slouched on the couch, but he saw nothing of what passed before his eyes. About eleven, the rattle of the mail-slot brought him out of his thoughts. In a desperate mood, he dragged himself off the couch and made his way to the little pile of mail in front of the door.

At the kitchen table, he looked through the stack. A flyer from a pizza parlor, a reminder about his dental appointment, a letter with no return address, and statements from his two credit cards. He opened the letter first; a mass mailing that shouted at him in large print: "I made

$37,000 in one week in my spare time! You can, too!" Right into the trash it went. Then he opened the first statement. He didn't want to look at it because he'd used the card a little too liberally the past two weeks. He stared at the statement without comprehension. He'd figured it would be $200 or maybe $250. But the total due was $13,743.67. For a moment, thoughts of Charlene no longer dominated his mind. This is absurd, he thought; there must be some mistake. He looked at the name and address; they were his. Then he looked at the itemized list of charges. K-Mart, the one over on Vander Boulevard, $172.53; the Gap, $238.92; Walmart, $103.17. The list went on and on; the realization came like an assassin in the night - Charlene!

"Son of a bitch," Henry screamed out loud. That fucking bitch, that " Desperately,

with shaking hands, he tore open the second statement. There, scorching his eyes, was the impossible total of $17,048.29. And every charge, he already knew, would bear the unmistakable stamp of Charlene.

The anger and pain that had marked the morning gave way to a rage as black as the crows that came daily to torment him. Henry tore the statements to shreds. He slammed the chair against the door and in his rage punched a deep divot into the refrigerator door. He'd have gone on and probably wrecked the entire house had it not been for the crows.

Somehow their shrieking cacophony had penetrated his tantrum. They were all around the house. The crows had come streaming up the street from their sanctuary in the woods and descended upon Henry's yard. They screamed in the maples in the front of the house and in the oaks and the apple tree in the backyard. They teetered on the wires and on the fence and squabbled on the grass. Their unending shrieking became the focal point of his rage.

Finally, unable to endure another second, he ran out onto the porch screaming. "Get out of here, you little bastards!" Dashing down into the yard he searched for anything to throw - pebbles, bits of twigs and broken branches. "I'll kill you, you little black bastards!" Clouds of crows rose into the air at the rain of pebbles and sticks that came their way, but they didn't leave. The intensity of their uproar increased as they flew in a great swarm over the house to circle and return to the trees from which Henry's tirade had driven them.

Henry stood in the yard, fists clenched, eyes bulging, the veins standing out on his forehead. The evil black birds continued to squawk and scold, mocking Henry until he could bear it no longer.

He ran into the house, to his bedroom closet where he rooted behind his shoes for the steel box that held his pellet gun. Pulling the box from the closet, he yanked it open and grasped the pistol. It bore a fair resemblance to a Smith&Wesson .44 magnum, and it was ready to go with a full complement of pellets and a fresh CO2 cartridge. Like Dirty Harry, he stormed through the house, out onto the lawn.

The crows all seemed to be watching him, their cries rising in tempo as he stepped to the middle of the yard and swung the pistol up to aim. Pop! And a crow toppled from the nearest maple. Pop! Pop! And two more fell heavily to the frozen ground. At first, the commotion among the crows grew louder, but as Henry aimed and fired - pop, pop, pop - and more crows went down to meet their maker, they grew silent. Henry managed to get off several more shots, bringing down two more crows, before they rose in a great black conflagration and flew away. He watched them disappear into the woods at the end of the street.

Henry stood in the yard, his arms fallen to his side, the pistol dangling loosely from his hand. All about him the ground was littered with crow bodies. Like the last British soldier standing as the Zulus fled, he stared with wide eyes after his departed foe.

But it was silent, the infernal racket of the vermin birds was finally stilled.

As Henry turned back toward the kitchen, he felt strangely jubilant. A minute ago, he'd been the victim of those fucking little black bastards and now he'd turned the tables on them. He stood for a moment at the back door; he could still hear them murmuring down the street, but they weren't shrieking in his yard. It would pass for silence.

He went into the kitchen and tossed the pistol onto the table. His thoughts, for several minutes diverted, returned to Charlene. The rage rose in him again, choking and twisting him. His mind began churning away, counting the transgressions she'd inflicted upon him, but when he came once again to this latest savagery, he snapped.

"That bitch," he screamed to the kitchen. "She'll pay for this."

Henry thought about the crow shoot and picked up the pistol. He knew that the pellets wouldn't have the same effect on Charlene as they had on the crows. But she didn't know that; one gun would look like another to that dumb bitch.

He spent the rest of the day planning, his black mood growing sharp and glittery like obsidian. As dusk approached, he put on his black jeans and a black sweatshirt. He stuffed the pistol into his belt, pulled on a black watch cap, and, picking up a roll of duct tape, headed out the door.

On the drive over to Brennermont, he realized that his mind was still, that the eternal agonizing over Charlene was, for the moment, ended. He parked around the corner on Cedar and walked back to 4727, the building next to Charlene's. The door was unlocked, but that did not surprise him. He was on a mission and the way would be cleared for him, he could just feel it. The door to the roof, too, was unlocked, just as it had been the other time.

Henry went to the edge of the roof and peered down at the lighted windows of Charlene's apartment. For a moment he watched and then he became aware of the sound. It seemed to come from some distance, but from every direction. He knew that sound, knew it very well. It was the crows. He glanced around and saw a few of them perched on the chimney and more on an old TV antenna. They didn't interest him anymore; he'd vanquished them.

Turning back to the building opposite, he was surprised to see Charlene step out onto the balcony. She wore her old white terry cloth bathrobe. Leaning over the railing, she thrust her hand out and peered toward the sky. Henry ducked, certain she'd seen him until he realized that he was dressed in black and that at worst she might have taken him for a crow.

Sliding up to the edge again, he saw her silhouette appear in the small window that must be the bathroom. Quickly, he carried the two slender planks over to the edge and maneuvered the first one out over the alleyway, struggling to direct its far end onto the balcony railing. It took all his strength to get the plank to its objective without dropping it into the darkness below. The second plank he slid across on the first until it cleared the railing and then he turned it over till it lay beside the first. It was nearly a foot shorter than the other and its purchase on the roof was tenuous. He would have to move carefully so as not to dislodge it and send it and himself plunging to the pavement four stories below.

Taking a deep breath, he stepped out onto the planks. Narrow as they were, they provided an unstable footing, but Henry, still calm and fearless, began his crossing, duct tape in one hand, pistol in the other. He was about halfway across when he saw the light go out in the bathroom and Charlene passed the door to the balcony. He froze in mid-step, waiting. A moment later the light came on in the kitchen; he saw her at the sink.

As he was about to take his next step, a tangle of crows came down the alleyway, cawing and screaming, passing so close to him that he could feel the rush of air. For a second, he teetered, and then, his focus back on the balcony, he moved quickly, and he was across.

Henry hopped down onto the balcony and reached for the door handle. It was open, as he knew it would be; he was on a mission. Quietly he opened the door and entered the little hallway. To the left, light from the kitchen illuminated his way. He stuck the pistol back in his belt, out of sight under the sweatshirt.

Charlene was at the sink, humming to herself. She'd shed the bathrobe and wore only panties and bra. The sight of her brought up the nerves and anger and the calm that had brought him this far sizzled away in the fire of renewed rage.

He crossed the narrow kitchen in a single stride and seized her around the neck, pulling her away from the sink and flinging her against a kitchen chair. She screamed as she toppled to the floor, but she recovered immediately and jumped up, confronting her attacker.

"You!" she spat at him. There was fear in her eyes until she realized it was Henry; her eyes filled with contempt and belligerence. "Get out of my apartment, you weasel," she said in a voice like steel shavings. She tried to push past him, but he shoved her hard and she fell back against the chair, nearly falling to the floor again. Before she could open her mouth, Henry had the pistol out and thrust it against her upper lip, forcing her head back.

"Shut up," he said, pushing harder with the pistol. "Don't say a word." He saw the arrogance flicker in her eyes as though fear might take over. He made her put her hands behind her back and quickly bound her to the chair with the duct tape, hands and arms, and then her legs, each taped firmly to one of the front legs of the chair. Her thighs were open and when he stood up, he saw the dark smudge of her pubic hair against the sheer fabric of her panties. He started getting hard and for a moment he considered raping her, of reaming her till she begged for mercy, Miss High and Mighty, Miss Bitch. But the thought of it made him angry.

She began to scream, and he slapped her hard. Grabbing a dish towel from the stove, he forced it into her mouth and wound tape around her head. Sound of any kind was now impossible for her.

Henry slumped back against the sink, his breath coming in ragged gasps. The hand that held the pistol was wet and slippery with sweat. He looked around the kitchen. It was a mess just as his had been when she was there. He hated her slovenly ways, the dirty dishes in the sink, the bottles of oil and vinegar, spices and condiments on the stove top, sticky with grease and spatters from cooking. The table, too, was full of bottles - wine, honey, water, and milk - sour no doubt.

His gaze returned to Charlene, and he saw her eyes flickering between fear and hatred. His resolution, his mission, so successful thus far, faded into indecision. He didn't know what to do next. For a moment he closed his eyes and when he opened them, he had just enough time to see the hatred flash like lightning in Charlene's eyes.

Somehow, she managed to launch her chair at him, hitting him in the groin. They crashed to the floor together and tumbled against the table. The pistol slipped from Henry's grasp as bottles and jars cascaded all over the kitchen floor. The honey jar broke, the wine bottle broke, and as Henry struggled to regain his footing, honey and wine covered his hands.

The chair hit him in the balls and pain flashed through his loins. He growled in rage as he slipped on the floor, his hand sliding through the honey and wine until it touched the jagged neck of the bottle. Without thought, guided only by his pain and his rage, his fingers closed around the glass, and he struck out at Charlene. In moments, the floor was slick with her blood.

Henry pushed himself desperately away from her. He slid into the corner by the refrigerator, unable to catch his breath, unable to move, unable to think. He watched the fear coagulate in Charlene's eyes and then slowly fade as her life ebbed away in the rivulets of blood pouring out onto the kitchen floor.

As if by osmosis, the fear soaked from Charlene's blood into Henry's being. He sat for a long time, paralyzed. Later, much later or a little later, he didn't know, he struggled to his feet. He tried to concentrate on what he must do to save himself, but it was so hard. First, find the gun; there it was on the floor near the refrigerator. He picked it up, sticky with blood, and wiped it off with some paper towels; he thrust it back in his pants. The duct tape. And the bottleneck. He'd flung it away from himself and it was harder to find, but he located it in the far corner of the kitchen behind the waste basket. He wiped the blood off as best he could then wrapped it in paper towels and stuck it into his pocket. There was a horrible feeling rising in him, a fermentation of bile and acid that clawed its way upward through his esophagus. His vision was blurred, and stabs of pain ravaged his brain. This was worse than before, much worse, and he had to get out of here, away from the blood and that . . . that thing he'd hated so much in life.

Fingerprints, he thought. He had no idea what he'd touched; grabbing the dishrag from the sink, he went frantically around the kitchen wiping at places that might bear his prints. He switched off the light and swiped the switch.

Out of the kitchen, into the dark hall. He swiped the door handle, flicked the deadlatch, wiped it, and stepped out onto the balcony. Had he touched the railing? He couldn't remember, his head hurt like crazy. A quick wipe and he tossed the dishrag into the alleyway. Unsteadily, he climbed up onto the railing and made his way onto the planks. His nerves were shot and his Knees felt like rubber as he began his journey toward the opposite roof. He was already shaking badly when the first swarm of crows came shrieking up the alleyway and beat their way past him so close he could feel their wings against his face. With the second wave, several of the black devils smacked against his body. He wobbled at the impact and the shorter plank tipped and slipped from the roof's edge.

Henry's left leg gave way as the plank plunged into the darkness. He managed to grab onto the remaining plank, clinging by his fingers to the cold wood. He hung there in space, gathering his strength. With much effort, he managed to pull his legs up and loop his ankles over the plank. He contemplated his next move when he felt a crow land on his shoulder. As it began to peck nastily at his ear, he heard the great cacophonous shrieks as more and more crows landed on the plank. A crow pecked at his exposed ankle and soon another and then another. Crows filled the air and lined the rooftop where he so desperately wanted to be. All around him they squawked and shrieked and mocked him. Then he felt the first piercing stab at his fingers, still sticky with honey, wine, and blood.

The crows pecked viciously at his ankles; he could feel his ear tearing, blood trickling down his neck, his fingers taking a nasty beating. He couldn't hold out much longer. He tried to move, to edge himself along toward safety, but the punishment the crows were dishing out sapped his strength and his will. A blackness, like the night and the bodies of his enemies swept through his mind.

His ankles gave way and his body dropped to dangle over the darkness. The crows swarmed close, pecking at his legs and torso. A profound weariness engulfed him as the pain in his fingers intensified. He longed for release, and finally his fingers, unable to endure any more punishment, gave him what he wanted. They released and Henry plunged into the dark alley- way, the sudden release of pressure jolting the plank from its lodging to follow him down. He hit the concrete wall that lined the passage to the basement entrance and toppled down into the pit, breaking his neck as he hit the stairs.

Above, the space between the buildings was filled with the frantic and victorious cries of the crows. Like a band of savages drunk on a vengeful victory, their raucous voices rose into the cold chill evening. They swirled through the alleyway and flew off into the night. Within moments, all was still. The darkness was complete, as black as crows.

The Green Green Grass of Home

Sandy Collins stared about, his eyes wide. What should have been the familiar walls of his bedroom were huge boulders and a dark blue sky, lightening now, the stars disappearing one by one. He lay on a grassy spot amidst large rocks, the chill of dawn causing him to shiver under a tattered, old blanket.

Somewhere off in the distance he heard a flat little pop, like someone puncturing a balloon, and then another, several more, and then silence. The sound brought it all back to him and he shuddered where he lay.

Stiff with the morning chill, Sandy threw off the dirty, old blanket and stood up. He gazed out toward Indian Ridge where the morning sky was turning pink and gold, an orange kernel announcing the coming of the sun. His place, he thought, should be down in the valley, going out to the barn to begin the day's work. His heart heavy, he doubted that he would ever again do that. His life had suddenly taken a totally unanticipated turn.

From the valley came the sound of an engine revving up. As the sound changed to an easy idle, it seemed familiar to Sandy, but he couldn't place it. He made his way carefully out onto the boulder from which he had a clear view of the valley. Looking again toward Indian Ridge where the hint of orange had grown to a brilliant flaming slash across the sky. And there was the eagle he'd first seen on the day that his life had veered off on this strange path.

Sandy Collins sat on the grandstand, the last person on the left side of the arc of dignitaries that graced the stage. At the microphone, Ralph Butterworth was jawing on the way those Chamber of Commerce types do. ". . . our forefathers who came here and sharpened their axes and put their muscles to the wheel to carve out a paradise that we enjoy today . . ." Sandy'd heard the speech before, often enough that he knew all the clichés by heart. He didn't care for Butterworth, who was always mouthing off about jobs and progress and development. They'd crossed swords several times have over the issue of industrial agriculture and there was no love lost between them. Sandy didn't much patience for this sort of hoopla and goings on. He was a farmer, plain and simple, with entirely too much to do to be wasting his time grandstanding.

Off in the distance, a quarter mile or so, above the feedlot, he saw an eagle circling. The bird had been there earlier, when the band was playing, and he'd imagined what the bird might have seen flying into the valley over the Broadgrass Hills to the west. He'd seen it himself, much the way the great raptor must be seeing it, the day Greg Thompson took him up in the crop duster. To the eagle, the Summerfield Valley High School Marching Band must have been nothing more than the thump-thump-thump of percussion from which the tinny tones of brass rattled on the wind. Sandy wasn't all that big on music, but he could make out Horace Miller's boy Irwin pumping out sour notes on his trombone and that cute little Sally Robbins pounding her drum off beat.

"The fertile land, protected from the harsh north winds by the sheltering hills..." Ralph's drone intruded for a moment on Sandy's reverie. The man loved to talk; he could have been selling appliances or burying his grandmother. Sandy turned his attention back to the sky, searching for the soaring bird.

The hills were rolling undulations, rising two to three hundred feet at their highest. They were thickly forested and looked soft and lush in the spring sunshine. In a long glide, the eagle swept down into the valley, passing over Jum Hendron's fields that ran up the east slope of the hills, mostly bright green in wheat this time of year.

Sandy's imagination had stayed right with that eagle, scanning the farms, each with its distinct checkerboard of fields and woodlots. The bird passed over the slash of glistening rails that bisected the valley, across more farms, and then over the feedlot. Beyond, stood the businesses and homes of Summerfield with its tree-lined streets, church spires shining in the morning sun, and the town plaza smack dab in the middle.

From that height, thought Sandy, everything looked right as apple pie. But the valley hadn't been spared the hard times that had come upon farmers in the past decades. Many families had suffered, and some couldn't make it and threw in the towel.

"Our farms are the muscle and vision of our great community," Ralph pontificated. Sandy checked his watch, disappointed that only eleven minutes had elapsed; to him it seemed as though an hour or more had passed. He'd stopped listening after the first few clichés. For Sandy the words faded away to the rush of wind as the eagle swept closer and closer.

"And now without further ado," Ralph said, leaning toward the microphone, "I want to introduce to you the man who will single-handed bring prosperity back to our valley, save our family farms - the backbone of our community. - and put Summerfield on the map in the process . . ." Sandy's attention was back on the proceedings. The "single-handed" remark grated on him. What was his role supposed to be? he wondered. Ralph had reached his high point to the accompaniment of a ragged drum roll. ". . . a scientist, a researcher, a businessman, and a great gentleman, the vice-president of Genecorps Enterprises, Dr. Ellis Scandor. Let's have a big hand for Dr. Scandor." The drum roll ended in a precipitous crash.

The audience, all of Sandy's neighbors, fellow farmers, and townsfolk he'd known all his life, offered up a generous round of applause for this remarkable man about to lead them to prosperity. The band struck up a rousing, if only marginally recognizable version of "Happy Days Are Here Again" as Dr. Scandor crossed the stage to the podium.

Dr. Scandor took a moment to gaze out over his audience before he began. His voice was strong, confident, as he rattled off greetings to the assembled dignitaries, the mayor, the assemblymen, "the eloquent and distinguished Mr. Butterfield," Representative Jim Cowell, and finally, the crowd. "A big hello to all you fine folks of Summerfield," he said. He could have been campaigning for governor. "We are here today," his voice sonorous, like a great orator of days gone by, "to inaugurate a new era for all of us, an era in which science and agriculture join hand in hand to take us to a new future of prosperity and plenty for all."

From the edge of the grandstand, a smattering of boos and catcalls greeted Scandor's words. A group of protestors, placards held high, were herded into a small knot by half a dozen of Summerfield's finest. In their midst, Professor Enders from the community college over in Murphysboro stood tall and defiant, his jaw thrust as he glared at the speaker. Gathered about him was a band of several dozen students, a few dozen women and a few men. Though the group was small and insignificant, the police stood menacingly, their peaked caps pulled low over sunglass-shaded eyes. The message was clear; there would be no shenanigans today.

Dr. Scandor peered down on the little group and smiled in obvious condescension. "Here before you, my fellow citizens, you see a fine example of the kind of misguided enthusiasm that has for so long held us locked in the jaws of ignorance. Oh, make no mistake," he said, leaning forward over the podium, gesturing like a father to his wayward children, "their hearts are in the right place. I'm sure they want what we all do; for things to turn out fine for all of us. Yes, their hearts are in the right place, but their minds are . . . shall we say, confused." Boos and catcalls arose anew from the little band as they waved their poster. Those close enough to the stage could see the fatherly smile of indulgence on Dr. Scandor's face, the faraway look in his eyes.

"Or perhaps the right word would be ignorant," he went on, his voice dulcet with sincerity, rising with conviction. "They think they know . . . but we in the industry are the ones who truly know. We, after all, are the experts, the scientists. We know we're right."

At the end of the arc of seats, Sandy shifted in his chair as he stared at Scandor's back. He was bored; he couldn't listen to much more of this speechifying. The sun was shining and there was work to be done. His gaze wandered over the crowd and off to his left where a truck was parked at the edge of the bandstand. Billy Smollet and two men wearing caps and shirts emblazoned with the Genecorps logo were working at the back of the truck. They were stacking crates on the lift gate when Sandy saw Billy slip, his foot twisting down between the truck bed and the lift gate. In his position, Billy was helpless to free himself. One of the Genecorps men stood at the controls ready to activate the gate, unaware of Billy's plight. A cry went up from several in the audience who saw what was happening. Sandy leapt from his seat, jumped to the lift gate and pulled Billy free just as the gate rose up level with the truck bed.

"Science has offered us a rare opportunity . . ." Scandor intoned, his voice rising once again in exhortation. On the lift gate, Sandy steadied Billy as a handful of people applauded. A ripple ran through the crowd and some of the celebrities stared in confusion.

At the podium, Scandor spoke on, oblivious to the disturbance behind him. "After all," he said, his eyes glazed, a fine sheen of perspiration on his face, "we have done our research and development, the testing and safeguarding. And here before us, lost and bewildered souls who, like the Luddites of other centuries, have a feeling" – he mouthed the word with deliberate scorn – "that this is not right."

There was a ripple of unease at the edge of the crowd as Ted Lewis and Walt Harris clapped Sandy on the back and shook his hand. Sandy climbed back up on stage and settled into his chair as applause broke out around the truck. All this attention made Sandy uncomfortable. He was nervous enough as it was. An uneasiness descended on him as he turned his attention back to Dr. Scandor, as though the incident had cast a shadow over the day's proceedings.

Sandy sat uncomfortably in his chair. He knew that soon the mayor would introduce him, and he'd have to say a few words. He wished he'd never let himself get dragged into this, but it was too late now. The sense of foreboding that had crept into him added to his growing desire to be elsewhere, back at the farm . . . or anywhere else. He looked down at the people crowding against the bandstand and there was Myrle. She'd intended to stand right below the podium to offer support while he played his part. But the commotion of a few minutes past had brought her to him. She waved, her face glowing with a smile of encouragement.

"It'll be alright. You'll do fine," she called. He couldn't hear her words, but he could read her lips and her mind.

Scandor was finishing up now, heading for the home stretch. "We, the men of science," he boomed forth, "sidestepping the cynics and naysayers who would keep us shackled to the past, have brought the future to this fair community. And a grand future it will be as we all join hands to step into as new age of agriculture." Scandor's voice rose as if he were a politician at the end of a whirlwind campaign.

As he spoke, Billy Smollet finished stacking sacks of seed onto a hand truck. Each sack bore the Genecorps logo and the image of a brilliant sun rising over a field of verdant grain. One of the uniformed men wheeled the hand truck up onto the stage and parked it near Scandor. "Today, friends and neighbors," Scandor said in a voice filled with emotion as he plucked a sack of seed from the pile, "like pioneers of old, we set out on a new adventure that will take us forward to a grand new future." The little knot of protestors booed and waved their signs, as a spattering of applause rose from the crowd.

Mayor Will Pedersen, who'd joined Scandor at the podium, turned, gesturing to Sandy and saying: "Our own Sandy Collins, all-American farmer and number one citizen of Summerfield." Sandy approached the podium, and the mayor shook his hand.

"Thank you, folks," he said, leaning close to the microphone so that his voice popped and crackled on the PA system. Dr. Scandor stood to his right thrusting a five-pound sack of seed at him. Sandy took the seed as Scandor stepped close to the microphone. Sandy noticed the beads of sweat on his brow and thought how he looked like someone who'd let his enthusiasm get the better of him.

"With this batch of seed, we officially inaugurate this program, making a giant step for American agriculture. Congratulations, Sandy Collins!" The crowd cheered and Sandy heard his name shouted over and over. He thought he'd be nervous here in the center of attention, but as soon as he accepted the sack of seed from Scandor, a sense of calm descended on him. He stood holding the sack, looking out over the crowd, smiling. Soon he was waving at his friends and neighbors as if he too were a seasoned politician on the trail of electoral victory.

As the ceremony ended, Sandy shook hands with Scandor, who leaned toward him and said above the blaring of the band: "Mark my words, son, in a year's time you won't know this valley."

Myrle joined Sandy on the stage as the mayor, several assemblymen, and Representative Cowell all pressed about to shake Sandy's hand. With the festivities at an end, the sack of seed cradled in the crook of his arm, Sandy felt very much at ease with the politicos and his new celebrity. Behind him, he heard Butterfield ask Scandor how they developed the new grain. The question interested him too, but the buzz of conversation and the commotion of the band all kept him from hearing a complete explanation. Like an elusive spring breeze, some words waffled past his ears while others went off in all directions. ". . . isolate traits we want   Shotgun, like a shotgun blast . . . . genes in the new seeds   " Sandy'd read about it, read the leaflet and the

reprints of reports that Genecorps had sent him, but still, it didn't make much sense to him. He glanced at Ralph and saw the look, almost of awe, on his face as he stood in the presence of greatness.

". . . testing has shown . . . ," Sandy heard Scandor plowing on, "of course, we're confidant, wholly confidant that nothing can go wrong."

Sandy didn't count himself among the slavish admirers of this new science. He'd seen and experienced firsthand too many infallible developments gone awry. Like the fertilizer of a few years ago that had boosted his wheat yield by nearly 15 percent, but had also managed to wipe out two thirds of his potato crop in the adjacent field. He'd had serious doubts about getting involved with this new grain. He'd talked it over with Myrle and his neighbors till they were sick of the subject, but in the end, the Genecorps representatives had convinced them all to go along with the new crop. And now, as he stood there smiling at Myrle, the sack of grain cradled in his arm, he had the feeling that this time would be different. He put his arm around Myrle and started edging her out of the crowd. Now that the hoopla was over, he was anxious to get started on this grand new future that awaited them.

They descended from the grandstand and threaded their way through the crowd. It was slow going as friends and neighbors offered congratulations, clapped Sandy on the back or insisted on shaking hands. They'd nearly made it through the dispersing crowd when they saw the Welbor brothers heading toward them. The Welbors passed for the local version of agri-business, having taken over a lot of the acreage from families whose farms had failed. They were tight with Butterworth and some of his crowd. They weren't well-liked in the valley, most folks looking askance at their short-cut procedures and their over-reliance on some very questionable chemicals.

"So, Collins," Earl Welbor said, blocking their path. "Pretty lucky, you bein' the only farmer in the valley to get this new-angled magic seed."

"I guess I am lucky," said Sandy.

"I don't see why you're the only one as gets the seed," Dick Welbor chimed in, the sour look on his face edging toward belligerence.

"I didn't make the rules," Sandy replied as Myrle grasped his hand. In fact, none of them knew why Genecorps had insisted on doing things this way. Sandy'd been chosen by lot to be the first. Nobody knew for sure what Genecorps was up to, but most assumed it had something to do with production difficulties of the new seed. "If it bothers you so much, you could complain to Dr. Scandor. He's right up there on the stage." Sandy pointed, and with Myrle in tow, edged around the Welbors.

"Well, it ain't right," whined Earl to their backs.

Sandy knew right from the moment he was chosen that there would be those who would resent him and begrudge him the honor of planting the first seed. He tried not to let it bother him, and now with the sack of seed in the crook of his arm, he felt hopeful in a way he hadn't felt in years.

The next morning at 7:30 the Genecorps truck drove down the lane and stopped in front of Sandy Collins' barn. Sandy'd just come down from the haymow as the driver climbed from the cab.

"Morning, Mr. Collins. Got your shipment of seed right here." Together they unloaded the sacks of seed and piled them on a pallet just inside the barn door. As they finished, the driver said to Sandy: "This should put a different face on the whole farming situation hereabouts. From what I hear there's talk they'll be trading in futures 'fore you've even got a crop up."

"That's good to hear," said Sandy, pushing his cap back on his head. "All of us farmers could stand a run of good luck."

"I'll be wishing you the best then," said the driver and drove off. Sandy stood in the barnyard and watched the truck disappear down the road. He'd been lucky to win the draw as the first farmer to get the seed. At least he thought he'd been lucky. At first, it had seemed too much of a gamble. All this science and technology stuff appeared to him to be pretty risky. He hadn't wanted to commit more than a small parcel of his acreage to the new grain, but the Genecorps people had put a lot of pressure on him, and he'd finally agreed to plant two hundred acres. He worried about that. Yesterday at the festivities, his spirits had risen, only to fall again once they'd gotten home. Now, however, with the seed in his barn, the fields tilled and ready for planting, he could feel his mood rising once again.

As Sandy stepped out of the barnyard, he saw Myrle coming down from the house. She joined him on the gravel, and he took her hand and led her into the barn to show her their future. "There it is, Honey."

Myrle shared Sandy's trepidations about the fast-talking hucksters of new technology. If anything, she'd had more reservations about this project than Sandy. As late as breakfast, less than an hour ago, they'd still been talking about their less than one hundred percent feelings about things.

As they stood by the stack of seed, Sandy related what the driver had said.

"You feel better about it now, don't you?" she asked. Sandy shrugged and said what's done is done, but she could see in his face that his mood had shifted. They were committed now, and they might as well make the best of it. Maybe, just maybe, things would be different this time.

Within a day, Sandy had most of the seed in, and nature, as if to bless this new departure, had brought a fresh spring rain to set it all in motion. Barely a week passed before the first signs of new growth showed sparkling green above the dark soil. The sprouts shot up rapidly and soon Sandy was walking amongst the burgeoning green stalks, standing jubilantly in their arrow- straight rows. In days gone by Sandy had again been visited by doubt. Now, as he walked amidst the shoots, so vibrant and alive, he had that wonderful feeling of what it was to be a farmer and to bring forth from the soil this exhilarating life. It was kind of what he thought women must feel when they became pregnant. He had to smile to himself at this poetic flight of fancy. The acres of green set him humming, despite his basically a-musical nature, a lilting little tune that could have been an Elizabethan ode to springtime.

As the weeks passed and the grain grew, Sandy still had his moments of doubt, but they were normally at night when demons and malevolent spirits were prone to prowl the darkness. Talk in town was always upbeat and folks had begun to banter around possible prices of the new grain, all of the estimates running well ahead of wheat futures. Several of the other farmers - George Kovacks, Henry Wilson, Ted Lewis – had received their shipments of seed and they too had sprouts up and were feeling hopeful about their future.

The grain grew higher than wheat, though otherwise, it looked pretty much like its more common and ancient relative. As the plants ripened,

Sandy took to walking the fields, brushing his hands across the growing clusters. This had a soothing effect on him, and he liked to think that it was the way farmers from time immemorial had felt as they walked amongst their thriving crops.

One day, as he cradled a cluster in his hand, he realized that the grain, though still several weeks short of harvest was already bigger than a wheat cluster. If its growth continued, by harvest time the clusters would be three, perhaps four, times the size of wheat or any other grain he could imagine. And with the projected futures prices running seven to eleven cents per bushel ahead of wheat, the prospects for a very successful year were enormous. He fumbled for a word to describe what he felt and all he could think of was joy.

As always, when he was in the fields, near the grain, he felt serene, confident, even joyous. Still, there were those times when he thought it was too good to be true. Somewhere, deep inside, he had these twinges of unease. He'd begun to feel the way he did when he was around fundamentalists who were one hundred and ten percent certain that Jesus would save them from any hardship. Or Ralph Butterworth when he was lit up on some chamber of commerce scheme. It was too perfect, too joyous, too serene to be real. And yet, here were the plants with their lush clusters of grain. He needed to believe in this grand sun rising in his firmament, he needed this windfall to put his farm back on a profitable track, and so he pushed down those thoughts. He let Ralph Butterworth's mindless boosterism have its way as he turned again to his marvelous crop. Only a fluke of nature, some unanticipated wild weather, or an unforeseen catastrophe in the economy stood between him and solvency. The farmer's dream was about to be realized.

As Sandy turned again to the grain, he felt that perhaps his positive feelings out here in the fields were some kind of psychological trick, but he had to admit that, trick or not, it was a future he needed to believe in. He walked along lost in thought, humming that tune that had first come to his lips a month or so ago. But it had taken on a fecund, almost earthy quality. Had he realized what he was doing, he would doubtless have laughed at himself, for Myrle had told him often enough that he couldn't carry a tune in a bucket.

With some reluctance, he headed up to the house for lunch. The past while Sandy had been in a euphoric mood that sometimes baffled him and delighted Myrle. She'd just come home from grocery shopping and was engrossed in putting things in the cupboard. Sandy came up behind her and kissed her on the back of the neck. The gesture surprised her, and maybe him as well.

"You're in a good mood today," she said. Actually, it wasn't just today, she thought. The mood on the farm had improved markedly since they'd planted the seed. The threatening cloud under which farm families lived had lifted and begun to dissipate with the prospects of a bumper crop and the financial rewards that would come with it.

"I just noticed something this morning," Sandy said. "I was down in the lower field and the grain is actually expanding. There's more plants than the seed could account for. It's expanding past the limits of the fields. We're gonna have an even bigger crop than we thought." Sandy sat down at the table and watched his wife putting away groceries. "It's really kinda hard to believe, isn't it? After all the troubles we've had."

"Let's just not think about that," Myrle said, turning to look at Sandy. "Let's just be thankful things are going as they are."

"I'll second that," Sandy said. He rose from the table and walked over to the refrigerator. As he opened the door, he began absently humming the flowing little melody that had so often in these past weeks found its way to his lips. Myrle turned again from the cupboard, a can of coffee in her hand. Setting the can on the counter, she stepped closer to Sandy as he stood peering into the depths of the refrigerator.

"What are you humming?" she asked. "Hmmmm?"

"What is that song you're humming?"

Sandy stood with his hand on the refrigerator door and stared blankly at Myrle. "I don't know. Was I humming something?"

"Yes, yes, you were. Just now when you opened the door you were humming this little refrain. It sounded like one of those new-agey tunes. You know, the kind that might be called "Woodland Solitude" or something like that." She stared sharply at him. "Come to think of it, I think I heard you humming it yesterday too."

"Aw, come on, you're kidding," he said, a you're-pulling-my-leg grin on his face. He couldn't imagine what she meant. But Myrle was serious; it was obvious from the set of her jaw, the clarity of her grey eyes.

"And what's more, you're not the only one. I heard Larry Hodgens humming it at the Shop'n'Sav not an hour ago." Larry was farming the old Wilton place over on Baxter Road and he'd just gotten his allotment of seed in the ground the week before. With the gentle rain they'd had at the beginning of the week, his shoots would be up about now.

"There he was, standing in the checkout line waitin' for Ethel to ring him up, humming that same melody."

"Damned if I know," he said, scratching his head. "I don't know where it came from. Hell, I didn't even realize I was doin' it. Musta been on the radio or somethin'." The look on Myrle's face said, "very strange", but she went back to her groceries.

Late the next morning, Billy Smollet came in the lane in the Agway truck with a load of fertilizer and a few other things for Sandy. As they unloaded the truck, Billy mentioned that he'd just dropped off a delivery of the new seed at Henry Wilson's place.

Sandy put down the sack of fertilizer and straightened up. "Henry got his seed already, didn't he? I thought he was the first one after me."

"Yep, that's a fact," said Billy, pausing in his labors.

"How could he get more seed?" Sandy asked, his brows drawing together.

"Well, ever'body else got theirs an' so now it's just available to anybody as wants to buy it. Tell the truth, I made a couple of deliveries the past few days."

Sandy stared at Billy, the puzzlement wrinkling his face. "How much seed?" Sandy asked, his voice rising nearly to a squeak.

"Twelve thousand pounds," Billy replied.

"Why that's more 'n enough to plant his whole damn place. An' he's already got . . . what, eighty acres planted?"

"Yup, I ask't him, Hen, I says, how come you want so much seed? Said he's gonna plow up his whole place 'n' plant ever' acre in this here new seed." Billy shrugged. "Seems kinda like a good idea to me. Price is up an' it's bringin' more 'n anything else he could raise over there, 'ceptin' maybe marrywanna." Sandy rubbed his jaw and thought for a moment. The idea struck him as strange, that he would plow up crops already up and growing and plant this one seed. Aside from the Welbors, most of the farmers in the valley shied away from one crop farming. But the thought kept on moving and within seconds, Sandy was nodding.

"Yeh, I guess you're right on that one, Billy. A man's got to look after himself and strike while the iron's hot." Having spoken the words, it made perfect sense to Sandy.

Later, at lunch, he mentioned Billy's remarks to Myrle, just in passing, as though it was of no particular interest. They were sitting at the table, bowls of soup in front of them. At Sandy's words, Myrle looked up, her soup spoon halfway to her mouth. "Henry bought that much seed? He'd have to plow up everything else he planted to use up that much seed." Now it was Sandy's turn to stop, spoon halfway to his mouth.

"Yeh," he said, "that's right. Figured he'd go for broke as long as prices are up an' all." He looked at Myrle, expecting her to agree with that line of thought.

"But if he plows up what he's already planted, he's going to lose all that he invested and that doesn't make any sense. That's just plain nuts!"

"Yeh," he said, a dim flicker of candle light emerging from the darkness that marked his countenance. "I hadn't thought about that aspect of it. Well, I did think about it " He let his words fade away.

"Sandy Collins, what are you saying? How on earth could you not think about that and if you did, how could you possibly agree with it? Just because you're a farmer doesn't mean you have to go all soft in the head when it comes to figures."

Sandy scratched his head. "I don't know," he said, "it just seemed so right and sensible when Billy was tellin' me. I didn't give it another thought. After all the hard times an' all," he finished lamely. He dropped his spoon clattering on the table, a bewildered look on his face.

Myrle stared at him, the unvoiced "what" ringing clear as a bell in the quiet kitchen.

"I just realized that when Billy left, I started thinking about plowing up the potatoes and planting some more seed."

"My god, Sandy, you are getting weak in the head. Plow up the potatoes!" They sat staring at one another, neither able to formulate a thought, the silence marred only by the clock on the shelf over the refrigerator. Sandy shifted in his chair, grown suddenly uncomfortable, and realized that a hard little grain of resentment had formed as he looked at Myrle.

The next morning, Myrle drove into town. When she came back, she went looking for Sandy first thing and found him in the barn. "I talked to Lola at the post office," she said without preliminaries. "I asked her about Henry plowing up his crops to plant more of this grain and she said, yes, Tess was in complaining about how Henry all of a sudden got it in his head and nothing she said could change his mind." She paused and looked hard at Sandy. There was a brittleness about her that he'd never noticed before.

"Well, I can see ," Sandy began, but she cut him off.

"That's not all," she said. "Seems like Ted Lewis, Tommy Barlow, George, a couple of the others have all come to the same conclusion. They're all converting every square inch over to the grain." Sandy turned away from her steady gaze and for several moments, neither spoke.

"Susie Barlow left Tom yesterday. Said she wouldn't be party to this. Mary Lewis and Barb Kovach are threatening to leave too. May even be gone by now."

He turned back to face her, spreading his hands in supplication, as if that could somehow make things right again. But before he could speak, she broke the silence.

"There's more." Her tone was hard and clinical as though she was a district attorney building a case. "A lot of the townsfolk have bought seed and are plowing up their yards to get a crop in. Seems like the prospects of quick profits have driven everybody insane." She paused and stared at Sandy. "Tess told me that a couple of reporters from *The Ledger* were nosing around asking questions. That guy, Larry Cummings, who writes the sidebar column poked around a couple of days ago, but after talking to some of the men, decided there was no story. Next day it seems a cub reporter – Sally Bellamy, I think Tess said her name is – talked to the women and then went to talk to the men and thought there was something weird going on. Nothing's been in the paper yet, but Tess said this Sally's going to write something." Sandy averted his eyes, staring at the barn floor, pushing some strands of straw with his foot.

"This obsession is going to lead to trouble," she snapped, her eyes striking fire in the dimness of the barn. "Wasn't one-crop farming one of the main reasons you and all the rest objected to industrial farming all these years?" Sandy nodded uncertainly, his mouth ajar as though he meant to say something. "Well, why are they all plowing up everything to plant this one crop now?"

"Well, maybe it just makes sense now," said Sandy. "Maybe "

"What's going on here, Sandy? What is it?" Sandy shrugged his shoulders and averted his eyes again. She was making him feel like a bad little boy and he didn't like it one bit.

"Look, Myrle," Sandy said, stepping forward to grasp her hands. "I've been giving this a lot of thought and I'm beginning to think maybe they're right."

Myrle pulled away in shock. "Sandy, have you been listening to me? Have you heard anything I said?"

"Of course, of course, I have. But maybe we should cash in too." He saw the look on her face, stunned as if he'd slapped her, and that hard little pebble of resentment he'd noticed yesterday when they talked began to grow. "In only one season we could be out of debt and "

Myrle yanked her hands from his grasp and backed away from him. Her eyes desperate, she turned her gaze to the stack of seed. Sandy saw the hatred. A jolt of pain shot through him and then, quickly, a razor-edged resentment. "Myrle, listen, . . ," he began, but she turned and ran from the barn.

For a moment he stood and stared after her, uncontrollable emotions rattling through him one after another. Soon though, he settled down, resolving that everything would turn out alright. He turned back to his work, humming to himself as he climbed up onto the tractor and drove out to the potato fields. Still humming, he surveyed the fifty acres of lush, dark green plants. He knew what he meant to do; he'd thought about it and thought about it and the time to act had come.

Turning back to the house, he saw the pickup headed his way, a plume of dust rising into the cloudless sky. Well, he thought, here comes trouble. He popped the tractor into neutral and swiveled in his seat as the pickup came to a halt beside the big machine. As the dust cleared, Myrle got out of the truck and came around to stand beside the huge rear tire. She looked up at Sandy and he could see that she'd been crying. The realization pinched his conscience, but it made him angry too. Myrle had been dragging her feet, trying to hold him back from the beginning and he'd had about enough. He loved her, he assured himself, but this had all gotten out of hand. He had to break free of her negativity. He stared down at her, his eyes hard, his jaw clenched.

"Sandy, I'm asking you not to do this. Please stop this nonsense," Myrle shouted over the throb of the idling tractor.

More of the same, thought Sandy, more obstructions and just plain thick-headedness. His face hardened against her even more, and for an instant he thought how much easier it all would be if she were dead.

"Stop this insanity. I don't know what's happening here, but you men all seem to have gone insane. It's madness to plow up the potatoes when they're almost ready to harvest. Please," she pleaded, tears appearing on her cheeks, "please stop this and come back to the house so we can talk."

"You're interfering," Sandy said, his face hard and determined. Cords of muscle stood out on his neck and his knuckles were clenched on the steering wheel. "Go back to the house and tend to your woman's work. I've got things to do."

"If you don't stop this right now, I'm leaving," Myrle cried at him, tears streaming freely down her contorted face.

In answer, Sandy turned away and slammed the tractor into gear. He pulled forward over the first row of potatoes and dropped the gang plow as he hit the throttle. He'd make short work of the potatoes and have the new crop in by dark. He turned for a moment to see Myrle standing by the pickup, her face a mask of sadness. All the starch was gone out of her, and she looked as if she were about to collapse in the dust like a Raggedy Ann doll. By the time Sandy made it to the end of the field and came around for his second pass, the pickup was gone. He looked back toward the house, but he couldn't see the truck and the matter went out of his head as he concentrated on the work at hand, that persistent melody meandering through his mind. But somewhere down deep, where his conscience wouldn't notice, a ripple of pain splashed against his heart.

It was nearly dark when Sandy parked the tractor in front of the barn. His joints ached and his kidneys and rear hurt from the vibration of the big machine. He'd plowed, disced, and replanted the potato field and he was filled with a righteous sense of accomplishment.

As he slipped down from the tractor, he noticed the pickup under the tree near the house. The house was dark, no light in the kitchen. Maybe Myrle was somewhere visiting or doing errands. Sandy stretched, trying to get the kinks out of his muscles as he walked stiff and bowlegged up the walk. He glanced around; the car was nowhere in sight.

As soon as he stepped into the kitchen, he knew she was gone. No supper waited warming on the stove, no sign of welcome, only an unmistakable emptiness. He was alone. Sandy slumped into a chair. Shock at the realization of her departure was followed rapidly by a profound sense of sadness, which soon gave way to anger and a rising feeling of betrayal.

He made a sandwich and opened a bottle of beer and after he'd eaten, he went out on the porch and sat in the rocker. As he looked out over the farmyard, past the barn, out to the fields of grain hastening toward ripeness he felt better. Out in the open, there was a sense of rectitude in the natural order of things, so he slept that night in the barn. All night long he dreamt of music, of a swelling upsurge of sound, dramatic and invigorating, that seemed to carry him along with it.

He awoke with the rising sun and didn't even think of Myrle until he went in the house to get some coffee. Somewhere behind the galling resentment at Myrle's flight, there was the irritation of a small nugget of sadness. He forced all thoughts of Myrle from his mind and for the rest of the morning, he busied himself around the barn.

Toward noon, he saw Al Templeton's station wagon with the U.S. Mail signs plastered along its sides at the mailbox. Sandy wandered out the lane and as he approached the mailbox, his neighbors, Jane and Ed Kestler pulled up beside him in their faded pickup.

"Howdy, Sandy," they called to him from the cab, their youngest, Fred, on the front seat between them. Sandy stared at the truck, heaped high with furniture and tools, everything tied down as though they were reenacting a scene from *Grapes of Wrath*. The two older boys, Ben and Tommy, were perched high on top of the load and Sandy waved to them.

"Hey, Ed, Jane," said Sandy, his gaze slowly returning to the occupants of the truck. "What's goin' on?"

"We're leavin', Sandy," said Ed. "Just wanted to say goodbye."
"Leavin'?" Sandy pushed his cap back and scratched his head.

"Yep. Jane convinced me that somethin' isn't right here anymore and we're gettin' out." "Not right at all," echoed Jane.

"I'm sorry to hear that. I think you're makin' a big mistake. You should stay around and cash in on this thing."

"Ed thought that too, but I talked him out of it," said Jane. Ed sat behind the wheel looking sheepish, as though he'd like to agree with Sandy, but needed to agree with his wife. Women again, thought Sandy. "So, we're leaving," said Jane, while Ed just sat and nodded his head. "Good luck to you, Sandy." Ed touched his cap to Sandy as he set the truck in motion and pulled out into the road.

"Well, I'll be damned," said Sandy as he stood watching the pickup drive off into the distance. He turned back to the mailbox, took the mail out, and riffled through the stack of envelopes. Mostly bills, as usual, he thought in disgust. As he turned to head back down the lane, he saw the glint of sunlight on the windshield of an on-coming vehicle. He watched the play of light and soon made out the green and white of Art Wolper's pickup. The truck drew to a stop beside him.

Art was at the wheel with Charlie Barnum riding shotgun. "Mornin', Sandy," they said in unison as Sandy stepped over to the passenger door. Art and Charlie had been the last of the valley farmers to receive their allotment from Genecorps, and their crop was a good two months behind everyone else's. Genecorps had had difficulty getting their seed to them, an unforeseen glitch in the gene modification process had delayed delivery of the last batch. Once that batch had come out, however, there had been an abundance of seed available. The two had quickly developed an underdog attitude and their complaints were well known across the valley.

"You heard about what's happenin' in town?" asked Art. "How folks are plowin' up their yards an' all to plant this new grain?"

"Myrle told me," said Sandy.

"She's still with you, then?" asked Charlie. Sandy shook his head. "She took off yesterday." "A lot of women folks have left," said Art.

"Good riddance to 'em," snarled Charlie. "Most of 'em are just plain obstinate, a pain in the ass. They're no loss, I'd say." He turned to Art and winked. "Some of 'em had to be put outta the way," he added. Sandy saw the look on their faces and for an instant he thought of the way he felt about Myrle when she objected to plowing up the potatoes. He wondered what Art meant exactly. Had Art gotten rid of Gladys? And how had he done that? For a moment, the questions dominated his thoughts, but slowly they faded away.

"You know, Sandy," said Art, leaning across the seat toward him, "Charlie and I ain't been too happy 'bout the way things worked out here. You 'n' some o' the others got crops comin' in way ahead o' ours, so you're bound to make more money than us."

Sandy nodded. He'd already put a good bit of thought into the nature of things; he'd even wondered whether Genecorps had deliberately planned it that way or if it was just a fluke in their process. "I know, I know, but it was the luck of the draw. I was just lucky, I guess."

"Yeh, well, that's all well 'n' good amongst us farmers. Nothin' we can do about that.

But his business of sellin' seed to the town folks is another matter."

Charlie nodded in agreement. "When I heard folks was rototillin' their yards to plant this grain, I drove into town to have a look, and sure as hell, that's what they're up to. Rototillers busy on ever' block."

"Ain't a square inch o' lawn left in Summerfield way I hear it," said Art. "Why even the lawn in front o' the post office and the VFW been plowed up."

"That ain't right," said Charlie, his face pinched and hard. "No, it ain't," agreed Sandy.

"Wasn't it supposed to be this new grain's for us? For us farmers so's we can maybe crawl outta the hole they pushed us in these past years? Ain't that the way it was supposed to be?" asked Art. Charlie nodded, Sandy right with him. "Way I see it, Tom Herman at the Agway's the cause of this. He's the one doles out the grain 'n' he oughtn't to be sellin' to folks that ain't farmers."

"All this craziness is gonna run the price down 'n' we're the ones gonna be holdin' the bag again."

"You're right sure enough," said Sandy, "but what are you drivin' at? What are you plannin' to do?"

"Maybe it's time we had a little talk with Tom Herman," said Charlie.

Sandy tugged his cap down over his eyes and squinted at the two in the cab. "That makes sense," he said, nodding his head slowly. "I'll go get my truck and meet you at the Agway."

Charlie and Art smiled without humor and pulled away as Sandy set out down the lane.

Twenty minutes later Sandy drove up to the Agway and swung around to park beside the green and white pickup near the loading dock. He saw immediately that matters had escalated to a very unfriendly situation. Art and Charlie stood belligerently on the ground gesturing at Tom, their voices loud and hard. The anger on the faces of the farmers was mirrored in their postures. Tom was red in the face, his own voice loud and edging toward loss of control.

"I got every right in the world to sell seed to whoever's got the money to buy it," he said, thrusting his finger at the two on the ground. Several other farmers and a few townsfolk had quietly joined Art and Charlie in front of the loading dock, all of them watching the proceedings closely. "And you," he shouted, "have no right to be telling me what I can and can't do."

Sandy walked toward them, the tension in the air sent a shiver up his back. The on-lookers had begun to choose sides and everyone seemed to be waiting for something to set them off. An image of on-coming disaster suddenly loomed up before Sandy and he hastened toward the crowd.

"I've had enough of this shit," screamed Art and dashed back to his truck. Some of the other farmers in the crowd had begun shouting at Tom while a couple of the townspeople loudly voiced their support. Sandy stopped dead in his tracks as Art rejoined Charlie, his shotgun in his hands. He wanted to do something to stop the terrible course of events, but he felt leaden, as though he was caught in something inevitable and unchangeable. He watched the barrel of Art's shotgun rise toward Tom's chest and in the next instant the noon air was rocked by the blast of the gun. Tom went flying in a spray of blood and collapsed against the wall.

After that nothing made sense. Sandy ran back to his truck and tore out of the parking lot. He sped out onto Main Street as behind him he heard shouting, screaming, and then the eruption of more gunfire. He hadn't gone more than a few blocks before people with guns began to appear on the street. He heard shots from the migrant workers' houses down by the tracks and then more shouting from the shady side streets of the Woodlawn section of town. The whole town appeared to be a powder keg that had just been waiting for a spark, a spark provided by Art's shotgun.

Just ahead of him, he saw Eddie MacKenzie who owned the Silver Circle Grille and a few of his regulars from the bar. They were in the middle of the street with guns, looking his way with what looked to him like evil intent. Sandy spun the wheel of the truck and shot down Chestnut, but that didn't work either. Everywhere he looked, people rushed out into the streets carrying pistols, rifles, and shotguns, shouting at one another and gesturing wildly. A bullet crashed through his windshield and another thunked like an angry bumblebee into the metal of the cab.

Off to the left, Sandy heard someone yell: "There's Collins!" Several more bullets smashed through the rear window. He tore down an alleyway lined with garages. He hadn't gotten but halfway along the alley when Ralph Butterworth appeared in front of him.

Butterworth had a rifle and he swung it up and fired at Sandy, the bullet punched another hole in the windshield. Swerving desperately to avoid the fire, the truck smashed into a utility pole. Scrambling out of the wreck, he heard more yelling and a fresh burst of gunfire from behind. With danger at either end of the alley, Sandy ran in a crouch rapidly crossing what had once been lawn, now a bed of new green shoots.

With little choice, he dashed into the kitchen of the house. The door was wide open, a lunch set out on the table as if the family was just ready to sit down to eat, but no one was there. Frantic, Sandy made his way up to the attic where he could keep some kind of watch. He realized the danger should any of the gunmen search the house, but matters outside had become so chaotic and random that safety had become an illusion.

Sandy hid in the attic, now and again peering out. In the street, several bodies lay motionless on the pavement. There had been sporadic shooting and much yelling and screaming all afternoon. Toward evening, however, silence settled over the neighborhood. The gunfire had moved north and now seemed to be coming from the area out along the railroad to the east. Sandy waited until the sun was low in the sky before making his way carefully down through the empty house and out onto the street. Keeping as best he could to the shelter of yards and shrubbery, he hurried toward the edge of town.

Finally, as the sun slipped down behind the ridge, he reached an old garage that served as an engine repair shop, the last structure at the edge of the fields. Crouching behind the dilapidated building, Sandy surveyed the scene before him. The wide main street passed into the state route with the wide shoulders and the drainage ditches beyond. All he had to do was cross that open space and get through the drainage ditch into the grain fields beyond. From there he should be able to reach his place by full dark.

Nothing moved in the street. The occasional sound of gunfire and engines, of vehicles moving, came from back in town. Gathering his nerve about him he stepped out into the street and ran, crouched over to lower his profile. He hadn't made the center line before he heard someone shout his name. He knew that voice, that malevolent growl, as belonging to Dick Welbor. A rifle cracked and a bullet sizzed by his head. Several more slugs pinged into the pavement as he ran full tilt across the shoulder and into the ditch. Out of sight of the shooters, he ran doubled over, along the debris and trash–littered bottom of the ditch.

Soon there were more shouts, although the shooting stopped, and then the sound of several trucks prowling the roadway above him. Night was coming and night would be his ally, but for the moment, a more immediate friend covered his retreat. He slipped into the grain that grew right into the ditch. The four foot height of the grain hid him as his enemies patrolled the road above, shining their headlights down where he'd been. He could hear the Welbors yelling back and forth, and several other voices he didn't recognize. Here amongst the grain, he felt safe and soon a now familiar melody rose in his mind.

He was in Will Cashman's field, he knew, and if he headed off to the southwest, he could cross the railroad tracks and make it home by dark. If he wasn't discovered. When he reached the tracks, he took great care, despite the dark, to crawl across the open space, before running again into the grain on the other side.

It took nearly an hour longer than he'd expected to reach his farm. As he crossed his own field toward the house, he saw that his plan was already thwarted. Several pickups, their lights glowing above the waving grain, were driving down the lane. Moving along in the grain, Sandy edged up toward the farm buildings where he heard voices. Rising up enough to peer over the grain, he saw half a dozen men with rifles searching, flashlight beams darting this way and that.

Moving back into the grain, Sandy felt safer. Safe, this evening, was becoming an increasingly relative term. Exhausted, he sprawled amidst the stalks and contemplated his next move. There weren't many choices. Out beyond the grain, he heard the angry voices of the Welbors and their henchmen. They might at any time, Sandy knew, begin a systematic search of the fields, and then they would find the track of his progress in the bent and broken stalks.

Sandy rested for a while before moving on, away from his own farm, heading for the high ground where there would be less likelihood of pursuit. He made his way through the field to the lane between his land and Jim Hendron's. Crossing from field to field, he saw the lights of vehicles a half mile or so off, heading in his direction. There was a glow of light from Jim's farm buildings, so Sandy kept on moving as fast as he could.

The tension and demands of the day were taking their toll on Sandy; he hadn't eaten since morning, and he wasn't used to running for his life. His nerves were frazzled and he was exhausted. It took a long time to reach the rising ground where the cultivated fields gave way to scrub and new-growth timber. Stumbling and clawing his way up the slope, he reached the old, line shack, approaching it carefully, even though there was no sign of human presence. He thought momentarily of spending the night there, but the trail leading up to the shack was still passable to pickups, rendering the site vulnerable. Inside the single room, he found two musty old blankets on the floor amidst a clutter of beer bottles and cans, cigarette packs, butts, and used condoms. He rolled the blankets and took them with him. Moving as fast as his fatigue would allow, he climbed steadily, emerging finally onto the promontory overlooking the valley. Carefully, he made his way out onto the great, flat boulder and stared into the night. Below, he saw lights, most of the farms in full illumination. A smoky, orange pall hung over Summerfield where fires burned in several parts of town. The Agway, he saw, was reduced to a smoldering pile of embers in the night. The night wasn't still. The lights of cars and trucks moved along the country lanes. Here and there were occasional bursts of gunfire, flat little pops, and even at that distance, he caught bits of shouting on the evening breeze.

Sandy edged his way off the boulder, back where a cleft in the rock offered a sheltered niche. He still heard the music in his head, but up here it sounded muffled and far away. Spreading one of the tattered blankets on the sparse grass, he lay down, covering himself with the other. It had been years since he'd last been here, with Myrle when they were newlyweds. They'd come for a picnic, and he'd made love to her on this very spot. It was, he realized suddenly, the first time in nearly twelve hours that he'd thought of Myrle. I've been kinda busy, he thought morosely, as exhaustion swept him into unconsciousness.

Sandy jolted awake several times during the night and always he heard in the distance flat little pops that sounded like someone puncturing balloons. Now, however, aside from the far-off chatter of the engine, all was still.

He'd heard the engine cough and start. As the engine revved up, it began to move across the morning landscape. Tracking the sound, Sandy realized what he was hearing. It was Greg Thompson's crop duster accelerating along the gravel runway in his lower pasture. The sound told him that the plane was now airborne, heading east. With the sun in his eyes, Sandy could not at first make out the little yellow plane. But Greg – or whoever was at the controls – was moving south now, heading into a climb that taxed the plane's engine. The plane was a barely perceptible speck in the sky, like an insect. The climb went on and on until the plane had risen high above the town, the valley, even the promontory. Then it turned over and dropped into a precipitate dive, the engine screaming as the plane plunged earthward. Sandy watched, spellbound, expecting Greg at any moment to pull out of the dive. But the dive went on and on until Sandy realized that there could be but one outcome. The little plane screamed into the earth just east of the feedlot and exploded in a ball of flame. Oily black smoke roiled and billowed up into the morning sky. All was silent. The sky was empty save for the black smoke from the crash, the thin wisps of smoke from town and from the farms that had burned during the night. And the eagle, the same one, Sandy thought, that had been flying around the day this all started.

Sandy stared out at the valley, at his home, and he knew deep down inside that he was alone. The absolute silence of the morning told him that he was the last man standing. He let his gaze sweep out to Indian Ridge and work its way back over the valley to the foot of the hills on which he stood. Slowly, amidst all that green, he saw something he hadn't seen before. The entire valley, all the open space, every bit of unforested, undeveloped land, was covered in rich, deep green. Most places, the green undulated like waves on the ocean, the grain mature, ready for harvest; some places it was a brighter, younger green. But everywhere, the grain had begun to grow over farm lanes, open spaces, even the railroad tracks. Again, he heard the music, but this morning it was strong and clear. The sound swelled in triumph, a rising anthem that reminded him of the old *Victory at Sea* theme. In horror, Sandy continued to stare at all the grain, waving in the light morning breeze. His head fell into his hands as he realized that Dr. Scandor had been right. It hadn't taken a full year, and the valley was unrecognizable. Here was our grand, new future!

II

Boys and Girls, Men and Women

Secret Smelteries of Backwoods Pennsylvania

"You'd better stop and ask," she said, careful not to sound as though she were nagging. They'd driven nearly thirty miles out of the way before he finally consented to stop at a run-down old gas station. By that time Danny and his brother and sister had lapsed into resigned silence, having long since despaired of getting there soon.

As Danny's father pulled in beside the pumps the children grew alert and began clamoring for candy. Already annoyed at his inability to locate the Lost Bear Campgrounds, he was in no mood for their begging. Had it not been for the intercession of his wife, he would have made them stay in the car.

"Oh, Frank, let them get some candy. It's been a long ride. Besides, you could get me a Tastykake krimpet. I'm hungry too."

So it was that Danny found himself standing in the dirty, greasy service station staring into a glass candy case trying to choose from among the array of candies. All manner of penny candy, boxes of Good'N'Plenty, Baby Ruth, Mounds, Milky Way, Tootsie Roll pops, and, of course, strings of red licorice. The station, standing by itself along the two-lane blacktop, was a dilapidated, flat-roofed building with one repair bay and a gravel apron. Two old men in greasy coveralls stood behind the candy counter. Outside, the towering forest lent a premature darkness to the day. Danny had a momentary feeling of familiarity, of *déjà vu* - although he wouldn't learn that term for many years to come. He looked at the faded green paint, the smudged and scratched glass, and shook off the feeling, the matter of choosing candy taking his full attention.

Back in the car, a box of Good'n'Plentys in hand, Danny's thoughts turned again to those two old men in the service station. In their greasy clothes, their hair and skin looking almost as dingy as their coveralls, he realized that they reminded him of two other very similar old men he'd seen in a run-down old service station perched on the side of a road in a sea of corn. That had been five or six years ago, and those old men had spoken with the heavy Pennsylvania- Dutch accents that were so prevalent around home. As with the station they'd just left, his father had stopped for gas and he and Bobby and Jeannie, who was little more than a baby then, had gone in to pick out candy. "Licwisch," Jeannie said, "I want licwisch."

They'd stood in front of the candy counter peering in at the shelves of treats awaiting their selection. On top of the counter were an array of greasy tools, a tattered, black-edged receipt book, some dusty old maps, and a stack of nondescript pamphlets. Danny had been contemplating the candy when he'd noticed the fuzzy grey photo on the cover of the top booklet.

Unwittingly, as if he'd fallen under a spell, Danny reached out and picked up one of the pamphlets. The photo was indistinct, but not so much so that he could not recognize the image as a stone chimney rising out of an old building. *Secret Smelteries of Backwoods Pennsylvania*, he read, the letters black on the buff cover. As if in a trance he began paging through the book. The printing was strictly amateur – even Danny could see that – and scattered through the book were more fuzzy photos of stone buildings and stone ruins overgrown with brush.

"What have you got there, son?" his father asked. Danny turned to look at him, holding out the pamphlet. He had the feeling in that instant of something falling into place, as of a gear or cog in some great machine.

As his father began to flip through the pamphlet, Danny knew that this crudely printed little book would become their polestar for years to come. Without even half trying, he could see the five of them, his father in the lead, eager, impatient; his mother, anxious to please; Bobbie, quiet as usual; and Jeannie, crying because she couldn't keep up. And, of course, himself, plodding reluctantly down some forest trail where the brush grew over the path and brambles grasped at the passerby. And on the path itself, the famous rocks of Pennsylvania seeking to trip and unbalance them at every step.

Since then, they'd trudged miles and miles through the forests in search of smelteries long since gone to ruin. Nestled in hidden vales or tucked away in the lee of mountain ridges lay the buildings and the ruins. Sometimes they were entire sites, the buildings intact, although overgrown, just beginning their decsent into ruination and wildness. Other times they were well along in the process, mere piles of rubble entangled in brambles and wild grape vines with saplings growing profusely from the floor where once men sweated and struggled to wrest pure metal from stone and rock.

Danny thought of how it had all come to pass, just as he'd seen it that day in that other old gas station in the corn. Even now the pamphlet lay on the dashboard of the car. Over the years it had guided the family to numerous sites in the wooded mountains and valleys of central Pennsylvania. The author had numbered the sites and each, as it was visited, had garnered a circle in red around the number.

The slow accumulation of circles pleased his parents. They annoyed Danny; to him, each red circle represented time wasted. It was his opinion that if you'd seen one smeltery ruin, you'd seen them all.

Before the pamphlet came into their lives, the family vacations took them on trips down the Skyline Drive, to the Finger Lakes, to Gettysburg, to the Jersey shore. All that, however, had given way to the dedicated investigation of smeltery sites. It was as though his father and mother had been drifting, directionless, when the *Secret Smelteries* booklet fell into their hands It brought focus and purpose to the family vacations, an order the children could neither see nor appreciate.

The matter puzzled Danny; he'd long ago lost interest in traipsing through the Pennsylvania forests in search of yet another fallen-down industrial site from some obscure past. He could not fathom what motivated his parents and he often regretted the day he'd picked up the booklet. In fact, he'd grown to hate it.

Over the years, his reward on these family adventures had been mosquito bites, poison ivy, scratches from brambles, and sprains and bruises from the rocky trails they'd hiked. Now that he was thirteen, He'd begun to experience moods and desires he didn't understand, impelling him toward situations that had never before interested him. He wanted their vacations to take the family to places where there were people and shops and things to see and do - Atlantic City or Avalon or maybe even Williamsburg; some place alive. But his parents remained single-minded in their pursuit of secret smelteries, and he had no choice but to go along.

When they finally found the Lost Bear Campgrounds, the sun was slipping down behind the distant hills. Lost somewhere in the wilds of the Endless Mountains, somewhere in that great Pennsylvania rectangle east of the Allegheny and north of the West Branch of the Susquehanna, the muddy river, the great crooked river. It was exactly what Danny had thought it would be. Somewhere in that vast expanse of wilderness, where the trees were plentiful and the roads were not, was this miserable clearing referred to as a campground.

A dusty lane led past a camp office, toilet and washroom facilities, an open-air shower, and a meadow of parched grass for ball games. Some of the fancier campgrounds they'd stayed at had a concession stand and one even had an amphitheater where they'd shown movies after dark. But that had been a very fancy one; Lost Bear wasn't in that category.

As the family car pulled into the clearing in the woods, marked by a wooden stake on which the number 13 had been painted in red, Danny's heart sank. The signs were all bad; a pile of stones that would serve as a grille and beside it a rusted trash barrel and a stack of half rotted wood. This was going to be some vacation.

By the time they'd situated the trailer and unloaded the car, day had given way to the utter darkness of night in the Pennsylvania woods. There'd been no time to go out and explore the camp. Aside from a trip to the toilets and washrooms, there'd been no opportunity to see anything.

Danny lay in his sleeping bag listening to the crickets, wishing he was back home. At least there he would have had something to look forward to the next day. Far off in the woods, barely audible, an owl hooted. He felt trapped.

If anything, the Lost Bear Campground looked better under the slanting red rays of the setting sun than it did in the full light of morning. Breakfast over, Danny felt a pressing need to get away from his parents. His father was still out of sorts and defensive over his navigational failure and his mother was in one of her sickeningly sweet, look-how-happy-we-all-are moods. He didn't feel like investigating the campground just yet; all there was to see anyway was the woods and the dusty meadow where the grass was dried up and brown.

He slouched against the trailer, kicking at a root when he looked up to see his father staring at him. The look on his father's face was as clear as the headlines of a big city newspaper. It was his you'd-better-shape-up look, and it made Danny angry. You ought to look in a mirror and see your own reflection, he thought.

Danny turned away and headed for the car, moving as though he'd just thought of something urgent he needed to do. He climbed into the back of the car and reached under the front seat. Carefully, he pulled out the great bulk of the Sears Roebuck catalog, which he'd hidden there before their departure. He plopped it onto his lap and opened the book. He'd always loved the catalog, especially the Christmas book with its pages and pages of toys. He liked too to look at the camping equipment, the BB guns and deer rifles, and the engineer's boots. But lately, he'd found himself turning more and more frequently to the lingerie section, lingering over the ladies and girls in their underwear.

Danny studied each picture trying to imagine each of the models freed of the restraints of brassieres and corsets. The pictures excited him, as though a million insects were scurrying about on his skin. He turned the page and stared at the girls, many of them little more than his age, modeling the training bras. The phrase made him chuckle out loud as he wondered why those little girl titties needed to be trained. For a moment he stared intently at the blonde girl in the lower right corner of the page, the smile on her face suggesting the pleasure she derived from being "trained" by her bra. I'd like to train you, Danny thought, licking his lips, not at all certain what he might have done had the opportunity presented itself.

As he turned to the next page where the full-figured women modeled full body armor, his focus faltered, and he sensed something intruding on his privacy. His head snapped up as he slammed the catalog shut.

"Watcha doin', Danny?" Jeannie said, peering in at him. "Why were you looking at ladies' underwear?"

"I. . . I wasn't," said Danny, his voice a trifle too loud, wavering for control. He avoided Jeannie's eyes.

"Yes, you were," said Jeannie, eyeing her brother with all the scrutiny that a seven-year-old could muster.

"No! No, I wasn't," insisted Danny. "I was trying to find the BB-gun pages." "Hmmph," she said in a grown-up way. "Mom wants you."

A few minutes later, a large jug in each hand, Danny was on his way for water. There were several standpipes scattered about the campgrounds and the one closest to number thirteen was out near the meadow. As Danny trudged along the dusty lane, he peered at the tents and travel trailers scattered about the woods. The people he saw were all old, his parents age or even older. Nobody my age, he thought, kicking stones down the lane.

Rounding the last clump of brush, he approached the faucet where several people waited to fill their own jugs. The last person in line, much to his surprise, was a girl about his age. She was deep in conversation with the burly, grey-haired man ahead of her. As Danny came up behind her, she turned to look at him and said, "Hi!" She stared openly at him with big, inquisitive, blue eyes. "Did you just arrive?" she asked. "I haven't seen you here before." Danny looked at her, but the expression on her face disconcerted him and he looked down. He saw she wore shorts, that her legs were long and slender and very tan, and that on her feet she wore buckskin moccasins with bright beadwork on the toes.

"Yeh," replied Danny, eyes downcast as though he were talking to her feet. "We got here around dark last night." He looked up at her face, at her clear eyes, the pig-tail braids that hung down to her shoulders. Standing there in front of him, her eyes so openly examining him, Danny felt ill at ease. He still felt tingly from looking at the Sears catalog and the embarrassment of being caught at it by his little sister. And now this inquisitive girl was staring so brazenly at him. "Wha . . . what are you doing here?" Danny asked after several seconds that seemed to slide silently toward eternity.

"We're on vacation."

"Yeh, us too."

"We were at Gettysburg and Valley Forge and Independence Hall. My parents thought I should see some of the history that made our country great," she said, her eyes opening as though they were expanding to take in all they'd seen on their travels. "We're on our way back to Ohio," she concluded, her eyes again focusing on Danny. "What are you doing here?"

"We're looking for smelteries," Danny said flatly. "Smelteries?" A perplexed look crinkled her face.

"Yeh," said Danny, "old-time smelteries... you know, where they made metal - iron or copper or something - out of ore." The look on her face suggested that she thought he was pulling her leg. It was obvious that she did not believe him.

"Oh," she said, trying to stifle her laughter.

"Seriously," said Danny, suddenly concerned that she doubted him. "My parents drag my brother and sister and me around looking for these old-time smelteries. They're always out in the woods and mostly they're just fallen down heaps of stone and stuff." She looked at him quizzically, as though he might be telling the truth.

"I bet you tell that to all the girls." She was laughing now.

"No, no! They've been doing it for years," he added, as if this bit of information must surely convince her that he was telling the truth. "It's not my idea. I'd rather be at home. My friends are digging a mine near our house, and I don't want to miss any of it. But if we have to go someplace, I'd rather go to the shore." She smiled at him in commiseration. Obviously, the idea of wandering around in the woods did not appeal to her any more than it did to him.

"OK, girlie, it's your turn," the man at the faucet said. "Don't get your feet wet." He glanced at Danny and winked conspiratorially.

"Thanks, Mr. Hammel. I'll be real careful," said Karen in a talking-to-big-folks voice. She pushed her jug over to the faucet with her moccasin-shod foot. As she turned to her task, Danny stared at her dark hair and the deep tan on her skin. He thought she was pretty, and he found himself peering at her chest, but her loose blouse revealed nothing about her breasts. He wondered if she was wearing a training bra.

She filled one jug, but before she began on the second, she looked at him again. "Are you going to the carnival tonight?" she asked, her face suddenly serious. He knew nothing about any carnival. "It's just down the road a mile or two and it's loads of fun. There are posters all over the campground. Get your parents to bring you. I'll be there. I could meet you."

Danny stared at her; she was serious, he was certain. She finished filling her water jugs and stood there, one in either hand. "Well, what do you say?" she asked, her face bright, her eyes wide. He hesitated, and she added quickly, "About the carnival."

"Oh. Yeh, OK." He felt a rush of energy through his body.

"Good," she said. "I'll see you there about eight o'clock. Near the Ferris wheel." She smiled, and it seemed to Danny that she was genuinely happy that he'd be there.

"By the way," she said, "I'm Karen."

"Danny," he said as she turned and headed toward her campsite, water sloshing from the jugs. As he turned to the tap, he watched to see where she went. Through the trees, he could just see that on her campsite set a real trailer, a bright shiny aluminum one and nearby stood a big shiny black car. No pop-up trailer made by her dad from plans in *Mechanix Illustrated*, he thought.

On his way back to campsite 13 with the water, thoughts of Karen floated through his mind. Her blue eyes, her tan, her smile, her dark hair. Again, he found himself wondering whether she wore a training bra, and he realized that he was in a good mood for the first time since they'd left home.

As he wandered along the lane, he saw a bright red poster stuck to a tree. "Carnival," it said. He pulled it down and crammed it into his pocket to show to his parents.

He expected them to reject the idea of taking the family to the carnival. As soon as he mentioned it and unfolded the poster, however, Jeannie squealed, "Yes, yes, a carnival. Can we go, daddy, please, please, can we go?" Bobbie, too had climbed out of the trailer, where he'd been lounging with a book, and added his voice to the urgings. Much to Danny's surprise, his parents had smiled and assured them that they would all go to the carnival that night.

The afternoon dragged on for Danny. He wandered around the campgrounds hoping he'd run into Karen, but she was nowhere to be found. He passed by the campsite where the shiny aluminum trailer stood - number 7 according to the red number painted on the stake - but the black car was not there. Next door, at number 6, he saw the man from the standpipe, Mr. Hammel, and they waved to one another. He moped around the meadow, the camp office, and finally campsite 13. Time passed as though each second was a penny doled out by an old miser. Finally, about 7:30, the family piled into the car and drove to the carnival.

The fields were already crowded with cars and his father had to park out near the road, a hundred yards or more from the gate. Through the thick dust, red in the rays of the setting sun, the family joined the throng of people headed for the lights and music. A high fence surrounded the festival grounds and people funneled toward the single entrance, a giant clown face painted in bright colors. The face was so large that people passed in and out through the massive open laughing mouth of the clown, and from somewhere behind the face, mechanical laughter roared out into the night.

Once inside Danny sidled up beside his mother and asked if he could go off on his own. Bobbie and Jeannie heard him and immediately clamored to go along. Danny feared they would ruin his evening with Karen, but to his great surprise, his mother let him go, keeping Bobbie and Jeannie with her.

Danny hurried into the crowds along the midway, making his way toward the Ferris wheel, anxious to find Karen. He threaded through the throngs of people, his senses bombarded by sights, sounds, and smells. He gulped it all in as though he'd just surfaced from a dive into the deep end of the pool. The night was ablaze with white lights along the midway and colored lights blinking and flashing from the rides. Off in the distance he heard the calliope from the carousel, gunshots from the shooting gallery, the voices of barkers and callers, and the hubbub of the crowds of people. His nostrils filled with the aroma of roasting meats, baking pies and cakes, and the smell of hot grease as great mounds of french fries, pierogies, and funnel cakes were deep fried. Here the sticky sweetness of cotton candy wafted away to be replaced at the next step by cigar and cigarette smoke, after-shave, and the pervasive odor of women's perfume. As he approached the rides, the smell was of machinery grease, thick and pungent, overheated by friction and mingled with the ozone crackle of electricity. Nearing the Ferris wheel, he could hear laughter and the nervous shrieks and screams of women and girls as the rides flung them through the air. The excitement of the evening tingled his blood. This was exactly what he wanted.

He walked into the masses of people around the Ferris wheel, his eyes darting anxiously, searching the faces in the crowd. His heart beat faster and his lips were very dry. He had to walk completely around the Ferris wheel before he saw her, but finally, there she was, standing off to one side near an ice cream stand. He'd been looking for a Karen in pigtails and shorts, but this evening her hair was down in a kind of pageboy and she wore baggy jeans with cuffs rolled up to show her bobby socks and oxfords.

It wasn't until he walked up beside her that he realized she was not alone. She appeared to be genuinely happy to see him and quickly introduced her companions. Swallowing his disappointment, he said hello to Karen's friend Betty, who was also staying at the Lost Bear Campgrounds with her parents. She was a blonde with a full, baby face, thick blonde hair pulled back in a ponytail, and eyes as blue as Karen's, but without the lively expressiveness. She wore a tight pink sweater that forced Danny to look at her large breasts. He was quite sure she was not wearing a training bra; her breasts appeared to be very well-trained. When she said hello to Danny, there was a hint of sullenness about her.

His heart fell at the sight of the girl. He'd spent much of the afternoon thinking about walking around the carnival with Karen and he was reluctant to let go of his fantasy. He wasn't at all sure what he would do alone with her for the whole evening - or even why he wanted to do it for that matter - but that's what he'd set his heart on. But Betty wasn't the end of it.

"This is Ray," Karen said, gesturing toward a muscular boy with dark hair slicked back behind his ears. He and another, smaller boy had been standing behind the two girls and now stepped forward to stare at Danny. "And this is Leroy." Karen waved at the smaller, tow-headed boy who appeared to be about Danny's age. He reminded Danny of a fox or maybe a rodent because of the way his face came to a point.

Danny's spirits plummeted as he nodded and said "Hi" to the two boys. They stood off a bit and Danny had the feeling they were checking him out. The bright light from the Ferris wheel flashed on their faces and he wasn't sure what he saw there; it made him uncomfortable. Danny wanted to talk to Karen, but Betty had staked a solid claim to her, and he was forced to stand there awkwardly, the two boys staring at him. Finally, Ray, who appeared to Danny to be sixteen or seventeen, asked where he was from. Telford, said Danny, but neither of the boys knew where that was, and Danny had to go into a lengthy explanation. That didn't seem to please them, especially Leroy who seemed to smirk at him.

The two were locals, Ray a quiet farm boy who spent most of his time working on his family's farm, which explained why he looked so much older, so muscular. Leroy, on the other hand, lived in the village. "With my uncle," he said, not bothering to comment on why he lived with his uncle or where his parents might be.

"So, what's Telford?" Ray asked. "Some kinda city or somethin'?"

"Naw, it's just a little town," Danny said. "We live right at the end of town next to Holzwalder's dairy farm."

"You got cows back east?" Leroy asked as if the idea were too preposterous to contemplate. "Sure," said Danny.

"You don' t look like you ever stepped in a cowflop," Leroy sneered. "Does he, Ray? Hunh?" But Ray was warming up to Danny. He listened attentively as Danny talked of Telford, a small town in a farming area where he spent a lot of time prowling around the fields and wood lots. Danny saw by the look on Ray's face that it wasn't as good as being a farm boy, but it sure was a lot better than being a full-fledged town kid. As for Leroy, Danny couldn't figure him out. He seemed always to be ready with some odd remark. He fidgeted and talked, saying dumb things when there was really nothing to say.

"Hey, let's go ride the Ferris wheel. We didn't come here to stand around talking," Karen said. "And then we can ride the carousel! I love the carousel."

Betty shrugged and muttered a "sure" devoid of enthusiasm.

Danny liked that idea until they got in line, and he realized Betty had snared Karen as her seatmate. Obviously, Ray and Leroy would sit together, which left Danny to ride alone. The carousel was a little better, but still he felt left out.

Danny managed to mount a red and orange circus pony just behind Karen. Beside her, Betty clambered onto the giraffe that rose and fell in counterpoint to Karen's pastel pony. Where Ray and Leroy ended up, he didn't know or care. All through the ride Danny watched Betty chatter incessantly to Karen, though over the roar of the calliope he couldn't make out a single word. Near the end of the ride, Karen swiveled on her gracefully rocking mount and smiled at Danny. She waved like a grand lady from *Ivanhoe*, infusing Danny's flagging spirits with renewed hope.

As the carousel slowed to a halt and the music died away, Danny slid from his gaudy charger and followed Karen out into the crowd. Betty was right at her side, and within seconds, Ray and Leroy materialized beside them.

"I do love the merry-go-round," Karen said, her eyes dreamy, lost in fantasy.

"Yeh, it's great," Betty said flatly as the boys shuffled their feet, less certain of their appreciation of the ride. Danny stared at Karen, trying to think of something to say, something to suggest that might turn matters more to his liking.

"I want some funnel cake," Betty announced, sniffing deeply at the heavy scent of deep fried batter thick on the evening air. "Come on, Karen, it's time for us girls to have some alone time." She grabbed Karen's arm and began pulling her toward the midway. Karen giggled, resisting half-heartedly. She looked at the boys, and for an instant, her eyes connected with Danny's.

"OK, OK," she said. "You boys go check out the sideshows or something and meet us at the bandstand in... oh, about half an hour." Then she ran off with Betty, leaving the boys standing in the dust as the crowd flowed past them. Danny felt as bereft as a scarecrow in the middle of a hundred-acre corn field.

"Whaddya think of the girls?" Ray asked, turning to face Danny.

"Yeh," Leroy said, "whaddya think of the girls?" somehow managing to make his eyebrows jiggle as if he were a puppet on the Howdy Doody Show.

"Karen's really nice," Danny said.

"Yeh," Ray agreed, his tone of voice making it evident he shared Danny's feelings.

"Yeh, she's OK," Leroy said, ignoring the mutual appreciation of his companions. "But that Betty! What a number! I bet she really puts out." Danny stared at him; he didn't know what he meant.

"I guess she's OK," Danny said.

"OK?" Leroy snapped. "OK? She's friggin' great. J'ya get a load of those headlights? Boy, would I like to get my hands on those."

"Aah, Leroy, you're such a little bull-shitter," Ray laughed. "You don't have a chance in the world of getting anything from Betty."

"Hey, cut it out, Ray. I got the goods right here." Leroy thrust his crotch out and strutted a few steps like a bow-legged banty rooster. "Right here," he repeated. "If I could get her alone, she'd roll right over for it." Ray shoved Leroy, nearly knocking him off his feet.

"Hey, come on, Ray. Cut it out," whined Leroy, regaining his footing. Ray laughed at him. "Leroy thinks he's a real ladies' man," he said to Danny.

For a moment the three stood quietly amidst the uproar of the carnival. Leroy fidgeted and then, badger-like, began talking in his rapid, clipped speech. "Hey, Ray, whattaya say we check out the *show*." Leroy wiggled his eyebrows and blinked his eyes.

Danny was perplexed by the boy's antics, and he looked at Ray for some indication of what was up. But Ray was silent, looking at Danny in that appraising way again. Then he smiled, a smile that struck Danny as strange, although he couldn't guess what it might mean.

"Come on," Ray said and turned toward the sideshows. Soon they were sprinting along, ducking through the crowds, wending their way down behind the row of tents. They ran along the fence in the semi-darkness until Ray slowed and slipped up to the corner of one of the tents. Leroy stopped next to him, almost pushing up against him, while Danny stood behind them waiting to see what would happen next.

"How is it, Ray?" Leroy whispered. Ray waved Leroy back as he carefully pulled the canvas flaps apart at the corner, just far enough so that he could peep into the tent. Leroy stayed right beside Ray, unable to keep still. For what seemed like a long time, Ray stared into the opening while Leroy whispered at him and tried to push him away. The boy grew more and more excited, unable to control himself, as he tugged at Ray's sleeve. Finally, Ray stepped aside, and Leroy flung himself against the canvas, pressing his eye to the peephole. Ray stood back, watching him.

"Let him look for a couple of minutes, then it's your turn," he said to Danny. Danny still had no idea what they were staring at. As the seconds ticked by, and Leroy began to moan and groan, Ray looked first one way down the row of tents, then the other. Danny watched him, noting the way his eyes kept moving.

"OK, Leroy, time to let Danny look," Ray said, tugging at Leroy's sleeve. But Leroy batted his hand away and hissed, "A little longer, just a little longer." Ray's glance darted right and left, and he slapped at Leroy's arm. Danny, in his uncertainty, began to grow nervous.

"Come on," Ray urged Leroy, tugging at him now to get him away from the tent. But Leroy resisted for several moments before finally letting himself be pulled away. "Your turn, Danny," Ray said. "Hurry it up."

Danny knelt to the hole and stared into the tent. Behind him he heard Leroy protest that he'd hardly seen anything, that he hadn't had enough time. Danny had a hard time focusing. Inside the tent he could see a crowd of men, their backs to him. Mostly what he saw was the backs of their heads. The light was none too bright, and a thick haze of tobacco smoke hung on the air. It was oddly quiet in the tent as if everyone was holding his breath. Beyond the men, he caught the flash of something white, something moving, and his attention riveted to the woman who stood on the stage high above the men. He saw her in profile, and for a moment he did not understand what it was that he was seeing. Thick dark hair crowned her head and her body seemed to glow in the dim light. Her full breasts thrust provocatively out from her chest.

A shock coursed through Danny's body. "She's completely, absolutely bare-assed naked," he said softly. At that moment she swiveled toward him. As if in slow motion, he saw her breasts jiggle with her movement. Slowly she bent her legs in an awkward crouch, reached down to her knees, and ran her hands up the insides of her thighs. As her hands slid over her white skin, electrical tingles flickered up Danny's limbs, tingles more intense by far than the insects generated by the Sears Roebuck catalog. Her hands continued to travel slowly up her thighs until her fingers tangled in the shock of dark hair that covered her crotch.

Danny's heart thudded as his blood pumped wildly. His skin came alive with a prickling heat as an erection strained in his pants. His eyes worked hard to take in the woman and all her marvelous and forbidden parts. Long before he had seen all he wanted to see, Ray began tugging on his arm, whispering at him, "Come on, come on. Let's go." He wanted to see more, to see the look in her eyes. He wanted to let his gaze linger on her breasts, her legs, her crotch. He wanted time to really see all of her at once. But Ray and Leroy were pulling at him and beyond their urgings, he heard a man yelling.

"Hey, you boys, get the hell away from there." And then they were running through the semi-darkness behind the tents, jumping and dodging the tent pegs and the guy lines, the man pursuing, falling behind, but still yelling. "You little bastards stay the hell away from here. Son of a bitch "

Darting around a tent near the end of the row, they emerged into the bright lights and commotion of the midway, their breath raging in their chests. Slipping between two booths, they collapsed in the shadows and lay quietly on the grass for several minutes.

"Boy, wasn't she the hot dog," Leroy said as they began to recover their breath. His speech was fast and high-pitched as though he couldn't wait for the words to come out in a natural order. "And what tits! Did you see, Ray? Didja?" Leroy pinched at Ray's shirt, his fingers moving constantly, nervously nipping the air.

Danny could sympathize with him because he felt the same way. Something like molten metal coursed through him, and he felt exhilarated and wildly alive. And yet, at the same time, he felt . . . dirty; like a sinner and he wondered whether the Devil had gotten a hold on him. His emotions were a roller coaster, raging up and down, until finally the adrenaline began to fade.

"I didn't know that women had all that hair," he said. Information like that was not available in the Sears catalog. Ray laughed at him, and Leroy snorted. "You dumb shit," he said.

"How about that other hoochie-coochie lady we seen last night," Leroy said to Ray. Danny felt as though he'd been dismissed, too ignorant to bother with. "You could barely see her hair, it was so light. Remember, Ray?" Leroy hurried on, talking so fast the words barely formed as they tumbled from his mouth. "But this one was better, wasn't she, Ray? She could really shake that thing." Leroy fell unexpectedly silent, but his body continued to twitch, his fingers pinching and grasping in the evening air.

"Anyways," he said, looking at Danny, "I already knew that . . . about their hair down there. I seen my sister. She's seventeen. She let me look and she's pretty hairy." The remark sent a shock through Danny; he'd peeked at Jeannie a couple of times, but she didn't have anything down there but a dimple.

"Get out, Leroy," Ray said, smacking Leroy's arm. "You're a bullshitter. You never saw your sister. Nancy never let you look at her."

"Yeh, yeh, I did," Leroy insisted, jumping to his feet.

A few minutes later they were at the bandstand where an old-timey band, the somebody family or something, were playing a mix of country and gospel music. A woman who looked like Dale Evans was playing guitar and singing a Hank Williams song, "Lost Highway." People stood around in clusters, swaying to the music, talking and eating. Some of the men drank beer out of paper cups.

As the song ended, Danny saw Karen and Betty heading toward them through the crowd. Betty leaned toward Karen as they walked, talking in her ear and Karen giggled as though they were sharing some wondrous joke. Danny felt a ripple of jealousy pass through him. He hadn't ever been jealous over a girl and here he was jealous *of* a girl as well. He wished that it were his words that were making Karen laugh.

"Well, what have you boys been up to?" Betty asked as the girls came up to them. She spoke in an exaggerated rhythm that made Danny think she and Karen knew exactly what they'd been up to. When the girls both giggled, he felt certain that that was the case. He thought he saw Betty square her shoulders and thrust her large breasts out as if to taunt them.

Ray said nothing, but a sly grin crept onto his face. He didn't have to say anything; Leroy began to chatter for all of them. His inane comments told the girls all they wanted to know, and they laughed openly. Danny turned away and stared at the bandstand where the mandolin player was introducing the next song, a gospel number, "Just a Closer Walk With Thee".

Leroy was still talking, and Betty was bantering coyly with him. Ray, too, turned to listen to the band. Danny looked at Karen; her attention was on Leroy and Betty so Danny felt free to stare at her. I wish I could walk close by thee, he thought. As he stared at her profile and her glistening dark hair, he found himself thinking of her in the nude. What would her breasts look like? Did they need training? Did she have hair on her crotch? As if his thoughts had somehow touched her, she turned to him and looked into his eyes, Danny blushed, certain that she knew what he'd been thinking.

Guilt washed over him for thinking about her in that way. Even as his blush deepened, utterly helpless to halt the thought, he wondered what she would look like with the animal look of abandon on her face, the look he'd seen on the face of the naked hoochie-coochie lady. He couldn't take his eyes off her, and he couldn't stop his thoughts. Her eyes were wide, inquisitive, as they had been at the water faucet. He wanted to look away, but she held him and her eyes darkened, grew serious, a reflection of some resolution forming in her.

Karen leaned toward Danny and kissed him gently on the lips. To Danny, it happened in slow motion, time fading to nothingness as it had done a short while before. The lights of the carnival, the old-timey string band, the shrieks and screams from the rides, all faded away. He floated in silence, a void where nothing of the material world any longer existed. Only Karen and himself, her lips on his, the faint scent of fragrant soap and young girl in his nostrils.

When she withdrew her lips, the world came slipping back into his consciousness. Light grew out of the darkness of the void, sounds filtered back to an intensity that hurt his ears, and the smells of hot grease, food, beer, and sweat washed over him. The clock began to tick again.

Karen smiled at Danny and turned to the other three. For what seemed to him like a long time he stood in the crowd alone, as alone as if he'd been on the moon. He could feel his heart thumping, but he couldn't feel his fingers or his feet in his sneakers. Everything he saw as he stood there and all he saw later along the midway seemed to him insubstantial, as though it was all a dream.

It grew late, the crowds began to thin, the evening coming to an end. Danny could feel it, a bewildering emptiness, a desperate need for more. His hopes of being alone with Karen faded to nothing, impossible now. The five of them stood near the shooting gallery, drinking a final root beer when Bobbie came running up to Danny and tugged on his sleeve.

"It's time to go," he said. "Mom and Dad want to leave." Bobbie looked at the others; they all stared at him. No one made a move, all of them as reluctant as Danny to call an end to the evening.

Betty poked Karen and gestured across the midway where Karen's parents stood waving to the girls to join them. A look of annoyance flitted across Karen's face. Finally, she said, "Guess we have to go, too." With these words Karen and Betty said their goodbyes and ran off to join her parents.

Bobbie tapped Danny on the shoulder. "Come *on*, Danny. We gotta go. Dad's gonna be mad." To Danny, it all happened in a daze. He watched Karen and Betty, a brief glimpse of tanned legs and tawny hair as they disappeared behind the Ferris wheel. Danny said a half-hearted goodbye to Ray, ignored Leroy, and, with a heavy heart, followed Bobbie.

Danny remembered nothing of the return to the campgrounds or his preparations for bed. He lay awake for a long time, his nervous system afire with hope and excitement, replaying the day's events. He thought about the carnival, the hoochie-coochie lady and Karen. When he did fall asleep, he dreamt furiously, dreams that further excited him.

The next morning, he raced through breakfast and as soon as he could get away, he dashed across the campground to campsite 7. As he approached, Danny saw that the shiny aluminum trailer was not there, but hoping against hope, he ran onto the campsite, his heart crashing in his chest. The trailer was gone and the shiny black car was gone. There wasn't so much as a scrap of paper on the ground.

Danny stood with head bowed, kicking the dry dirt of the campsite. He looked up as Mr.

Hammel, the man from the neighboring site, walked up beside him.

"They're gone, son. Left early this morning. Said they had to get back to Ohio before the sun goes down." Danny felt the man's eyes on him, and he felt embarrassed by the disappointment that must have shown clearly on his face.

Danny dropped his gaze and turned away. The future, so rosy a few seconds before, crashed like a Jap Zero caught in a barrage of American anti-aircraft fire. His fantasies of spending the coming days with Karen and all the possibilities he'd imagined went down into the sea trailing a plume of black smoke. Instead, the coming week opened out in the tedium and drudgery of searches for lost smelteries.

The man put his hand gently on Danny's shoulder. "It's tough," he said, "and I know it won't help much, but there'll be lots of other girls. You'll see." He gave Danny's shoulder a little squeeze, turned and walked away. He'd nearly reached his trailer when he stopped and turned back toward Danny.

"It's good to get your mind off things," he said. "If you're interested, we'll be heading out to look for some of those secret smelteries this afternoon. You're sure welcome if you'd like to come along."

Strawberry Sun, Raspberry Moon

Rose awoke to find the room brilliant with sunshine. Her sister's bed was empty, and she knew she'd overslept. She rolled over and stretched, languorous in the warmth of early June. Her thoughts tumbled lazily like the brook in the meadow, but when they reached Steven, she sat bolt upright in bed. Heat coursed through her body, and she felt her cheeks flush.

Flopping down on the bed, she buried her head in her pillow, and in the soft darkness, she saw again the thick black and purple sky of the previous evening and the ragged forks of lightning ripping across the horizon.

They'd sat huddled on the porch swing, hugging and kissing in the darkness between the glaring flashes, watching the storm come. Steven was supposed to have gone home, but he lingered as the lights went out in the house. For a time, they sat silently, motionless, watching the storm roll closer, feeling the rising of the wind, warm and seductive, murmuring of places and things they'd never known. As the thunder rumbled closer and the lightning flashes grew brighter, Rose felt as though the oncoming storm had infected her with a touch of its wildness.

She unbuttoned Steven's shirt and began to caress his chest. Soon her blouse too was open and her bra was undone and for the first time she felt a boy's skin press nakedly against her breasts. Delicately he fondled her, kissed her nipples. Delicious, exciting, blissful: they kissed and touched, entranced as time passed, a moment, minute upon minute, forever, until the wind turned cold and the lightening flickered dangerously across the horizon and the thunder rolled belligerently in their direction.

Steven tugged his shirt together and buttoned it, and after a lingering kiss, dashed off into the night. Rose waited in the rising wind, icy on her feverish skin, watching down the street to see him in the lightning's glare, running pell-mell through the intersection at Chestnut and then he was gone. The rain held off just long enough for him to reach home before the thick, cold drops began to splat down in the dusty street and the dry grass of the yard.

Without buttoning her blouse or refastening her bra, feeling wicked and delicious, she slipped off to bed. As the storm crashed over the house Rose drifted into a deep sleep.

Rose peeked from beneath the pillow and flung it from her head. She jumped up and dressed and headed down the hall to the bathroom. On the way out of the room, she grabbed the copy of *How Green Was My Valley* she'd begun a few days ago. A few minutes later she came down the stairs into the hall. In the kitchen, she heard the radio on the windowsill: ". . . fighting continued today on a broad front across northern France . . ." and the voices of her mother and sister.

". . . just a couple of bookworms " she heard Lilly say in her grown-up, authoritative voice.

". . . held against heavy German attacks . . ."

". . . out on the porch in that storm . . ."

". . . stand and fight to the death,' proclaimed General . . ."

"Even bookworms . . . given the right circumstances," concluded her mother. Rose stopped dead in her tracks. Lilly stood in front of the refrigerator peering into its depths, while their mother stood by the sink drying cups and saucers. Rose looked down at the book in her hand and hastily slipped it onto the what-not shelf. Though her mother had not yet noticed her, Rose saw the look on her face which clearly said that her words, though meant for Rose, applied equally to Lilly. Lilly's eyes grew large in the innocence of a rag doll, and she was about to protest when she noticed Rose in the doorway.

"Good morning, Mother," said Rose, coming into the kitchen.

"Well, late night last night?" asked her mother. Rose felt the color begin to rise in her cheeks.

"Yeh, what were you bookworms up to out in that storm?" added Lilly archly. "You weren't up to anything naughty, were you, Shoes?"

"Mother," Rose whined, "make her stop calling me that." "Lilly, you stop calling your sister names."

"I didn't say anything," snapped Lilly, her voice as bristly as the thistles that grew in the alley behind the house.

"Yes, you did. And anyway, even if you hadn't, I know your evil ways. You're an expert at tormenting your sister. And you, Missy", she said, turning to Rose, "you could stand to get your nose out of the books now and then and learn to stand up for yourself. At nineteen you should show a little more spunk. You don't think I would have caught your father if I hadn't shown some spunk." Rose stared at her mother, her mouth fallen open.

"You tell her, Maw," Lilly giggled from the other side of the kitchen.

"You just be quiet, young lady," she said to Lilly. "And you, Rose, fetch the milk. It's been so busy around here this morning, I plumb forgot to bring it in."

Rose, the color now high in her cheeks, was only too thankful for the opportunity to get out of the kitchen before one of them noticed. With great relief she stepped outside, pretending to admire the splendid morning while she calmed herself and the flush faded from her cheeks. There was no reason to pretend; the rain had made everything green and magical, and a fragrant wind rattled the leaves. She picked up the two bottles, the necks, shaped like baby's heads, filled with thick, yellowish cream.

As Rose came back into the kitchen, her mother began to detail the chores she wanted them to tackle after breakfast.

"Oh, Mom, we can't do chores this morning," Lilly moaned. "We have to pick strawberries." She looked at Lilly, pained and exasperated, but before she could speak Lilly plunged on.

"Mr. Wyckoff told us to pick the strawberries in. "

"Mr. Wyckoff? Where did you see Mr. Wyckoff?"

"At the Post Office," Lilly said, the exasperation in her voice making it evident that she could not believe how obtuse her mother could be. "Remember - you sent us to the Post Office yesterday afternoon? Well, we ran into Mr. Wyckoff, and he said he didn't have time to pick the wild strawberries in his upper field - they're the very best wild strawberries anywhere around, he said - and he hated to see them go to waste so we should come pick them and they're near the end, so we have to go today." Lilly drew a deep breath, staring at her mother as if to say: this explanation should not have been necessary.

The girls' mother sighed. For a moment she drummed her fingers on the edge of the sink, measuring odds and options. "OK," she said finally, "you can go pick strawberries this morning, but this afternoon I have things for you to do."

Lilly turned to look at Rose, a sly, victorious grin on her face.

Several hours later Rose and Lilly climbed over the stone wall into Mr. Wyckoff's meadow. Rose stood for a moment on top of the wall, staring up at the sky. It was an unusual day, a day of unexpected brightness even though the blue of the sky was pastel and filled with an unending flow of clouds, cottony and outrageous, that streamed from horizon to horizon. The world seemed bright and diffracted to Rose, wild in a way she hadn't noticed before, an essence that dovetailed precisely with the kittenish effervescence coursing through her body. It was a feeling of freedom and wildness new to Rose. She breathed deeply the scents of fresh grass and new-mown hay curing in the heat of the sun, the honeysuckle, heady and intoxicating. Under those dominant rhythms of scent was a counterpoint of forest blossoms and wild growing things.

Rose sprang from the wall, landing in the thick meadow gras, and knelt in search of the little berries. She saw the serrated leaves and as she parted the leaves and grass, there they were, like rubies, or cranberries at Christmas time. Not far away Lilly was already down on her knees, engrossed in the search. The berries were irresistible. Rose picked several and ate them, savoring their intense sweetness, their distinctive flavor. Quickly she plucked and ate several more. Her fingers grew red with the juice and soon her lips too took on an exaggerated redness. For a moment she was lost in the pleasure of the berries, sitting in the grass, savoring the taste.

"Hey, Sis, what do you think? Aren't these strawberries the greatest?" Rose was yanked from her reverie by her sister's words. She nodded, feeling no need to say anything, the look on her face the clearest testimonial. "Wouldn't it be great to take our clothes off and roll around in all these berries and get all red and juicy and sticky," Lilly cried, waving her arms in the air.

"Oh, Lilly," Rose exclaimed, in much the same voice that their mother might have used. But somewhere inside herself, she was surprised to find a sentiment very similar to that of her sixteen-year-old sister.

The girls set to work picking berries, working their way down along the stone wall and into the meadow. Rose picked steadily, her mind as busy as her hands. She thought of Steven and the way his kisses had excited her. Perhaps it was the storm that had made her act as she had. But she thought too of Lilly's remark about rolling naked in the strawberries and how somewhere inside of her, the bonds and ties of her reserve were beginning to weaken and fray.

Rose sat back in the grass, the nearly full pail beside her, and brushed her hair back out of her face. All around her, the air was alive with birdsong and high above, in the cloud-strewn brightness, she saw a hawk circling lazily. She imagined the freedom of that great bird and for an instant, she thought that she too might possess that kind of freedom.

Rose dropped her gaze to the stone wall and was surprised to find someone standing there staring at her. It was a boy - someone about her own age - that much she could discern, but in the brightness of the day she could not make out who it was. He waved and she thought that it must be Lilly's current beau, Bobby.

The boy jumped down from the wall and headed in her direction. He was a well-muscled and tanned farm boy wearing a straw hat. Rose watched him approach, expecting his features to resolve into Bobby's, but they didn't.

"Hello," he said as he came up to her. "Picking strawberries?" Rose nodded; squinting to see whose face was in the shadow of the hat. "I'm Carl Wyckoff," he said and for a moment Rose feared that he would challenge their presence in the meadow. "Abe's nephew," he added. "I was headed over to Liberty's to see about borrowin' some shear pins for the sickle-bar." He pushed his hat back on his head and Rose could see his face clearly. She had no idea what he'd just told her, but his face was pleasant, and he obviously had no intention of chasing them off.

"Hello," she said as she got to her feet. She introduced herself and then gestured to Lilly who sat in the grass about forty feet away, her hand shading her eyes, staring at them.

"Hello," called Carl, waving to Lilly who waved back. She too got to her feet and began to walk in their direction.

"Nice day for berry picking," he said, smiling at Rose. She nodded, thinking she should explain that his uncle had given them permission to pick the wild strawberries. She could see now why she'd thought at first that he was Bobby. There was a strong physical resemblance, but this boy had a nicer smile and bright, lively eyes. She felt his gaze on her, and it made her feel even hotter than the sun did.

Carl asked where they lived and after Rose explained that they'd come out from the village, he offered the information that he was working for his uncle and would be spending the summer. Rose could sense that Carl was about to say something about seeing one another again when Lilly began to scream. They turned and stared at Lilly who was dancing frantically in the grass a few yards away,

Carl ran to her, and she threw herself into his arms. "A snake! A snake!" she screamed. Carl pulled himself from Lilly's clinging arms and peered in the grass nearby. He bent over and came up holding a small green and black garter snake. It curled contentedly around Carl's hand as he held it out for her to see. Lilly backed away, frightened, still jumping up and down, frantic, while Rose stood where she had been, staring first at Carl and the snake and then at Lilly.

"It's only a little garter snake," Carl said. "It wouldn't hurt you." He held the little snake up and peered at its head. "It's got strawberry juice on its lips. Just picking berries like you." He held it out for Lilly to see, but she danced backwards and keened as though he were thrusting a sidewinder, business end first, in her direction.

Carl turned to Rose and said again, "A garter snake." Rose stared at Lilly, her mouth open. Carl stood for a moment, uncomfortable in the silence. He glanced at the nearly hysterical Lilly and then at the snake. "I'll put it over on the other side of the wall."

He climbed over the stone wall and carried the snake off forty or fifty yards into the new-mown hay and let it go. When he returned, Lilly was calm. She looked at him with huge eyes as he re-crossed the wall.

"Oh, god, I'm so frightened of snakes," she gasped. Rose was still silent, still staring at her sister. "I'm so thankful you were here. But how could you stand to touch it? Ughhhh!" Lilly shuddered.

Carl stood a little taller as he said, "It was just a little garter snake. It'd never hurt anybody. They're real sociable. An' anyways it just wanted some strawberries just like you do." He smiled at Lilly.

"Well, thank you so much," Lilly said, stepping forward, laying her hand on Carl's arm. She gazed fondly into the eyes of her defender and very nearly let a wondrous sigh escape her lips. Carl smiled and looked at Rose. He seemed a bit confused.

"Well, I've got to run," he said, straightening his straw hat. "Pleased to have met you. Hope to see you again." He made a jerky, halfway little bow to Lilly, tipped his hat to Rose and headed off across the field.

Lilly ran suddenly up to the top of the wall and peered into the distance, watching Carl. When he finally disappeared through the hedgerow and was gone, she turned back to the meadow where Rose still stood in the grass. She took in her sister's wide eyes, shrugged and jumped down from the wall, returning to her berry picking.

She hadn't been long at her task when she looked up at Rose who was still staring at her. "What?" she said, defensively.

"Oh, god, I'm afraid of snakes," sneered Rose. "A snake! A snake!" she parodied. "I couldn't believe my ears."

"Well, it surprised me. Sometimes I do get scared when I'm surprised like that."

"Oh, suuure." Rose rolled her eyes. "Suuure! The girl who put two garter snakes in Mom and Dad's bed when she was twelve is all of a sudden afraid of snakes. Uh hunh!"

"I told you, I was surprised." "Right. You thought it was a cobra."

"Oh, fiddlesticks," said Lilly, turning away and beginning once again to pick berries. "I'm not even going to talk to you."

"I thought you were going to throw your arms around him and kiss him." Rose had no intention of letting Lilly ignore her no matter how hard she might try. "You were flirting like... like... an axe murderess," taunted Rose. Lilly tried not to listen, but she couldn't help herself.

"Oh, so what," snapped Lilly, jumping up from the grass to confront her sister. "So what if I did? At least I'm not an old prune like you. I gave you every chance to flirt with him and you just stood there like a moon-eyed cow flop. It wouldn't hurt you to flirt once in a while. It would do you good."

Lilly stalked off into the meadow and went back to picking berries. Rose too returned to her work, her feelings in turmoil. Part of her was shocked at her sister's forwardness and part of her envied Lilly's ability to be so brazen. She'd never thought anything like that before and the thought startled her.

Soon she heard Lilly humming a song they'd been hearing on the radio. Lilly began ad-libbing, making up nonsense syllables and words, throwing in words with ridiculous rhymes, just to match the melody. Rose tried to blot out Lilly's voice, but she was annoyed by Lilly's antics and her voice refused to be blocked out. Soon Rose began hearing words that sent her anger soaring as Lilly made up verses to the tune of *You Are My Sunshine*.

"She is my sister," Lilly sang, "my sister Two-Shoes . . . Miss Goodeee Two-Shoes . . .

She doesn't know howww . . . to kiss a . . ."

"Stop that! Stop singing those things," Rose screamed as she ran toward Lilly. Lilly looked up from her berry picking, staring at her sister, pained that her little ditty should be so rudely interrupted.

"Sis," Lilly said softly, calmly, so reasonably, "whatever are you getting so upset about?" Rose stood before Lilly shaking her fist, sputtering: "You . . . you . . ." Lilly's eyes were huge, her lips parted, the soul of amazement and reason. She was about to add something, sweetness and light, thought better of it, and let the expression slip from her face.

"Oh, Rose, you're such an old maid. And that Steven of yours is such a bookworm. Even worse - he's just a worm. I bet you've never even kissed him." Indignation swept through Rose, mingling with her anger, rendering her speechless. Lilly went back to picking berries, adding as if to herself, "I'm sure you've never let him touch you. If he ever thought of such a wild and crazy thing."

Lilly's words brought a hot flush to Rose and she felt the memory of Steven's hands on her breasts, his lips on her nipples. She wanted to flee back to her kettle of berries before Lilly turned once again to look at her. Lilly was still chattering, more or less to herself, "I wonder if your panties have ever gotten wet . . .," when Rose's silence registered. Her head snapped up and she looked at Rose. The red flush on Rose's cheeks extended down over her shoulders and chest.

"Ohhhh-my-gawd," Lilly drawled. "You're blushing! My sister Two-Shoes is blushing." She jumped up and spun around and grabbed Rose by the arm. "You have done something, you and Steven, haven't you? What did you do? What did you do? It must have been good for a blush like that."

"I am not blushing," shouted Rose, trying to pull away from Lilly. "I am not . . . it's . . . it's just sunburn."

"Oh, Rosie Two-Shoes, tell, come on, tell me. What did you do? Please, pretty please, what did you do?"

But Rose clamped her mouth shut, pulled her arm from Lilly's grasp and, in her turn, stamped back to her kettle of berries and knelt to her work. Behind her Lilly continued pestering her to tell, but she said nothing. By the time the kettles were full, Lilly had given up, yielding to her sister's stubbornness and they walked home in silence. That was the end of the strawberry picking. The next day the meadow was mowed, and strawberry time was past. Despite Rose's adamant refusal to tell her sister anything, Lilly went on alternately pestering and teasing her. And Rose went on feeling both guilty and empowered by her expanded romantic activities with Steven.

But there was a strong element of confusion to this wild and willful season. She watched her sister closely, seeing in her exuberance a sensuality and a daring that alternately horrified and enticed her. There was a part of her that wanted more from her slow, soft Steven. But there was a part too that was frightened to step off into deep water.

Carl Wyckoff added yet another thread of confusion to Rose's life. He took to stopping by sometimes in the evening and even though nothing happened, Rose knew perfectly well that he was interested in her. But the confusing part was the reciprocal feeling that grew in her.

Lilly tried, whenever she could, to be present when Carl came by. Rose knew, that had the opportunity presented itself, Lilly would have grabbed Carl for herself. And then what would she have done with Bobby, Rose wondered. So, she paid close attention to the two of them whenever she saw them together. Sometimes she saw things that astonished her, as on another warm, sunny day about a week later.

Rose and Lilly sat on the porch off the kitchen shelling peas. From the radio on the windowsill came the voice of Gene Autry singing "Back in the Saddle Again." Lilly hummed along and Rose was deep in thought when the gate creaked, and they both looked up to see Bobby coming up the walk.

"Hi, Rose," he said. "Hi, Sweetpea," bending over to kiss Lilly on the cheek.

"What are *you* doing here?" Lilly cooed. Rose watched them noting the change in Lilly, her response to Bobby's blatant maleness. She looked at his tanned skin, his muscled arms, and shocked herself by looking at his crotch, where she thought she saw more than she'd wanted to see.

"I was helping the Yost brothers an' now I'm headed home for lunch. And you, Baby Cakes, are right on the way." Bobby seemed to be afflicted with nervous energy as he stood by Lilly. Lilly, in her turn, seemed to be a transformer or maybe an amplifier that took in Bobby's energy, stoked it up, and sent it right back out to him. She smiled coyly.

From the kitchen, Gene Autry was cut off by the excited voice of an announcer: "This bulletin just in: German National Radio this morning announced the fall of Paris to German troops. Fighting continues . . ."

"Did you hear that?" Rose said. "The Germans have captured Paris!" Lilly looked at her sister with a long-suffering look, as if to inquire who could possibly care.

"Those Germans are really good fighters," Bobby said, admiration evident in his voice. "They beat those Frenchies in nothing flat."

"But why must they fight?" Rose asked, looking pleadingly from one to the other as if she truly expected an answer.

"Oh," Lilly snipped, "it's just those dumb old Europeans. That's all they ever do is fight." "Yeh, but those Germans are sure good at it," Bobby said. He was staring at Lilly's legs

and that was his last word on the matter. "Hey, I got to get home or my maw's gonna give me hell. Besides, I'm starving." He stooped again and kissed Lilly a loud smack on the cheek. As he turned to go, Rose was astonished to see her sister pinch him on the rump.

The special announcement over, the station returned to music, something by the Andrews Sisters. Lilly began to hum along dreamily as she continued shelling peas. As the song ended, she looked at Rose.

"Sis, what do you think of Bobby?" "What do you mean?"

"Well, do you think he's cute? Do you like him? As a boy, I mean." Her normally animated face was blank, offering no clues as to what might be on her mind.

"Oh, he's good-looking, I guess," Rose said, "and he's nice enough - if you like farm boys. But he's sure not my type." Lilly looked at her, a puzzled look on her face.

"Not your type? He's a boy with a great body. He's any girl's type. What do you mean not your type?"

"Well, he's not interested in anything but farming and hunting," Rose said. "He doesn't read." Lilly's eyes narrowed and her lips edged toward a grin.

"He doesn't have to read," she said in her superior, girl-of-the-world voice. "He kisses like crazy."

The moon was growing full, and Rose felt that in some crazy, imprecise way she too was growing full. She had no idea what that meant, but that was how she felt. The confusions still plagued her, but more and more she was seized by the wildness that characterized this unusual June of her life. As the month surged and ebbed toward July, the days continued hot and clear, and a hot wind swept across the countryside. The weather worked its wonders on the trees and bushes and on the farm fields around the town. Rose had already noted how the heat or the wind, or the weather in general seemed to have a strange effect on people as well as plants, as though it blew exotic scents and exotic thoughts from far-off places.

Behind the house, the garden patch grew luxuriantly and at the edge of the yard, the raspberries ripened with the swelling of the moon.

The moon had always been magic for Rose and on the night of its fullness her body was flooded with nervous energy. She sat for a long time, looking out the bedroom window after Lilly had fallen asleep. She hoped that Steven would be tickled by the same romantic feather that fluttered about her and would come sneaking through the moonlight. It was late, nearly midnight and she'd about given up hope when she saw movement out in the yard. Someone in a white shirt stood near the raspberry bushes. Silently she floated down to the kitchen and slipped out onto the porch.

She could see him down near the end of the garden, waiting. She edged from the shadows of the porch and dashed out into the garden, the grass still warm and dusty on her feet.

As soon as she came into his arms, she knew it wasn't Steven. She felt the thick muscles of his arms and chest, the thick cords of his neck as she nuzzled against him. He smelled of sunshine and soap and the night. Carl.

It was Carl. She was excited by the romance of it - a strong, sensual male creature in the moonlight - by the idea of proving her smart-aleck sister wrong even if she would never know, and by the flicker of guilt at doing something forbidden, something deceitful.

She was quiet, letting her lips find their way up his neck, along his jaw until his hand grasped her neck and willfully turned her head to his. Their lips met and she let herself fall into his kiss. He held her for a long time till she thought she would run out of breath. The kiss was forceful, deliberate, not at all like Steven's kisses. Steven could excite her there was no doubt, but his kisses were like the flutter of a butterfly's wings. This was different; hard, sensual and somehow wild and crazy.

This is how Lilly must feel when she kisses Bobby, she thought as the kiss ended. She leaned back in his arms, savoring the moment, fire on her lips, heat on her skin, the buzz of her blood coursing through her body. He was going to speak, she could sense it, and she stopped his lips with her fingers. She did not want words to interfere with the romance of the moment. From the raspberry bushes that tickled their elbows, she plucked several soft, ripe berries and held them to his lips.

He took the raspberries in, licking his lips at their lush sweetness. Grabbing her fingers, he licked the juice from them. In the next instant, his fingers were in her mouth, pushing soft, moist berries against her tongue. Like drunkards, they staggered through the raspberry patch, plucking berries, feeding them to one another, cavorting in the summer night. As they danced, she noticed the shifting wash of moonlight on the planes of his face. This face, so close to her own, looked like a mask, not like the face that she remembered as Carl's.

But by now, he too was caught in the heat of their play, intoxicated at the sweetness of the berries and the sweetness of her lips, lushness of fruit and body. His hands came up under her nightgown and grasped her firm young rump, squeezing and playing; they found their way to her breasts. She could have stopped him, grasped his hands, but she didn't want to stop this moonlight stranger from touching where no one had touched before.

They spun about in the moonlight like dancers on a Grecian urn and the ivory light fell full on his face. Rose stared at her partner, now totally aware that he did not look like Carl. But it was no trick of the nighttime, no misperception on her part. This sensual creature with whom she played was not Carl. For an instant she thought to pull away, realizing who her playmate was. It was Bobby! Her sister's beau, doubtless come creeping around hoping to entice Lilly to come out to play. Just as she'd hoped Steven would do. And there she'd come, skipping nonchalantly into his arms and . . . and he thought she was Lilly. Or did he?

Rose let his sticky fingers fondle her backside, pondering what she should do. She heard her sister's taunts and teasings, her voice calling her Shoes. She thought of Lilly's wanton ways and all she'd doubtless already done with Bobby. So, she pushed the thoughts from her mind, and forced herself to forget what she now knew. She liked the idea of taking revenge on her snippy sister in this way, but she didn't want to think about Bobby. So, she assigned him a new identity; he would be her phantom lover in the moonlight.

With a wantonness all her own she drew his face down to hers and kissed him as he'd kissed her. She could feel his arousal pressing against her belly and she wanted to touch him, this phantom in the garden in the moonlight, but she feared that was going too far. There was danger there and perhaps her sister was ready for that, but she knew she wasn't. She savored the feeling of playing the bad girl, but there were limits.

She felt delirious, wanton, utterly willful, as though she were possessed of a sensual power that could transform everything. The power she held could make this boy moan and groan and - if she wanted - to grovel. He would do that, she was certain. He would grovel and beg at her feet for the privilege of her flesh, for the intoxication of her . . . she thought maidenhood, but the word no sooner formed than it dissolved in the presence of another more powerful word: womanhood. Her body and her blood yearned to let go of all caution, to fall fervently with this boy into the grass and let their bodies do what they would.

As they kissed and touched, the moon passed through its zenith, and as if by design, the hot wind that had blown for the past week blew on over the horizon. The air was still, the night silent but for the slip of skin on skin. Rose, drunk with the moon, did not note its passage - its precise arc across the heavens - nor did she notice the sudden departure of the wind. But she knew that something had changed; she could feel it deep inside herself. Her mind, besotted with romance, cleared sufficiently to impose a brake on her body's headlong immersion in lust. Her mind insisted on peering over the moonlit garden into the bright light of the coming day. Where she saw in utter clarity a picture entitled Consequences.

Rose sensed the intense need growing in Bobby. She had no idea what liberties Lilly might have allowed the boy, though she had her suspicions - much stronger now than they'd been an hour ago. But she knew her moonlight sojourn as a bad girl had run its course. She kissed him hard, one last time, her sticky fingers raking down his chest and then she pulled back, out of his arms. He stood stock still, his arms outstretched, like a statue in an ancient garden. But she turned and dashed from the garden, across the yard, and into the house. Her heart pounded wildly as she closed and locked the door. She'd been a very bad girl and it had been crazy and delicious as if the raspberries were some thick, luxuriant liqueur. She'd been as wild and carefree as her sister, and she'd done it with her sister's boyfriend. And she didn't regret a moment of it.

Slipping silently into the bedroom she saw her sister's face in the moonlight. She looked almost angelic. Rose smiled a smile that would have made the devil blush and slipped into her bed.

Her blood was hot, and her nerves sizzled, and it was a long time before sleep came. As she finally felt the drowsiness stealing over her, she wondered what Steven would say if she were to kiss him the way she'd kissed her phantom lover in the moonlight.

Rose awoke early, coming straight up out of a wondrous sleep. She yawned and stretched, savoring feelings of fullness and contentment. Rolling luxuriously over in her bed, she sat up to find Lilly staring intently at her face.

"Sis, what's wrong with your face? Didn't you wash before you went to bed?" Rose's eyes grew wide as she touched her face, still slightly sticky. She looked at her hands, at the berry stains and she realized that the wild and wondrous dream in the moonlight had left its telltale signs. A desperate embarrassment washed over her, and she jumped out of bed. She wanted to rush directly to the bathroom and wash away those signs of her guilt, but Lilly too was out of bed, blocking her way. Before Rose knew what was happening, Lilly peered in the top of her nightgown where other dark stains met her eyes. Lilly's face wrinkled in confusion and then opened in awe.

"Shoes, you devil," Lilly drawled, tugging at Rose's nightgown. Rose turned away, trying desperately to hide the purple splotches she knew covered her breasts and hips. "How, oh how did you get Steven to treat you like that? You must know more than I gave you credit for." Lilly danced around Rose, trying to see more.

"Leave me alone! Stop it, Lilly!" Rose yelled. But Lilly persisted, pursuing her across the room.

"Or was it Steven?" Lilly said suddenly, getting a closer view of the fingerprints on Rose's chest. "Those prints look awfully big to be Steven's. It was Carl, wasn't it? You devil! You absolute devil, you." Lilly danced around her sister, clapping her hands, her eyes quick with the delight of her insight. "I never thought you had it in you."

"Girls, girls, what's all that commotion up there?" their mother called from the bottom of the stairs. Lilly and Rose fell silent, Lilly contracting into a nervous ball of energy, trying to stifle her delight.

"Oh, mom, we're just fooling around. We'll be right down," Lilly called. Their mother's interruption had altered the flow of events and Rose felt the embarrassment fall away. She felt suddenly grown up, in control, and for once, holding a much better hand than her sister. She pulled up her nightgown and candidly examined the purplish splotches on her bottom. She peered in the top of her nightgown at the stains on her breasts. All the while Lilly danced like a demented nymph smothering her merriment and pointing at Rose.

"It was Carl," she squealed, on the edge of hysteria. "It was Carl! I'm going to have to stop calling you Shoes."

Rose smiled at Lilly and for a moment she imagined she knew how the Mona Lisa must have felt.

The Girls of Summer

for G.M.

Sometimes her lack of attention annoyed Roger.

Sometimes a hard nugget of resentment grew in him until he didn't know what to do with himself. And sometimes it didn't matter, those times when he was just happy to be with her, the way it had always been.

That quiet sense of acceptance had marked their drive north yesterday and spread gently to the morning at Fort Ticonderoga and the ferry ride across Champlain. The lake breeze had riffled his hair as he watched the soft rolling hills of New York pass from deep green into a hazy turquoise, the hills of Vermont reversing the process to emerge in sharp green relief. It occurred to him how the image mirrored his feelings, changing, and changing yet again, only to remain the same. But he wasn't sure how long that would last.

It had been a day of blue and silver, one of those late July days when the sky was filled with thick white clouds that somehow seemed to intensify the brightness. They'd driven north into the hills of Vermont quilted in green crops and hay and the gold of ripening grain. The journey had been leisurely with plenty of time to think, punctuated now and then by Meg's sudden interest in an antique shop, a local craft-shop, or a yard sale.

And Roger had thought; he'd thought of himself as the lake, his emotions placid on the surface, but running down deep to dark and unknown places. He'd thought, too, of himself as the sky, with the clouds of his thoughts streaming by. And though the day was beautiful, the scenery splendid, underneath his serenity, a streak of dissatisfaction threatened to rise unpleasantly to the surface.

Late in the day they'd turned west, back toward the lake and the hotel where they were to meet Matt and Denise. By the time they'd checked in, freshened up, and gotten back out onto the hotel grounds, the tone of the day had shifted, its brilliance muted by the approach of evening. The spell that had lulled them into their meditative state was slipping away.

They stood for a moment surveying the grounds, looking out across the lake, the afternoon light changing, but still crisp and clear. All around the hotel, paths led off in various directions - to the tennis courts, the pool, the golf course, the stables, and out along the lake shore. Wherever they walked they could always see the great hulk of the hotel, deep red in an emerald and hunter setting.

"Doesn't this remind you of the area around Bucknell with the hills and the Susquehanna," Roger said as they strolled along.

Meg looked around at the lake, the hills, the greenery. "I guess so," she said, "there are mountains and trees and water." She tended to see things in general whereas Roger, in his travel, as in his business, was a man of detail. Where she saw a landscape of farmland and wood lots, Roger saw a gnarled old tree, a stone wall fallen into disrepair, a wooded glen where a stream gurgled down over large rocks. In her woods and fields, he saw oak, maples, hemlock, hay, wheat, and potatoes. She hadn't paid much attention to the landscape when they took Michael out to Lewisburg. Roger drove the car and scrutinized the terrain while Meg dozed.

It wasn't terrain, Roger knew, that the mention of Bucknell brought to Meg's mind - it was their youngest child.

"I wonder how Michael's doing," Meg said, as much to herself as to Roger.

Roger smiled. "He's fine," he said. "You need to lay off the mother thing for a while and relax." Meg looked at him. Roger saw the change in the shade of her eyes, the flattening of the arch of her eyebrows, the little tucked-under look at the end of her lips. In serious mother-mode, he thought. He could read his wife the same way he took in the details of the landscape. Somewhere deep inside he felt a twinge of irritation. Roger had been hoping that this vacation might break her free from her intense mother role, that she might for once turn her attention to romance.

"I worry that he's taken on too much trying to manage a double major."

"I keep telling you that there's no need to worry." Roger glanced at Meg, suppressing the thoughts that threatened to bubble to the surface. She looked flushed and beads of sweat stood out on her forehead and upper lip.

"Another hot flash?"

"It'll pass in a minute, I'm sure." Roger handed Meg his handkerchief. She wiped the sweat from her face and waved the folded cloth like a fan before handing it back to him.

"I worry about Frances, too." Frances, the middle child, was spending a year as an art intern in Florence, away from home for the first time.

"She's fine."

"But she's such an innocent. And you know how those Italian men were when we were there. I know, I know, that was a long time ago," she said, drifting back into the memory of their youthful summer in Italy. "Those wicked men would pinch my butt right out on the streets, and they were always trying to rub against my breasts. You don't think things have changed, do you?"

"And do you think that our daughter is so innocent that she can't take care of herself?" His words brought a sudden look of concern to Meg's face.

"Do you know something I don't?" she asked, her voice teetering on a potentially slippery slope.

"No, no," Roger said, chuckling, reaching for Meg's hand. "I don't know anything. I just think Frances is a capable young person who can take care of herself."

"Well, I worry," Meg insisted. "What if some worldly older man . . . some sophisticate . . . a dirty old man . . ." She let her remark slip away as Roger put his arm around her and hugged her.

"Am I making too much of this?"

"Yes, dear," Roger said.

"It's passed," she said, "They're so annoying. I wish this was over and done with."

Below them, further down slope, a young woman, a girl perhaps - Roger was never sure when a girl became a young woman - passed across their field of vision. She wore a black swimsuit and like all the young these days she was slender, tan, and beautiful, sharp and crisp like the light. Roger's eyes followed her until she was lost in the shadows of a stand of pines.

It had been a long time, a decade or more, since Roger had looked at young girls with any kind of interest. He'd always enjoyed beautiful women, regardless their ages, but for the most part he tended to notice women close to his own age. Nor had it ever been a prurient or obsessive ogling. It was rarely the woman as a whole that caught his attention. It was the moment that enchanted him; a matter of details: tanned skin, slender delicate fingers, the flow of shoulder to upper arm. It could be a graceful foot in a strap sandal, the way a girl's hair framed her face or an earring dangling from an earlobe, a bare mid-riff, a knee momentarily revealed. Not that he was immune to the wonders of breasts and derrieres and beautiful faces. It was just that these observations rarely led to the kind of fantasies that men were supposed to have about women.

He'd occasionally thought that there might be something wrong with him, that perhaps some hormone wasn't going where it should, some gland wasn't performing as designed. He'd listened to his men friends talk about women and he felt left out, lacking in some essential male quality because he had no interest in appraising women in that way, bantering in locker rooms and barrooms. His sexual relationship with Meg had remained strong and intense and doubtless, that was why he remained aloof to the allures of other women.

But lately, the last year or so, Roger had begun to look more frequently. It bothered him sometimes, that impulse to stare. At least he wasn't obvious about it as some men were. Certainly, he didn't think Meg was aware of his growing need to look at other women.

Meg, however, was the reason for it. He didn't want to blame her, it wasn't her fault, and yet there was an uncomfortable edge to his experience of her change of life. The old Meg, who'd always met him toe-to-toe in their sexuality, was missing in action. In her place was another Meg, a moody woman who complained of the physical changes and worried about aging. A woman who, over the course of six months or so, had lost interest in sex. Roger hadn't seen it coming and at first, despite Meg's protestations, he'd thought it was him, that she no longer found him attractive or perhaps that she'd found someone else. He'd had a hard time accepting that proposition and he still, now and then, thought that she might not be being completely honest.

It wasn't easy for Roger to separate himself from his own needs and desires to see the truth of the matter. True, circumstances had now and again altered their love life – most notably Meg's pregnancies. But this was different. And even after he'd accepted the situation, there was still that residual resentment, as though Meg was doing this to him. He didn't want to give up his beautiful and erotic wife; he didn't want to surrender his sexuality. He'd tried talking to her, but somehow, she didn't seem to understand. After those talks, the frustration and resentment stuck like bile in his craw. To him it seemed she'd made up her mind without considering his feelings and there was nothing he could do about it.

And so, he found himself looking more frequently, staring at women in supermarket check-out lines, women walking on the street, young girls - young women, he supposed - playing frisbee or walking their dogs in the park. Here in this holiday atmosphere of leisure and fun the opportunities to appraise the beauty of women expanded exponentially.

Taking Meg's hand in his, Roger put his thoughts aside and turned them toward the lake where canoes and rowboats nestled around a wooden dock. Ahead of them near the end of the dock, a young woman worked on one of the canoes. She wore a wine-red shirt, open like a jacket, which, along with khaki shorts, constituted the informal uniform of the hotel grounds staff.

As they walked out onto the dock, the girl rose from her work and came toward them. Her blonde hair was piled in a disorderly tangle on her head, strands of it trailing around her face. Like all the other girls of summer, she was slender and graceful and tanned a honey gold. Under the wine-red shirt, which was much too large for her, a man's shirt on her slender frame, she wore not khaki shorts but a red bikini. Her name was Tracy, or so the blue stitching over her left breast proclaimed.

"Hello," she said, smiling, "can I get you a canoe? Or a paddle boat?"

"No thanks," Meg said. "We're just looking around. Maybe tomorrow." The girl nodded to Meg, her eyes moving on to Roger. Her eyes sparkled and the smile that lit up her face seemed genuine, not the polite smile-for-the-guest that he'd already seen several times elsewhere this afternoon. There was in her face one of those moments that caused Roger to stare. It wasn't that she was an outrageous beauty; she wasn't. More a girl-next-door type. He'd seen several girls earlier that day who were more beautiful.

Meg was already turning away, nearly bumping into him as his gaze lingered on the girl's face. It took a conscious effort to break free, to turn away and follow.

Roger and Meg walked back to the terrace where they spent the rest of the afternoon prolonging the meditative quiet of the day. The sun slid down the western sky, the blue and silver day tinged now with a deep red iridescence, a quality of light that hinted at autumn sunsets. The heat of the day abated, and a breeze came in across the lake.

"It's about time those two showed up," Meg said, sipping her martini. "I'm getting hungry."

A grin wrinkled Roger's face. "What?" Meg demanded.

"Oh, knowing Matt, I'd bet he took the wrong turn off the interstate, and right about now they're either back in Albany or else crossing the state line into New Hampshire."

"I wouldn't be surprised," Meg said. "Matt certainly doesn't have the best sense of direction." She slipped her hand into Roger's. Together they rose from their seats and turned just in time to see Matt and Denise emerge from the lobby. They both wore pale yellow polo shirts, white shorts, socks, and tennis shoes. Their attire contrasted sharply with the deep tan that colored their faces, arms, and legs. They looked like the perfect suburban couple arriving at the country club. Matt waved, his action seeming to engage the whole of his six-foot-three frame.

"Roger, you old dog," Matt hailed as he crossed the terrace in robust strides, Denise hurrying to keep up.

"We thought you'd gotten lost," Meg said.

"Lost!" Denise said. "You don't know the half of it." "Where did you pick up the interstate?" Roger asked.

"We didn't come on the interstate," Denise replied. Matt grinned sheepishly.

"Then how in the world did you get here?" Meg and Roger exclaimed in unison.

Denise rolled her eyes. "A native guide," she said. "No, seriously, my direction- challenged husband, after much driving around, did manage to stumble onto the right road." Matt shrugged.

"Actually, we did get here on the interstate," he admitted. "That's the road I stumbled on, as my dear wife so quaintly put it. About ten miles south of Burlington." Roger and Meg laughed at Matt, while Denise, in imitation of her husband, shrugged her shoulders.

"Oh, well, you made it," Meg said, "and just in time too. I'm starving."

"At least you don't look any the worse for your trials," Roger said to Matt, knuckling him lightly on the upper arm.

"Him?" Denise said. "He's not the one to look worse for wear. He's Mr. Cool-and- Natural. I'm the one who's got three more grey hairs."

Meg looked at Denise's thick dark hair; she was wearing it long this year. It was very becoming and made her look younger than her years.

"Speaking of which," Matt said, "the old grey has certainly crept up on you, hasn't it, Rog?" Matt returned the knuckle jab to Roger's shoulder, a bit more vigorously than he'd received.

"Oh, you should talk," Denise said. "Just look at you. Grey all over. Besides, Roger looks very distinguished, doesn't he, Meg? I bet there are lots of women checking him out." Meg's eyes were soft on her husband, her reply, a smile like the scent of honeysuckle on the summer air.

"How are the kids?" Meg asked, turning her attention to her friend. "Oh, they're the same as always. Kim is away in Europe and . . ."

"So, Rog, how's it going?" Roger was anxious to talk to Matt, but it was man-to-man talk and he realized that now was not the time. Timing was an important factor, for Matt had always maintained a cool, suave demeanor upon meeting, but sooner or later he'd slip into the comradery of fraternity brothers. And when he'd had enough to drink, he got downright lewd. It was not at the level of fraternity buddies that Roger wanted to talk about his concerns, and that bothered him.

So, Roger bided his time, and they talked as old friends do upon meeting after a prolonged separation - of their jobs, old friends and acquaintances, of odds and ends, bits and pieces of personal information that tied them one to the other. Their conversation, which at first paralleled that of the women, soon drifted off to that pervading interest of men: sports.

As their conversation turned to the Phillies, Roger's "team" - an affinity not shared by Matt - a knot of young people, boys and girls together, crossed the terrace headed for the lobby. They were all in shorts and several of the girls wore filmy, revealing tops. Roger noticed Matt's eyes shift from his face to the group of young people. Had they been alone, Roger might have watched the girls, but he did not want to be obvious. Matt, however, did not share Roger's reserve. He grew silent and Roger turned to follow his stare. When he turned back to face Matt, he saw that his friend was still staring intently at the girls. As the group filed into the hotel, Matt brought his attention back to Roger.

"Whew," he said. His eyes were bright with the images of young female flesh. It seemed to Roger that his face was flushed, though it might have been the effect of the sinking sun. It lasted only a moment and Matt's focus was back on Roger and he picked up the threads of what he'd been saying.

As Matt talked on, Roger found himself following superficially, his mind working on what he'd just witnessed. He didn't recall ever having seen anything like that in Matt in recent years. Back in their college days, before they'd married, yes, but not recently. Within him several different emotions tangled uncomfortably; a sense of embarrassment at Matt's behavior, which seemed to Roger to be almost juvenile, college frat-brat at the very least. Or maybe just low class. There was something in it too of a basic male instinct, the emotions tangled like honeysuckle and wild grape on a wooded hillside.

Roger noticed during dinner as the two couples lingered over their meal and later, in the bar, how Matt looked at the waitresses, how his eyes ranged over the room. Roger was both puzzled and excited by Matt's behavior. Nervous energy flickered through him. He looked at the slender young women Matt was checking out and much as he didn't want to admit it, they stirred his interest as well.

Roger looked at Meg. It was true; she was no longer the slender woman he'd married. The years and the children had added weight to her. He glanced at Matt, looked at Denise.

They'd all thickened, no longer the slender young people they'd been; even Denise, though she was at least five years younger than the rest of them. He saw it in himself as well - whenever he took the time to look. They were no longer young.

He was still thinking about it the next morning when he found himself alone on the terrace. Meg had opted to stay in bed with a novel - a luxury she said she'd been looking forward to, just this one morning. Matt and Denise were off at the tennis courts and Roger was on his own. He would rather have stayed in bed with Meg. Ever since they'd made their plan, he'd hoped that the change in scenery might strike a romantic spark in Meg. But that hadn't been the case. Roger had made several subtle romantic gestures, all of which Meg, in her practical fashion, had simply not noticed. He'd been disappointed at her lack of attention and this morning the disappointment was crystallizing into sharp little slivers of resentment.

He sat on the terrace looking out across the lake at New York, soft and indistinct in the brilliant sunlight. It had been a long time since he'd been alone like this with nothing in particular to do. Especially in a more or less exotic place he didn't know. He settled back in his lounge chair and let his mind drift. For a few moments, his attention snagged on the fluffy, high- altitude clouds skimming across the lake. They were like his thoughts and soon they carried him away, skipping from one association to another until he came back to Meg. And from Meg, it was only a short skip to the nature of their marriage as age began to make its first inroads on their lives. He wondered whether Matt and Denise were experiencing the same thing.

Probably not; Denise still had that intense beauty of the mature woman, as yet untouched by the withering hands of time. But Matt Roger thought about the blatant way he'd looked

at the waitresses last night. Perhaps he too was facing that same problem. Or some variant of it. There was an undercurrent that emerged now and then in the remarks of Matt and Denise, suggesting hidden rocks, rifts, and eddies in the stream of their marriage. Roger was momentarily thankful that his emotions were not so dominated by the visions of young women. Girls? His mind went blank, and he felt the need to move, to be up and doing something, something that was not thinking.

He could wander over to the tennis courts and watch his friends play, but quite frankly, he found tennis boring. He could walk around the grounds or, looking out towards the lake, he could take a boat out. He thought then of the girl on the dock, the girl in the red bikini. A pretty girl, a very pleasant girl, he recalled. As if that thought resolved the issue, Roger set out for the lakefront.

As Roger approached the dock, he saw the girl in conversation with a blonde woman. The way they stood facing one another suggested to Roger that this was not a friendly encounter. The woman, who appeared to be in her late thirties or early forties, wore a fashionable teal and sea green swimsuit, beige pumps and a wide-brimmed straw hat. A large towel was wrapped around her waist like a sarong. At her neck, the sparkle of a gold chain; more gold on her wrist. Roger wasn't close enough to hear their words, but he could see by the way the woman held herself that she was not at all pleased. Tracy stood on the dock with her head lowered. Like a schoolgirl called before the principal. She looked up, past the woman's shoulder, and saw Roger. Anger and embarrassment commingled on her face.

The woman turned and glanced at Roger. She turned back to Tracy for some parting remark and then abruptly stomped up the dock toward him. She walked with a studied self- importance that spoke volumes. Regardless of who she thought she was, Roger recognized her as a bleached blonde, once as willowy as Tracy was now, thickened by the easy life as an executive's wife. The diamond encrusted engagement-wedding ring ensemble burdening her ring finger only served to underline the obvious. He knew these things because she looked exactly like Hank Willoughby's wife when she was annoyed.

Roger moved aside to let her pass and as she did, she looked at him and said sharply, "Impudent little bitch." As Roger made his way along the dock, he saw Tracy trying to compose herself. She looked up at Roger, eyes shifting to avoid contact, her face forced into a smile she obviously didn't feel.

"Hello," she said, her voice unsteady.

"Hi," Roger smiled. "Was the fine lady giving you a hard time?" Tracy's eyes grew wide, and Roger watched the forced composure slip away and true emotions emerge.

"That woman," she snapped. "Every day it's something else, some stupid demand that. . . ."

"I wouldn't let it get to me," Roger said, watching the flush of anger in her face, the sharp

glint in her grey eyes. "I know her type. She's just like the wife of one of my business associates. Never happy unless she's lording it over somebody." Tracy's face had gone blank, neutral, as though the world had changed right before her eyes. "Want to know the best way to deal with people like her? Go along with whatever she says, and then, as soon as she's gone, have a good laugh at how ridiculous she is."

"I'm sorry," Tracy said. "I shouldn't have said that."

"It's OK. Perfectly understandable." Tracy leaned back against the piling, the tension slipping from her body. Today she wore the khaki shorts with her bikini top. They stood for a moment gazing out over the canoes, out onto the lake. The silence made Roger uncomfortabl, and he searched for something to say. Grasping at the first thing that came to mind, he asked - logically enough - about school.

"I'll be a senior at the U. this fall," she said. To Roger's next question, she replied: "Veterinary medicine. I love animals. At home we have horses, sheep, ducks, and chickens. And, of course, cats and dogs."

Roger smiled at her; of course, he thought. "You must be a real country girl."

"Oh, I am. You can almost see our farm from the front drive of the hotel. You know that sugarloaf with all the boulders sticking out in the middle? We live at the base of that mountain." Roger knew what she was talking about; he'd already noted the outcropping as the most unusual feature of the local landscape.

"We live in suburbia and have one cat," Roger laughed. Tracy smiled and asked about the cat. It pleased and surprised Roger because, unlike most people who would have ignored the remark or asked rhetorically, it seemed to him that she was genuinely interested.

He thought that they would soon run out of things to say to one another. That's the way it was with the young. Even his daughter, he regretted to admit. But that wasn't the case at all, and he soon found himself immersed in a conversation about Tracy's family, her interests, her animals. When he thought about it later, he realized that talking to her had been as easy as talking to Meg. She spoke like a real person, not like most of the young people he'd encountered who spoke some patois that bore only the slightest resemblance to English.

There was, nonetheless, a quixotic aspect to her talk as she slipped easily from the serious to the frivolous. Rather than bother him as he might have expected, Roger found himself charmed and delighted by her youthful zeal and good humor. A warmth grew in him, a warmth that he'd not experienced in a long time. He found himself thinking of that old song from his teen years, "Do You Believe in Magic". He couldn't remember the words, but it was something about magic and a young girl's heart.

As she spoke, he was aware of her spontaneity, that youthful tendency to see life as boundless and magnificent. Watching her face, animated, unaffected, he was happy simply to look at her. Standing on the dock in the heat of the morning sun, the lake breeze fresh on his face, he had the feeling that in some mysterious way she was giving him something he'd been needing. The realization surprised and unsettled him.

She was probably the same age as Frances, and Roger wondered what he was doing here. He was having a hard time of it, trying not to look at her breasts, her legs. Concentrate on her face, he thought, the little dimples at the corners of her mouth. What really surprised him, however, was that they were able to sit in the sunshine and talk as equals. Her hair, in its unpredictable tangles around her face, made him think of the freshness and innocence of Meg before they married.

Lost in his thoughts, caught in the magic of the moment, barely aware of what she was saying, he caught himself just as he was about to lean over to smell the sun and breeze in her hair. Disconcerted, he looked away, glancing at the canoes and the paddle boats. One of the canoes had come loose from its mooring and was floating away from the dock.

"You've got an escapee here," he said. She stopped in mid-sentence, her face wrinkling in query.

"An escapee . . . ?"

"That canoe." Roger pointed and Tracy uttered an oh. She knelt to the dock and reached out for the rope that trailed in the water. The canoe was just out of reach, her fingers missing the rope by inches. Roger offered his hand, and grasping hold, she was able to lean out far enough to snare the rope and haul the canoe back to its berth. Roger tugged her arm, pulling her up from the dock. Rising, she stumbled and fell into his arms. The sudden presence of this girl in his embrace shocked him. Tracy took it in stride, smiled, then laughed at their inadvertent contact. Roger felt an uncomfortable heat spread thru his body. He was disconcerted, uncertain whether it was the touch of her flesh or their respective reactions that had unsettled him.

For a moment a sense of incompletion permeated the space between them. Before he realized what was happening, his mind had made a dangerous leap. He didn't want this to happen, he knew that it would loose a flood tide of emotions and desires he didn't want to deal with. But he couldn't help himself, he couldn't stave off the thoughts that pressed into his mind. He saw her naked, her face flushed with desire, saw himself kissing her, touching her breasts, her sex, pushing urgently between her slender thighs. Like gate crashers at a soccer match, the thoughts pushed and swarmed into his consciousness, revelers at a debauched Mardi Gras. Roger shuddered, aware that once free, there would be little chance of catching those thoughts and once again confining them to some cage in the back of his mind.

"Thank you," she said, stepping back, still smiling, her eyes telling Roger of her pleasure and amusement at what had happened.

"I'm sorry," she said, "I should have introduced myself. You probably saw my name on the shirt. I'm Tracy. Tracy Green. Like the Green Mountains." She laughed, thrusting her hand out to Roger.

"I'm Roger Lathern," he said, grasping her slender hand, his thoughts elsewhere. He was still thinking of what had just transpired. Certainly, he'd touched other women over the years, women he'd embraced in greeting, women he'd danced with. But never, aside from Frances, had he touched the bare skin of a young woman, a girl. All manner of strange feelings flashed and flickered through his mind, but the sound of voices approaching brought him back to the moment.

"You have very kind eyes, Mr. Lathern." She looked almost angelic, open and fresh, and for the second time in minutes he thought of Meg as a newlywed. His mouth opened to speak, but for a moment he could say nothing.

"I'd better let you get back to your duties," he said finally. "It's been a pleasure talking with you."

"The pleasure has been mine, Mr. Lathern," she said, sounding mature and worldly beyond her years. "I hope we get to talk again." As he walked away Roger had the feeling that she meant what she said.

Matt parked his car on a side street up the hill from Burlington center. Under the blazing sun the two couples followed their tourist map the several blocks to Church St. When they turned into the pedestrian mall, all four were astonished at the large number of people on the street. Even in the heat of the afternoon the street was alive with activity. The pedestrian mall stretched for blocks, lined with restaurants, clothing stores, jewelry stores, gift shops, and much, much more. It looked far more European than

American. People bustled along the street. Tourists, students, shoppers, business people, and locals, all strolling along, chatting on corners. The young and the elderly, talking, smoking, watching the crowds drift by. There was an atmosphere of vitality that suggested some other time and place, before technology isolated people in their private cocoons. With the lake visible at cross streets there was a holiday feel to the town, almost as if they'd stumbled into an Italian town in the lake district.

"Well, what are we up to?" Matt asked as the four stood at a street corner surveying the possibilities.

"I don't know what you boys intend to do," Meg said, "but we girls intend to do some very serious shopping."

"Very serious," Denise added, as she turned to stare at a shoe store across the way.

"I know what that means," Matt said, "and I want no part of it." He turned to Roger. "Why don't we just walk around, go down to the lake, find a nice watering hole?" Roger nodded in agreement, although he would have had no problem accompanying Meg had they been alone, but he'd been waiting for an opportunity to talk to Matt alone. "Sure thing."

Denise looked around, her eyes taking in a trio of teenage girls wearing short shorts and tank tops that left little to the imagination, a pair of tall, well-dressed young women who looked like legal secretaries, a scantily clad co-ed on roller-blades. She turned to Meg, a look of dissatisfaction on her face.

"It's kind of like letting a pair of foxes loose in the hen house," she said to Meg. "Or better I should say wolves."

"Oh, I don't think our boys are anything like that," Meg said in her sincere way. "Are you, Matt? I know Roger isn't. He likes to look, I think, but there's no harm in that. Why don't we all meet in two hours. . . ," she looked around and pointed to a café with tables out front and umbrellas for shade, "there." Details settled, the women went off arm in arm, heading for the shoe store that had caught Denise's eye.

Matt and Roger strolled along the street, weaving languorously in and out amidst the flow of pedestrians. Unlike the women, they'd already run out of small talk, so they walked in silence, waiting for a worthy topic to present itself. That worthy topic was on the tip of Roger's tongue, but he was hesitant to broach the subject here. There was likewise a flicker of doubt about how Matt would respond, so he concentrated on the sights. Roger had watched Denise check out the women on the street when she'd made her remark about wolves, and he could see easily why she'd said it. There was a continuous parade of young women, an incredible concentration, in fact. Everywhere he looked his eyes encountered firm, tanned skin, long slender legs, bright eyes. After a while he noted that they seemed to dress in a vague uniformity: spaghetti-strap top in some silky fabric in black, white, orange or wine-red. With the top, a contrasting skirt or shorts - skirt usually - and sandals or clogs. Never did a man need to turn his head to follow a beautiful woman, he thought, for one no sooner passed than several more came into view.

Roger was trying his best to be circumspect, he didn't want to fall into the position of validating Denise's remark. He glanced at Matt who didn't seem to mind; his eyes were very busy checking out the feminine wonders of Burlington, Vermont.

The two drifted to a halt in front of a clothing store where lacy bras and panties were prominently displayed. They stood silently staring in at the exotic under things as if entranced.

"A lot of nice things to look at in this town," Matt said. Inside the store several young women looked through the racks of clothing. "Look at that tall girl with the long dark hair." Matt elbowed Roger in the side. "She looks like Nastassja Kinski." Roger peered into the shop and, yes, the young woman did look like the European actress. Roger remembered her from years before when she was barely more than a teenager. He thought she'd been involved with some well-known movie personality - Polanski maybe.

"I always had the hots for her," Matt said. "Did you see her in *Cat People*? I watched that movie dozens of times just to look at her." Roger stared at Matt, his nose practically pressed against the glass. He had a hard time comprehending what his friend had just said. The man had a beautiful wife he could look at any time; not only look at, but touch - a real woman. Why would he become so obsessed with an actress?

As they turned from the window, Roger glanced at Matt, following the movement of his eyes to a slender blonde, her hair a golden mane in the afternoon sun. In a white suit and spaghetti-strap high heels, she could be nothing less than a goddess of the modern world. Roger watched the woman for a few moments, admiring the grace of her stride, the sinuous flow of her hair in motion. Then he turned away, not wanting to stare, but conscious nonetheless of a none- too-subtle stirring somewhere deep inside.

"Are the girls more beautiful than when we were young?" Matt asked, turning abruptly to Roger. "Or is it my imagination?" The question came as no surprise to Roger, for it had occurred to him as well that women of this modern age appeared more beautiful than had the girls of his youth. Maybe it's just age, he thought, though he didn't want to admit that, and in any even, he would not say that to Matt.

"Maybe it's because of the food, better nutrition," Roger said finally, his mind seeking some rational explanation for the phenomenon. Matt stared at him, a blank look on his face. "Or maybe it's just money. Kids have so much more money available to them than we did. Or maybe," he went on, recalling several scantily clad nymphets he'd seen earlier, "it's just the styles. They're so much more daring than what girls wore years ago." Matt said nothing, his eyes still blank, as if Roger's words had gone unheard.

"How do they affect you?" Roger asked, feeling foolish the moment the words left his mouth; he could see how they affected Matt.

"They drive me nuts. I can hardly stand it." The intensity of Matt's reply surprised Roger.

He had no doubt that his friend was being utterly truthful with him. "But you've got an absolutely gorgeous wife."

Matt looked at him, his eyes wide. "What does that have to do with anything?"

Later, the afternoon sun edging down toward the horizon, Roger and Matt sat in a café on the public docks drinking beer. As they watched the coming and going of people and sailboats, Roger toyed with the coaster under his beer glass.

"What's up, Rog? You have a faraway look in your eyes."

"Uhhh . . ." Roger hesitated. "Nothing. It's nothing. Just a passing thought."

"I don't think so, buddy. What's on your mind?" Roger was no longer sure he wanted to tell Matt what he'd been thinking, but the words burst forth despite his reluctance.

"It's this menopause thing. Meg's starting her change of life."

"Uh oh," Matt leaned back making the sign of the cross with his fingers. "Yeh, right," Roger said. "To tell the truth, it's really got me down."

"I don't think I want to hear about this, but go ahead."

"Meg's lost all interest in sex," Roger said, sitting back in his chair and sighing. "We always had such great sex and now it just stopped."

"Stopped? No sex at all?"

"Well, now and then, yeh, but I can tell her heart's not in it. I feel bad . . . to lose the passion, of course, but because it bothers me so much, too."

"I guess it would bother you. It'd bother the shit outta me, let me tell you." Matt hunched over the table and said in a flat voice: "It's bad enough as it is, but I know that's just down the road." Roger looked at Matt and for a moment he thought of one of those Bill Malden cartoons he'd seen as a kid. Two bedraggled GIs in a foxhole in the rain. He shrugged the thought away and downed the last of his beer.

"Let's go," he said, "Too much thinking isn't good for us."

That night they returned to Burlington for dinner. In the cool of the evening with throngs of people in the streets, the carnival atmosphere was far more evident than it had been during the day. The night was alive with the noise of the crowds, laughter, music from one night spot competing with music from other night spots, the sense of merriment, of holiday. Again, the image of some Latin or southern European city passed through Roger's mind.

It didn't take them long to find a charming little French restaurant. As the waitress served drinks and took their orders, they made small talk. The conversation wended its way here and there until Meg said something about getting older and, for whatever reason, Denise returned to her observation of the day before about Roger's distinguished looks.

"I can't get over it, Roger, how that little streak of grey at your temples changes your looks."

"Yeh," Roger said, "it makes me look older." "Not older, Roger, better."

"Oh,oh,oh, here's my wife flirting with my best friend," Matt said. The remark was accompanied with a chuckle, but Roger thought he detected an undercurrent of something hard and sharp.

Denise went on as if she hadn't even heard. "Really. You've always been a good-looking guy, but that grey somehow sets you off. I don't know. It adds a depth of character or something. Don't you think so, Meg?"

"It doesn't add character," Matt quipped, "he's always been a character." Matt leaned across the table to give Roger a comradely cuff. The women ignored him.

"You're absolutely right," Meg said. "I've noticed that women look at Roger differently the last while."

As Denise nodded in agreement, Roger tried to protest this line of talk, but no one paid him any mind.

"Yeh, maybe even the young ones," Matt said, following up his remark with a Groucho Marx imitation.

"Oh, Matt," Denise said, "you can be such a dirty old man at times." "Dirty old man? Me?"

"Yes, you! You think I don't see your eyes wandering when one of those slinky young things goes prancing by."

"Well, yeh, maybe I look, but that doesn't make me a dirty old man, does it?" There was a note of puzzlement in Matt's voice.

"If you're looking, you're thinking too," Denise said, turning to share a knowing look with Meg. Roger was silent, waiting to see where this was going, fearful that he might be dragged into something of which he wanted no part, fearful of the unpleasant potential.

"Oh, come on," Matt moaned, obviously aggrieved at the direction the talk was taking. "Come on is right! I know you well enough to know what's going on in that head of

yours. You're certainly not wondering how those bimbos are doing in school." Denise's voice rose as she spoke, and Roger watched a sudden flush of color come into her face. He looked at Meg, seeking to catch her eye, but her attention was on Matt.

"How would you define a dirty old man?" Roger asked, his voice level. The emotions around the table were rising, Matt growing defensive, obviously feeling attacked. He tried to remain calm, asking to understand, even as a presentiment of guilt began to claw its way up his spine.

"A man ogling a girl young enough to be his daughter," Denise said as Meg nodded agreement. Roger didn't like the drift of things, this all too easy polarization of the genders.

"You mean looking alone is enough to condemn a man? He wouldn't even have to do anything?" Matt persisted, a strained quality to his voice.

"Ogling and thinking about young girls? Of course, that's enough to earn you a dirty old man rating," Meg chimed in.

The dissatisfaction with the women's remarks shadowed Matt's face. Roger wore a mask of objective neutrality, but inside his emotions moved toward chaos. It bothered him that Meg swung so easily into the attack, her face taking on the high color that marked Denise.

"You mean that if I just look at a young girl, I'm guilty?" Matt asked, an aggressive edge creeping into his voice.

The women were leaning in over the table now, an uncomfortable tension flickering about the four of them. The women's eagerness for battle, their willingness to tar and feather any man who so much as looked at a young girl unsettled Roger. Of course, men looked at young girls; why wouldn't they? He looked too. He looked at beautiful women regardless of age, wanting to add, however, that he rarely thought about them naked or what it might be like to touch them. But his train of thought derailed abruptly as he came upon his reaction to Tracy just a few hours before.

Even though it was Matt who was taking all the fire, Roger knew that it was him they were talking about. Even by his own standards, he had to admit that he qualified. He felt the heat sweep up over his cheeks; his facade of neutrality beginning to crumble. He recognized the testiness in Matt's voice and part of him felt the same way - belligerent and self-justifying. But somewhere deep inside guilt roiled and twisted in his guts.

At least, he thought, I wouldn't actually do anything. The thought died aborning as an image of Tracy swam into his consciousness. Suddenly he wasn't sure what his body might force him to do. Denise's gaze, now sharp and probing, fell on Roger. The look on her face changed momentarily from determination to surprise. Her eyes didn't linger for long, her attention returning to Matt.

"Of course," the women agreed. They exchanged a glance that said: Duh! What other answer could there be?

"That's a pretty hard-assed opinion," Matt said, his word choice serving to underscore the irritation in his voice. Roger agreed, but he said nothing. He feared that Matt's line of reasoning would not be his and he could end up condemned to the scaffold without a trial. For his own part, he could see nothing wrong with looking at a beautiful young girl. How could there be anything wrong in looking at a thing of beauty? But he also understood in his bones what Meg and Denise meant; that looking at young girls with longing was in a very real way a dishonor towards them. He knew that he had already gone well beyond that innocent line. Roger remained silent, wanting in no way to participate in this potentially lethal discussion.

Matt launched into a defense, his blood rising with the volume of his voice. Roger's annoyance deepened as he watched the women gird for battle, apparently ready to tar and feather any man who so much as looked at a young woman – or girl. It bothered Roger that the women were so eager for battle, so willing to attack any man who so much as looked at a young girl.

"You are so absurd, Matt," Denise said, the steely ring of anger invading her voice. "You don't for one moment think that I'd believe that a man who was ogling wasn't also undressing the woman and thinking about her sexually." Her remark cut through Roger's thoughts, and he knew that neither Denise nor his wife would ever believe him were he to voice his thoughts.

"Big deal," Matt snapped, his voice matching hers. "So now and then I have sexual thoughts about a woman . . ."

"Isn't that what I just said." Denise turned to look at Meg. The two women had that guilty-as-charged look on their faces. It made Roger feel like a member of a vanquished race dragged into the court of the victors. There was a sour feeling in his stomach.

"If you got the chance, you'd fuck those girls you drool after," Denise said, the anger out in the open now. That word, flung so suddenly into their midst, chastened them.

They fell silent, an awkward tension settling like a chill mist over the table. Roger wanted to say something, something witty, clever and transcending, but he felt as though he'd fallen into a ditch and didn't know how to crawl out. He looked at Matt, his face sullen, close to anger. Meg and Denise were silently communicating some woman thing that he could easily guess at. Finally, as the silence dragged on, Matt shrugged his shoulders and let his breath out in a great sigh.

"Oh, well then," he said, "how about another drink, Rog? You seem to be down to the rocks." Roger breathed a sigh of relief, and it seemed as though the mist lifted from the table. Meg and Denise sat back and began discussing shops they'd been in earlier in the day and Matt sat back in his chair. Roger looked at Matt and saw in his eyes in huge letters: Whew! Close call.

It was late when they left the restaurant. They stood outside the door for a moment to get their bearings. The sidewalks were still crowded, and the carnival air of the night pulsed on unabated. Roger heard someone call his name and as he looked up Tracy, arm in arm with a handsome young man, emerged from the crowd.

"Hello, Mr. Lathern," she said, the pleasure at seeing him evident in her voice. Roger, caught off guard, was barely able to croak out a greeting. "This is my friend, Jaimie." Roger began to extend his hand, saw that the boy was not about to reciprocate, and aborted his movement. The casualness of youth, he thought. Before anything else could be said, the press of the crowd carried the two away, Tracy waving gaily as they disappeared.

When Roger looked at the others, he found them all staring at him. Each face held its own questions about what had transpired. Meg's face was puzzled while Denise's expression spoke of secrets revealed, of a suspicion confirmed. And on Matt's face, Roger found what he expected; the conspiratorial grin of a fraternity brother. The women said nothing as they headed off into the throng,

Matt hung back a momen, and when Roger moved to follow the women, he leaned close and said, "You dog, you."

Roger knew what he was thinking and thought to attempt an explanation, but saw immediately the futility of any such effort.

Meg was in the bathroom preparing for bed. In an effort to short circuit his mind, Roger slumped in the wing chair and flicked on the TV. He surfed the channels, seeing nothing of what passed before his eyes. Meg had said nothing about Tracy, but the air between them had grown uncharacteristically strained. They'd ridden home in the back of Matt's car and when Roger reached for her hand, she'd withdrawn it.

Roger was confused by his reaction to Tracy, unprepared for the sudden rearing up of need that she had unleashed. As if his life were nothing more than a line of dominoes; with the near argument at dinner, seeing Tracy, and the ride back to the hotel matters began to topple toward turmoil.

The stirring in him was a bedevilment. It walked right in and sat right down as if it meant to stay. It flickered along his skin and invaded his mind. It possessed his muscles and wrapped its claws around his heart. And always, peeking around corners and hiding in the shadows, was the guilt. He could just imagine the disdain and anger with which Meg would greet any confession he might attempt. She would be contemptuous and hurt. He could hear her voice as plainly as if she'd spoken: "The very idea! A girl, a mere girl!" She would be severely hurt, so much so that their relationship probably wouldn't survive. It was the hurt that plunged the dagger of guilt deep into his soul.

For the first time in many, many years, Roger realized that he was afraid. He didn't know whether the fear emanated from a sense of what he might do or what he might not do. It was not the clear, cold fear of confronting an enemy; it was a clammy sensation that, like a fifth column, spread insidiously. Maybe it was Meg, the way she would react that scared him.

And now it all pushed at him, and he had to admit that he'd been denying his feelings. Thoughts of Tracy danced thru his mind, and he thought that perhaps he'd fallen in love with her, but he knew it wasn't true. It was lust, plain and simple. He'd been caught out in the open with no place to hide. It was an obsession that drew him deeper and deeper into forbidden thoughts. He was being ridiculous, yet he could not help himself.

Roger knew that even then, in his mind, he was being unfaithful to Meg. He wondered whether he might slip into being unfaithful in the flesh should the opportunity arise, and the thought plagued him like a pebble in his shoe. He didn't want to think about it, but thoughts of Tracy, nude, responding sexually began to slip over the stockade walls of his consciousness and make their silent way like shadows past the indifferent guards.

When Meg came out of the bathroom, she crossed to the bed without looking at Roger and slid under the covers, her back to him. Roger stared at her for a moment then went into the bathroom. He took his time, his mind grinding away at the unpleasant experience of the dirty old man episode at dinner. That had annoyed him in ways that he couldn't exactly identify. Rightly or wrongly, he felt that the women were somehow to blame for the strange and uncomfortable twist the evening had taken. And now his wife, his loving, understanding wife, was giving him the silent treatment because a young girl had said hello to him.

When he came out of the bathroom and settled into bed, he lay stiffly, Meg tense beside him, not touching, Roger knew what was up, but his annoyance kept him from speaking out to defuse the situation.

"Who's Tracy?" she asked after several moments of silence. She made an effort to sound natural, easy, conversational, but it was brittle, strained. An unfamiliar bolt of heat shot up through Roger's chest.

"Tracy? Are you mad at me because some young girl said hello to me?"

"Of course not," Meg protested, the catch in her voice making obvious her deceit. "I'm . . . I"m just curious, that's all. How is it that some young . . . chick . . . knows your name like you're old friends?"

Roger sighed. Of course she had every right to know about Tracy, but he couldn't help being bothered by the way she was going about finding out what she wanted to know. It was but another aspect of how she'd changed over the past months. She didn't usually take this tone with him.

Resentment, a reluctance to tell her anything, rose up in him in response to her posture. He hesitated for a moment then pushed his feelings aside. Patiently he explained to her about his chance encounter with Tracy, how they'd fallen into conversation, and how she happened to know his name.

"You know what surprised me the most?" Roger said. Meg didn't say anything. "How easy it was to talk to her. She talked just like a human being." As the words tumbled from his mouth, he suddenly had the feeling that he was making a big mistake. But Meg seemed to accept what he'd said and the tension between them faded away. Roger was thankful for that, but a sense of dissatisfaction remained knotted in his chest. He wasn't ready for sleep. He needed some kind of resolution to vanquish the feelings that troubled his soul.

"What did you girls talk about all day?" "What did you boys talk about?"

"You girls." Meg laughed, then settled into silence. The need for connection was still strong in Roger and he searched for something else to say. He blurted the first thing that popped into his mind. "Did Denise say anything to you? About her and Matt?"

"What do you think she might have said?"

"I don't know, but it seems to me that something's going on. They're different, both of them."

"Something is going on," Meg said. Roger was silent, the question in the air between them. "The usual. She thinks Matt is running around on her."

"Hmmm."

"Did he say anything to you?"

"No, but he's different. Filled with some kind of nervous energy or something."

"I sensed that too. Anyway, Denise says she has no proof. Just a bunch of circumstantial stuff."

Roger rolled toward Meg and slipped his hand under her pajama top, letting his fingers rest gently on her belly. He was still hoping that here, on vacation, away from the everyday, Meg might be inspired to be more romantic.

"You men are all alike, aren't you?" Meg turned to Roger and kissed him lightly on the lips. "All except my Roger. Goodnight, dear." Meg settled into her pillow, her breath soon slipping into sleep rhythm.

Roger sighed and lay back on his side of the bed. His mind would not be still, and he found himself thinking about Meg. For the twenty-five years of their marriage, Meg had kept herself in good shape. Age was just beginning to show on her face. There were wrinkles and her skin wasn't as tight, her flesh as firm, as it had been. But over the past year, hints had begun to suggest a different story. Menopause had galloped into her life and with it came fears and anxieties she'd never before known. She'd gained ten pounds and at first he hadn't even noticed - not until she'd begun to complain about it.

Roger thought back to a night in March when he'd lain on their bed watching Meg undress. The light was soft and diffuse, romantic like the mood that enveloped him. She had her back to him, a beautiful back - he'd always thought so. His eyes drifted down over her buttocks, down to her thighs. He saw the cellulite and around her knees and on her calves, he saw varicose veins and the blemishes of aging. He'd seen them before, of course, but somehow that night it was different, as if he was seeing something he'd never seen before. A great sadness settled over him and he mourned for his wife and for her fading beauty. He mourned, too, for himself. He mourned at the knowledge that the beautiful woman who had shared his bed for all those years was slipping away in age.

He rolled over to his side of the bed and closed his eyes. He'd been waiting for her to come to bed because he wanted to make love to her, but he found himself now disinterested, his passion and arousal drained away. His thoughts carried him back over the years of their marriage from the heady infatuation of first love that had lasted much longer than it did for most couples. It was only with Meg's first pregnancy and the birth of Billy that the rhythm of their lives had changed. The children had imposed a rigid routine and even though the children were no longer at home, the routine still held them in its grip. The sacrifices – and, of course, Meg would never consent to think of their family life as sacrifices, Roger thought – had all been for the children.

Roger thought back on how he had willingly enough surrendered the spontaneity for family life and how he had agreed to let the passion slip away because it took too much energy. But he'd come now to look upon the routine that he'd so willingly allowed into their lives and to question what he'd done. Routine equaled security. But had that really been the wisest choice? Maybe a little insecurity and a lot less routine might have given them better, richer lives. Had it all been worth it, he wondered now. Had he sold out too cheaply?

The next morning, Meg and Denise went off for an early swim, leaving Roger and Matt to breakfast by themselves. They'd no sooner settled at a table on the terrace, mugs of steaming coffee before them, when Matt got right into it.

"That was a mighty close call last night," he said. Roger, who'd spent a troubled night, was uncertain as to which close call Matt had in mind. The blank look on Roger's face prompted him to add: "The dirty old man thing . . . . Or was there more? Did Meg give you shit about the girl?"

"Not shit exactly, just a little of the old cold shoulder. But we talked about it.

Everything's OK now."

Matt looked quizzically at his friend. "It felt a little chilly in the car on the ride back to the hotel." He took a sip of his coffee.

"I don't know," Roger said. "I don't think she'd have reacted that way a few years ago. I think it's this menopause thing. Things get on her nerves. And the aging. She talks about it a lot these days."

"I get enough of that nerves shit without the menopause or the aging."

Roger looked at Matt, his thoughts for a moment adrift. "Yeh, it kind of depressed me the way the women assumed they knew exactly what was going on."

"Speaking of what's going on, what's with the young blonde?"

"Tracy? She tends the canoe rentals down by the dock."

Matt nodded, the beginnings of a smile playing about his lips. "And?" he said.

"And nothing," Roger replied. "I wandered down there yesterday and we got into a conversation, that's all. We had a nice talk, end of story."

"Uh huh," Matt said, again the leering fraternity brother.

"No, really. That's all there was to it. I haven't given her a thought since," Roger lied. Matt smiled and settled back in his chair. He sipped his coffee for a moment and then sat up again, leaning toward Roger. "She's a pretty nice looking little piece," he said. "You think she puts out?"

"Matt, what kind of question is that? I didn't even think about that. We just talked."

"They do though," Matt said, ignoring Roger's response, easily abandoning his interrogation of Roger to pursue this more exciting topic. "These young ones. They get started early. They're pretty wild. Like those two over there." Matt gestured with his eyes, adding emphasis with his coffee cup. Roger looked across the terrace as two young girls, both in short shorts, tank tops, and sandals, headed toward the tennis courts. The one was blonde, lithe, girlish. Her companion, however, was dark with the full lush body of a woman. They were close enough that Roger could see her eyes rove with a predatory air more likely to be seen in a young male. Roger knew immediately why Matt had pointed her out. She was ripe; it was obvious in her demeanor, either about to become sexual or already in the first blossom of sexual opening. Roger glanced at Matt, at his wide eyes and flaring nostrils, like a stallion picking up the scent of a mare.

"The dark-haired one. A total vixen, ready for it. Look at the way she moves. How she sticks those boobs out. Mama mia!" Matt's eyes narrowed, his smile sliding toward the lascivious.

Roger looked back at the girls and for a moment he thought of her in the heat of passion, her bedroom eyes glazed with lust, her body open, demanding. It wasn't hard to do; she practically invited it. Perhaps Matt was right, he thought, perhaps these girls are wilder, more daring, promiscuous.

For a moment Roger wondered whether his sons were experiencing the benefits of these young girls, these young women. Unwittingly, his thoughts went on to his daughter and he had to ask himself if she too was licentious and wild. She didn't seem that way, but how would he know, really? But this was tricky territory, and he didn't want to think about what Frances might be doing. Denied the freedom to think about his daughter, his mind turned back to Tracy. God, he thought, my thoughts are a mine field today.

"But they're all crazy," Matt said, interrupting Roger's churning thoughts. "I wouldn't trust any of them further than I could throw them. And that includes my own daughter."

Roger glanced at Matt. "You talk like a man of experience."

Matt didn't answer. He stared at the two girls as they disappeared around the hotel. Then slowly he turned to Roger, that wicked smile still on his face, and winked.

Once again Roger found himself alone. Meg and Denise, after their swim, had decided to take the full spa treatment, an event that promised to consume the entire afternoon. Matt had gone off to Burlington on another business-related errand, leaving Roger to amuse himself.

He already knew what he was going to do although he tried hard to deny it to himself. Setting out on the network of paths around the hotel - for a brisk walk, he assured himself - he was soon headed for the dock. Thoughts of Tracy played an erotic game of hide'n'seek in his mind. He knew it was absurd, a function of having to face his fading youth; the thoughts of a dirty old man, as Meg and Denise would point out. But reason was no match for the heady stuff that flowed through his veins.

Coming down the slope toward the dock, Roger saw Tracy deep in conversation with a young man. At that distance he couldn't tell for sure, but he thought it was the same person she'd been with in Burlington last night. Jaimie, wasn't it? As he drew nearer, he saw that whatever they were talking about was freighted with emotion. Their body language was every bit as clear as it had been yesterday when he'd interrupted the unpleasant interchange with the haughty blonde.

Slowing his pace, Roger found a bench with a view of the lake and settled there to watch. He was close enough now to see the aroused expressions on the faces of the two, see the muscles tightened in disagreement. For several minutes, he watched until the young man threw up his hands and stalked away. Before he cleared the dock, he stopped, went back and gestured angrily at her, and again stomped off.

Roger turned his attention to the clouds over the lake, not wanting to walk up on Tracy after another unpleasant encounter. He sat for what he thought was a long time, which in truth was probably no more than a few minutes. Then he stood up and walked leisurely down to the lake.

"Hello, Mr. Lathern," Tracy greeted him as he came out onto the dock. As yesterday, she was making a determined effort to mask her emotions. But today it was clear to Roger that the turmoil was something other than anger, something deeper. She made a valiant effort to hide what she was feeling but he saw the tears in her eyes, almost ready to spill over.

"Hello, Tracy. I was thinking of taking a canoe out this morning." Roger wanted to go on amiably making small talk, but tears began to roll down Tracy's cheeks.

"Boyfriend?" he asked, pulling a handkerchief from his pocket and handing it to her. "Why don't we sit down over here." He led her to the edge of the dock, taking her slender hand in his, and they sat on the edge, their legs dangling over the water.

"I just broke up with him," she said, her voice cracking, the tears beginning to flow faster. "He's really mad at me. He said a lot of really nasty things." An image of Jaimie and Tracy flickered uncomfortably in Roger's mind. For a moment he resisted and then a flood of warmth for this girl inundated his body. He put his arm around her shoulders and drew her close. Had he thought about it, he would have expected her to resist. For that matter, had he thought about it, the restraints of age and decorum would have prevented his action. Instead, she pressed against him and let the tears and sobs flow unimpeded.

They sat like that for several minutes until she gained control of herself and straightened up, slipping from his embrace, wiping her face with his handkerchief.

"I'm sorry," she said. "It seems every time I see you, I'm in some kind of state." "Do you want to talk about it? I'm a good listener. It might help to talk about it." "It wouldn't do any good. It's all so hopeless."

Roger sat beside the girl and stared at her slender legs, her young knees. Only minutes before his body had been erotically charged at the thought of her. Now though, that troublesome and irritating sensation had drained away, poured out through the soles of his feet into the lake. He felt odd; he could have been sitting with his daughter, this girl could have been his daughter. It was something else, some subtler, more elusive connection that might easily find a home in the concept of friendship. He felt instinctively linked to Tracy, deeply concerned for her welfare.

"Oh, I don't think it could be as bad as all that," he said.

"Do you love him?"

"Yes," she sobbed. "Yes, I love him. That's why it's so hopeless." She blew her nose and mopped at her eyes.

"No," Roger said, "that's where you're wrong. You're not thinking straight. If you love him, it can't be hopeless. Unless he doesn't love you." For a moment, Roger's thoughts veered to Meg and his own feelings about their relationship. "If there's love, there's always a way to work things out." Tracy turned her tormented face to Roger. He saw a flicker of something else, a hint of hope, perhaps.

"How could things work out? He's so angry and he said some very hateful things," Tracy moaned. Roger's mind was still on Meg though the girl's words had sidled up right beside the thoughts of Meg.

"Did you argue about events, things that happened, or about your feelings?" Roger asked. His voice sounded automatic, robotic even, because he was thinking about how he and Meg rarely argued. They talked about feelings; that's how it had always been. "Did you tell him how you feel?"

"N-nnno."

"Maybe you should. Maybe you should forget about what happened, the nasty things that were said. Maybe he thinks you said nasty things, too. Maybe you should just tell him how you feel." Maybe I should just tell Meg how I feel, Roger thought. Maybe I'm making this all too complicated. "Why don't you try that? If things are as bad as you say, what do you have to lose?"

Tracy stared at Roger, the torment slipping from her face, still sad, still serious, but opening now to some other possibility. "OK, Mr. Lathern, I'll try, but I don't think it will do any good. He is so angry."

"Tracy, try it. Trust your heart." Good advice, Roger thought; I ought to listen to myself more often.

"OK. OK, I will try." Tracy looked at Roger, the harsh lines of her face softening to a smile. She wiped the last trace of tears from her face and handed the moist handkerchief back to Roger. She grasped his hand and squeezed it affectionately. They sat in silence, serene in the sunlight, the lake breeze and the scent of water and pine.

From the end of the dock, the sounds of young girls reached their ears. Tracy let go of Roger's hand as she glanced toward the shore.

"Here come my girlfriends," she said as she began to rise. There was a sweetness in the moment as her fingers slid from his. Behind him the girls' talk was an excited banter that could have been a foreign language. Roger heard Tracy's voice rise to the level of her friends. For a moment he regretted the girls' appearance, their intrusion, but he soon realized that his moment with Tracy had come to an end. He watched the gentle ebbing and flowing of the lake and thought of the feelings that had filled him when he came down to the dock. All those absurd fantasies about Tracy were gone now, replaced by a serenity much like the understated power of the lake. He nearly laughed at the spectacle he might have made of himself. Behind him the girls' chatter filled the air as he got to his feet. The girls all looked at him and fell silent.

"I think I'll skip the canoe today," he said to Tracy. "You take care of yourself - and listen to your heart."

"Thank you, Mr. Lathern." The two girls looked at Roger, looked at Tracy, their eyes filled with questions.

Roger headed back toward the hotel.

Roger carried the last two pieces of luggage from the room, made one last tour of inspection, and stepped out into the hall. Meg had already gone down and was settling up so that they could be on their way.

When he entered the lobby with the suitcases, he saw Meg at the desk. His attention was immediately distracted by movement from the left.

Tracy, in her too-large, wine colored shirt and khaki shorts rushed up to him. Her face looked serious, and Roger had just enough time to wonder what was happening. But she burst into a smile and grasped his hands.

"I just want to thank you for talking to me yesterday, Mr. Lathern. I would have made a huge mistake if we hadn't had our little talk." Roger was surprised, but he recovered quickly. From the corner of his eye, he could see Meg watching from the desk. "It was great getting to know you, Mr. Lathern. I won't forget you." She reached up and hugged him and planted a kiss on his cheek. Stepping back, her eyes aglow, she squeezed his hands and dashed off toward the terrace. Roger was aware of people looking at him; he turned toward Meg, then picked up the luggage and walked out to the car.

His mind was full of Tracy, of the magic in a young girl's heart. He felt alive and present in a way he'd nearly forgotten, as if it were but a function of youth. As they drove out of Burlington on highway 7, he realized that Tracy had been his teacher every bit as much as he had been hers. They'd shared a moment and the experience had changed him, had opened his eyes to a wisdom he hadn't anticipated. Resentment and dissatisfaction had drained out of him into the lake along with his silly fantasies about Tracy. Rather than focus on what he'd lost he would stand with Meg as he always had.

The clouds streaming across the sky reminded him of an essential truth of life: all is change. So the possibility existed that Meg might one day awaken and ask herself, what have I been doing? It wasn't only in the young, he thought, that hope springs eternal. It was time to focus his energy on reaffirming the love that had shaped his life with Meg.

They were a good way south of Burlington before Meg said anything. There was none of the insecure annoyance that had marked her previous reaction to Tracy, merely a genuine curiosity.

"OK," she said. "What was that all about? Were you having a fling with that girl?"

"A fling? With Tracy? No . . . no." Roger chuckled. He pondered for a moment, his attention drifting to a herd of black and white cows all facing east. "Oh, I'm not sure," Roger said, his voice soft and distant. "I guess you'd have to call it a case of spontaneous affection. Yeh," he said, more positively now, "Spontaneous affection."

III

What Did You Expect?

A Very Grey Day

He awoke to find himself alone in the dark room, alone in the bed. It had been over a year now, and that early morning realization of his aloneness still distressed him. He thought at first that he'd grow accustomed to it, get used to it in a few months, but that had not proven to be the case. Just as his sleep continued to be fitful, uneasy, so too the loneliness persisted.

He pushed himself up in the bed and rested his head against the headboard. There was no need to open the shutters; he knew what time it was. He could tell by the sound of the traffic on the street and the sounds from the produce stand and the charcuterie just below. It was morning, time for him to get up. There was no pressing reason for him to arise, but in the past year he'd made it a matter of policy to act as though his was a normal life. He arose in the morning hours, dressed with meticulous care, shaved, and sat down to breakfast as though there were a real purpose for doing so. Aside from preserving his sanity, there was none. But sanity was a strong inducement, and he knew that. Were he to let go of the normal functions of life, he would descend rapidly into some deep, dark place where chaos reigned.

But this morning he wasn't ready. He lay with his eyes closed and let the memories flow. He always tried to contain the memories, releasing them one or two at a time so that the emotions would not engulf and threaten to drown him. The memories could have swept him away every bit as quickly as the chaos that lay beyond the forms of living.

She came quickly and filled his imagination, just as she had that summer three - or was it four? - years ago when they'd gone to Les Baux de Provence. She'd worn a light summer dress that day with her hair pulled back like a young girl. She'd looked so young, much younger than her years, for they'd both already been old. Physical age counted for little though; they'd both had that youthful aura about them. The sight of her coming through the high meadow grass, the picnic basket on her arm, the vivid light, the smell of the lavender, and the country air all made him feel again as though he were twenty years old and just starting out in life. He loved her very much that day and he wanted to make love to her there in the grass, but he was sure she'd refuse, so he kept his passion to himself.

This memory, a reverie, played out in his mind and he relived the feelings of that day: love, desire, delight. But in the end, he realized that they were only memories and inevitably the pang of that realization brought him back to his dark bedroom. For a few more moments he was still, allowing himself to slip deeper and deeper into his sadness. He might have lost his way in the grey fog, had not a black streak flown across the bed. A second later it was back, a dark bundle that raced up the blankets, coming to rest almost on top of his face. Yellow cat eyes stared from the black face, the message clear.

Some, said the cat without uttering a word, may think they have the leisure to linger about in bed, but there are important matters that need attention. "Yes, yes, my dear Minouche. I know you need to be fed." The cat, as if she'd understood every word, raced from the room as swiftly as she'd come. So, he grasped the rope of salvation that the cat had brought, as he invariably did, and pulled himself wearily from his bed, padding disconsolately to the apartment's tiny kitchen.

In the years that the cat had been there, aside from purring, she had made no sounds beyond an almost inaudible miaow, and that only infrequently. She communicated with her eyes and by flitting about like a little black ball of lightning. As he mixed some leftovers with milk, she alternately twined between his legs and then leapt up onto the sink, nearly stepping into the bowl. "Yes, yes, Minouche," he said, placing the bowl on the floor as the cat dove down to her breakfast. For a moment he watched her eat, wishing that he could once again feel even a fraction of the vitality that the cat regularly exhibited. It was as if, he mused, the cat lived for both of them; he only went through the motions. Finally, he turned away and made his way to the little washroom to get ready for the day.

Peering into the mirror that hung over the sink, he saw an old man looking back at him. Grey hair and grey skin, rheumy eyes. In the past year, the lonely year, he'd passed into old age, the youthfulness of his earlier years wilting away, fading like the mists of an October morning.

His disheveled hair, the white stubble on his chin and cheeks, made the wrinkles more prominent. An ache rose up in his breast and a sigh passed his lips: memorials to the losses of his life. When he'd first noticed how he'd changed, he was astonished at his decrepitude. But as time passed, the visage became nearly invisible, and in his loneliness, he rarely remarked the old man in the mirror. For some reason, today, he noticed again.

In the front room, he raised the shutters and looked out on the street below. The day was dull, grey, a day to get through, not a day to invigorate. A day, he thought, to match the feeling in his heart. A chill breeze flowed into the room when he opened the window. Yesterday had been such a splendid day, a day of brilliant sunshine and summer heat. But today the summer had fled, and the chills of autumn fastened themselves on the city. He looked again into the street, and it seemed as though the people hurried along, eager to complete their errands and to be back inside. In the little kitchen, so cozy when she'd been there to share breakfast with him, he prepared a bowl of café au lait, found the day-old end of baguette and sat down to his own breakfast. He ate slowly, dunking the bread into his coffee. If it weren't for the coffee, he might not even have been aware of eating.

Minouche came to join him, climbed onto his lap, and demanded attention. The cat, intent on the immediacy of her needs, had no time for an old man's musings. He had no choice: pay attention or be tormented by this black devil's incessant clamoring. If he chose to ignore her, he knew she would stand up in his lap, press her little cat face to his, and breathe her little cat breath into his face until he relented. Or she would clamor onto his back, sit on his shoulders and tousle his thinning hair, licking his ears with her scratchy cat tongue. So, he relented, left his grey world, and joined Minouche in the moment of her needs. As he stroked and fondled the cat, as she stretched and rolled languidly on his lap, while his mind wandered far away to the time before. He stayed there a long while, but eventually Minouche was satisfied and began to settle down for a nap. He picked her up gently and placed her on the chair. Empty and meaningless as his life was, today at least he had a purpose.

He dressed slowly, choosing his good dark grey slacks, a starched white shirt and a matching silvery grey tie. The memory of the chill air made him go to his wardrobe and search for a wool vest, which he put on. Then he chose a suit jacket of dark prince-de-galles wool, no longer stylish, but well-tailored and seldom worn. Black shoes and his dark beret. Minouche, fresh from her nap, twined between his legs as he examined himself in the full-length mirror of the armoire.

A well-dressed old man looked back at him. A grey old man dressed all in grey for a very grey day. He needed some note of color, he knew, a little note to lift him ever so slightly above the depths where he seemed so much to dwell. A boutonniere, a pink or yellow flower for his lapel. That was what he needed, he thought, as though it were a decision of the moment.

He knelt to pet the cat.

"Now, Minouche, you must stand guard while I'm gone. Don't let the mice take over." The cat looked up at him as though she'd understood every word and would proudly stand guard over the premises. A final stroking of the silky black fur and he left the apartment.

The bell over the door tingled as always as he entered the shop. The scents of many flowers, of dampness, and fecundity filled his nostrils. That commingled scent brought him a tangle of feelings: of calm and order, and at the same time the disorder of sadness, of loss. He had a few moments to savor this sensation before the florist came from the rear of the shop.

"Ah, good day, Monsieur Gismond," she said. "How are you today? I missed you yesterday. You always come on Wednesdays. Were you ill?"

"No, no, Madame Ney," he replied. "I'm quite well. For some reason - I don't know why - I went yesterday to walk in the Bois de Lancy. Perhaps it was the wonderful weather. So today I must go in the chill and wind. " He let the sentence fade away.

Madame Ney, of course, knew where he was going and went to fetch the flowers she knew he wanted. He'd come every week for the past year and every time his request was the same: a dozen white roses and a single pink carnation for his lapel. She wrapped the white roses in cellophane and tied them carefully with a ribbon. Reaching behind her, she took the carnation from a bunch on the shelf, snapped off the stem and leaned over the counter to gently affix the flower to the buttonhole on the lapel of his jacket.

"Voilà, Monsieur!" she said as he paid her and picked up the roses. She saw the closeness of tears as she did so often when he came in and her heart opened to this man before her. Later she would think rationally that a year was long enough and time he got over it. Nonetheless there was always a part of her that commiserated with him in his grief.

Monsieur Gismond left the flower shop and crossed the busy street to wait for the tram. He was thankful that the wait in the chill breeze was short. During the twenty-minute ride to the Place Jean Jaurès, he let his mind wander aimlessly. He tugged open the wrapping and sat looking at the roses, letting their scent rise to his nostrils. Better not to think about anything too intensely as the tram rattled its way along the streets.

At the Place Jean Jaurès, he exited the car and headed across the street toward the grand, stone archway. His sadness thickened like a knot in his breast, because he was thinking about happiness - how happy they'd been. He was, however, even in his grief, realistic enough to realize that, yes, they'd been happy, but mostly it had been contentment. They'd shared their lives, they'd been content, satisfied to travel life's path together. Oh, yes, there'd been times - but he mostly couldn't even remember them now.

And then that day, that terrible day. He could still feel his astonishment at how, all through the dreadful week, she'd appeared to become younger and more radiant, as if she would soon be a young maiden again, just out of the lycée. Until that Friday when the illusion crashed, and she was old and haggard and so dreadfully sick. Within hours she was dead. He felt again the pain, the despair, the utter hopelessness. He'd pleaded with God, he'd argued with God, and finally he'd cursed God, but nothing helped. The pain simply went on and on.

Eventually, the pain did diminish, growing dull and wearisome, although it flared full- fledged every time he approached the stone arch of the Cimetière de Notre Dame des Martyrs. But the loneliness, the loneliness - that never relented.

And so, alone as always, Monsieur Gismond made his way along the path lined with plane trees, past the tombs, monuments, crypts, and sepulchers to the intersection of the lateral lane. He turned left and soon came to the pathway that led to his wife's grave. As he approached the gravesite, he noticed a man kneeling there. A mourner at an adjacent grave, he thought, slowing his steps, not wishing to intrude upon such a moment. He knew how he'd feel if someone came around while he knelt at his wife's grave, just as this man knelt at the grave of a loved one. He would wait until the man had finished so that he could be alone with the spirit of his wife.

As he walked slowly along the pathway, with the wind whipping at the foliage so that all the trees looked frosted, he thought how the loneliness only abated when he was here at his wife's grave. Ahead of him, the man, wearing a navy blazer and a beret very much like his own, showed no signs of leaving. Monsieur Gismond slowed his pace even more, to mincing little steps, bringing the roses up to his face to inhale their perfume as he dawdled along.

Finally, the man rose, but instead of leaving, he stepped toward the gravestone and began to arrange a bouquet of pink flowers in a vase. Monsieur Gismond was by this time close enough to notice that the man appeared to be about his own age. When the man removed his cap, apparently standing in prayer, he revealed hair as grey as the hair on his own head.

There was something about this man and his proximity to Madame Gismond's grave that unsettled Monsieur Gismond. He couldn't quite put his finger on it, but he suddenly felt disgruntled, bristly, on the verge of anger, his loneliness and sorrow for the moment forgotten. The man was slender, almost youthful in build, but when he moved, his age was obvious. As he bent over to arrange the flowers, Monsieur Gismond saw his profile clearly. A bolt of recognition shot through him. But no, he thought angrily, this could not be. Impossible! The recollection of this man poured into his mind, and he wanted to scream in anger. They'd met but once before and the encounter had not been pleasant.

Monsieur Gismond was just about to turn off the path, to wait somewhere out of sight until that man had gone, when the man, obviously aware of eyes watching him, turned and looked directly at Monsieur Gismond. Despite the years and the distance, the recognition was immediate. The man stood facing Monsieur Gismond, instantly on the alert like a hunter in the presence of some wild beast. Monsieur Gismond could do nothing; he was seen, pinned to the ground. To turn away now would be to lose pride, almost an act of cowardice.

He hesitated a moment, standing in the path as still as his opposite stood there by the grave. There was no point in delay, nothing to do but go ahead, so Monsieur Gismond walked warily up to the man and stared at him. He noticed immediately that the man wore a single white rose in the lapel of his blazer.

"You," said Monsieur Gismond. The man wasn't standing at the grave next to his wife's, but directly beside it. Monsieur Gismond looked at the grave. Anger shot through him as his eyes fell upon the bouquet of pink carnations in the vase at the head of the grave. "You," he said again, this time in anger instead of astonishment.

"Yes, me," said the man arrogantly. "What do you mean to do about it? Drive me off with a stick?" The two men stared at one another, each appraising the other, noting the similarity of build, age, attire. They seemed to sink into the posture of wrestlers circling one another, looking for an advantage, an opening.

"Wha...what are you doing here?" The question almost hissed from Monsieur Gismond's mouth. He looked again at the rose in the other's lapel, at the carnations in the vase. He knew this man, this Reynaud, and in his anger, he knew how the man would answer.

"What am I doing here? I am here to pay my respects to the woman I loved!" Reynaud drew himself up in fragile defiance. An audible gasp escaped from Monsieur Gismond's lips. For a moment he was speechless.

"The woman you loved?" snapped Monsieur Gismond, the words bursting from him. He shook his bouquet of white roses at Reynaud, the cellophane wrapping making a crackling sound. "The woman you loved," sputtered Monsieur Gismond again. Reynaud stepped back in the face of this onslaught. He looked off-balance, as though he'd stepped onto rough terrain and was unsure of his footing.

"You're a sneak and a scoundrel," shouted Monsieur Gismond. "Marie never loved you!" He continued to shake his bouquet, totally unaware of what he was doing.

"Sneak?" snapped Reynaud, beginning to recover his confidence. "I was no such thing. I made no secret of my love for Marie." The words sent a shock through Monsieur Gismond and he began to lose control.

"Get out of here," he shouted, "leave us alone! You have no right to be here!" The two men looked like teenagers in a schoolyard posturing over their territory. But unlike two teenagers, they were slow moving and impotent. So, they continued to bully each other, Reynaud contending that

Marie had loved him and only stayed with Gismond out of convenience. Gismond sputtering in response that it was he, Reynaud, who was the interloper in an otherwise idyllic marriage.

They bickered and postured at one another until Reynaud finally shouted: "Enough! I'm finished here. I've paid my respects. But you can bet I'll be back next week. And you can't stop me!" With that Reynaud turned on his heel and strode away as fast as he was able. Monsieur Gismond was so angry that he stopped waving the roses and flung them to the ground. Realizing what he'd done, he bent and picked up the bouquet. He yanked the carnations from the vase, losing his grip on them as he did so, and they flew all over his wife's grave. He stared for a moment at the pink blossoms scattered about, not liking the look of that. After putting the roses in the vase, he gathered up the carnations.

He knelt distractedly at his wife's grave and tried to pray for her, but for the first time since her death, he had to search for that connection that had always been automatic. His mind was full of Reynaud. He rose from the grave and walked slowly out of Notre Dame des Martyrs, dropping the pink carnations in the refuse barrel that stood near the stone arch. He had been there barely fifteen minutes rather than the hour he usually spent beside the grave.

On the tram he thought only of Reynaud and the intense anger that he felt toward him. The interloper who had enticed his wife. But of course, there was something there that he didn't want to look at. Part of him knew that, and all of him accepted this deliberate blindness. He knew, of course, that his wife had entered willingly into that affair with Reynaud. He'd always known it, but he refused to look at that simple fact because it seriously threatened the carefully constructed image he'd made of her. He'd raised her to heaven at her death and he was not about to contemplate anything that threatened her sainthood. Yet here was this Reynaud, suddenly appearing to make him look at things he didn't want to face. His anger perked like a pot of coffee simmering on the front burner.

When he reached his apartment and walked in the door, Minouche came bounding out of the salon to twine about his ankles and convince Monsieur Gismond how much he loved her. He knelt cautiously and scooped up the supple little creature. Carrying her cradled in his arm like an infant, he went distractedly into the salon and sat down at the table. He was still thinking about Reynaud.

"Yes, Minouche, I went to see her, and that dreadful old man was there." In his mind's eye he could see Reynaud standing by the grave, his grey hair, the lines in his face, the sallow skin. An old man, thought Monsieur Gismond, failing to recognize in this description his very own being. "What nerve for him to come and put flowers on Marie's grave! Pink carnations!" he said derisively, thinking of the bouquet in the vase and the single white rose on Monsieur Reynaud's lapel. The man's mind must be going. He has no memory. To think that Marie favored carnations over roses!" Monsieur Gismond said that dramatically, lifting the cat until they were nose to nose. "The old fool...." He fell silent, Minouche curled in his lap. He wondered again how Marie could have become involved with Reynaud, when it suddenly occurred to him that for well over an hour he hadn't thought about his grief or his loneliness. He bristled at that realization, as though some precious keepsake had been stolen from him. For a second a thought flickered on some remote level of his consciousness: Reynaud would be there again next week; he'd said so. Well, if he is, his conscious mind responded, taking up the thought, I'll have to drive him away. He felt as though he was flexing his muscles and posturing like a vain, twenty-year-old. Minouche nestled more soundly into Monsieur Gismond's lap and dreamt cat dreams.

And being a creature of habit, as cats are wont to be, Minouche noticed on the following Wednesday that her devoted human did not leave her alone for hours as he usually did. Instead, he left her alone on Thursday and came back muttering and spouting, but with a more vigorous spring to his step and a hint of a sparkle in his eye.

Mud for the Dreamer's Temple

Madeleine came out of the station into the summer sunshine. Grasping her valise tightly, she went by the old black men waiting by the freight wagons, their faces brown and wrinkled. Down the stairs she went with the others who'd come into town on the 1:25 from Pittsburgh. On the sidewalk, she stopped abruptly and stared with annoyance at the avenue before her. The rain of the previous night had turned the street into a quagmire of mud and puddles which the intense heat of the sun had only begun to dry out.

The last hansom was splashing down the muddy street and no other carriages were to be seen. Across the way, Madeleine saw several teamsters and their wagons. Lifting her white skirts to her ankles, she carefully picked her way across the street heading in their direction. In the puddles, she could see the reflection of the blue sky and the clouds racing by high above her. Looking up, she saw one of the teamsters watching her, staring at her exposed ankles; she flushed at the thought, but there was no help for it. She managed to reach the other sidewalk without soiling her skirts, although her white shoes were spotted with mud.

She dropped her skirts and went directly to the teamster who'd watched her and inquired about a carriage. The teamster was a gruff, talkative sort, who gestured broadly and stated what Madeleine had already observed. There were no carriages available at the moment. She suspected that he meant to hold her in conversation as long as he could, no doubt, she thought, so that he could continue to ogle her at close range. He did, however, ask her destination, and at her reply, he reluctantly pointed to a wagon down the dock. It was headed, he said, not just in her direction, but to her very destination. As he told her this, she could feel his eyes wandering to her bosom. As she'd expected he tried to detain her in small talk, but she succinctly took her leave and hastened along the dock to the wagon he'd indicated.

As Madeleine approached the wagon the teamster came out of the freight office. A big, unkempt man, he proved to be as taciturn as the other had been loquacious; he listened to her request and without a word motioned toward the wagon, helping her up onto the seat. Checking the horses' tack as he went, he circled the wagon and climbed up onto the seat next to Madeleine. With a snap of the reins they set out, turning into the main street and the traffic of downtown.

They made their way slowly through the bustle of the commercial district, out into the residential areas. The sun beat down mercilessly and Madeleine's small straw boater with the artful arrangement of grain stalks woven into it did little to keep the sun from her head. In the heat she was uncomfortably aware of her proximity to the wagoner. She drew breath cautiously. The smell of horses she did not notice; that was, of course, an omnipresent scent of the age. The smell of the man who sat beside her was a different matter. He exuded a thick, musky, unwashed smell that made her nose wrinkle. Perhaps, she thought in her discomfort, it would have been better to have waited for a carriage rather than accept this ride with the teamster. It was, however, too late to concern herself with that, and in any event, she realized, she would have begrudged the time spent waiting.

Madeleine tried to focus on the interview to come and so she did not notice their passage through the city, the traffic in the streets, the tidy stores and houses, or the farms at the edge of town. She thought of Chester whom she'd seen only once before in her life. She'd been seven years old when she'd gone with her parents to visit Aunt Helen and Uncle Ferd. She wanted very much to pull the papers from her valise and check them once more, although she'd already done so at least a dozen times. So, she concentrated on the script she felt sure she could impose upon the interview; the little white room, cool in the big building, Chester, withdrawn, distant, but nonetheless pliant to her purposes.

The heat was oppressive, and she struggled to stay awake. The sway of the wagon, the steady clop of the horses' hooves, and the jingling of traces and harness conspired to rob her of consciousness. A drowsiness stole over her, and she began to feel as though she and everything about her was somehow insubstantial, as though the teamster, the team and wagon, and she herself were but toy figures. Finding it increasingly difficult to keep her eyes open, she feared she might pitch headlong from her perch on the wagon seat.

Madeleine's head drooped forward, and her chin touched her chest; she started and looked straight ahead. The scene before her was dim and murky as though she was looking through a film of muddy water, everything bathed and tinted in earth tones, subdued yellows, browns, and greens. She ran through a thicket, a dark, wild place of uninhibited nature. Tree branches, vines, giant tropical leaves, and brambles tugged at her clothing as she pushed her way desperately through the dank greenery. There was an urgency in her, as though she were fleeing from someone or something. Or, perhaps, merely a need to get through the thicket. Yes, the realization came slowly, that was it; she wasn't fleeing but charging desperately toward something. Ahead she could see brightness and in a moment, she emerged onto a lawn that sloped gently up to a country house, an almost familiar white house with porches around the front and side and gingerbread decoration at the eves, the gables, the porch posts.

Hurrying up the lawn Madeleine knew that when she came around the house, she would find her father cajoling her mother, and her aunt and uncle into a game of quoits. Her cousin Chester would be there too in his short pants, an almost clean white shirt, and wide-brimmed straw hat. He would be standing pressed against his mother, his fingers pinching the fabric of her skirt as though someone might snatch him away from her - or her away from him.

"Madeleine, come play with your cousin," Madeleine's mother called to her. She came closer, and looked at her cousin standing by his mother like some frightened little creature. They were the same age, the same height, with the same curly brown hair. In his face she saw not the fear she'd expected, but an amused inquisitiveness and a pair of remarkable blue eyes that would be her singular memory of Chester. He let go of his mother's skirt and extended his hand to Madeleine.

Madeleine, the seven-year-old, went off with Chester while Madeleine, the grown woman stayed to watch the scene on the lawn. The four adults no longer looked familiar to her although she knew without a doubt who they were. The man who was her father was now a tall slender man, clean-shaven with close cropped hair. He wore light, brightly colored clothing such as she had never seen before. In his hand, he held a black box which he pointed at the others while peering into the object. Uncle Ferd too wore strange clothing; a brightly colored shirt and shoes made of leather of two different colors. He'd become a swarthy man, his black hair oiled and slicked back.

It was the sight of the women, however, that most amazed Madeleine. Her mother wore her hair down, falling in a gentle wave on her shoulders. Aunt Helen's hair too was in a strange style. Both women wore flimsy frocks that clung revealingly to their bodies, the skirts shockingly short, barely covering their knees.

They were all laughing and cavorting childishly about the lawn. Madeleine saw them laugh, saw her father's mouth move as he directed the others, but no sound came to her; all was silent. She watched the man who was her father gesticulate and hold the black box up to his eye as he pointed it at the other three. He seemed to be sighting through it, watching as they apparently followed his instructions. Madeleine's mother and Aunt Helen put their arms around one another and swayed together, their hips bumping while Ferd, dancing behind them, put his arms around their necks. He kissed first one then the other and all four of them laughed and stumbled drunkenly on the grass below the house.

An unpleasant anxiety flooded through Madeleine as she watched them. They danced, embraced, and kissed, while her father pointed that strange object at them. In shocked fascination, she watched Ferd grab her mother and kiss her on the lips. Even more astonishingly, her mother offered no resistance, opening instead to Ferd's kiss. When the kiss ended, Helen too kissed her on the lips and slowly began to unbutton her sister's dress, exposing her sister's breasts covered only in a silky chemise. Drawing the fabric aside, she slipped the dress off her sister's shoulders and pulled down the chemise. Ferd bent over those exposed breasts and gently kissed them.

Madeleine was hot with shame at what she'd seen. She felt the heat flash over her body, and she clamped her eyes shut in the face of the scandalous scene. For several moments she stood still, breathing raggedly, trying to control her emotions. When she opened her eyes - tentatively - the two couples were as they'd been, her father and mother, her aunt and uncle talking as any adults might as Uncle Ferd took his turn tossing quoits at the stake across the lawn.

Madeleine blinked and found herself in the barnyard where her seven-year-old self was crouched at the edge of a mud puddle. A city girl, the sights and smells of the barnyard intrigued her and in some small way frightened her too. She sat with her skirts pulled up about her to keep them from being soiled as she watched her cousin. Chester poked in the puddle with a stick. Neither said a word as Chester looked up from the mud and stared at Madeleine. There was a strange look in his blue eyes, as though he was looking through Madeleine at something far away. Dropping the stick, Chester reached into the puddle and grasped a dripping handful of mud and unceremoniously plopped it onto Madeleine's white smock. Chester looked on impishly as Madeleine began to cry.

Starting violently Madeleine nearly lost her balance on the wagon seat. She shook her head, embarrassed at losing consciousness, amazed at the vividness of her dream. Fearful that she'd made a spectacle of herself, she looked cautiously at the wagoner, but there was no sign that he'd noticed anything. Groggy and embarrassed, the dream, the heat and the smell of the teamster conspired to make her feel nauseous. She felt as though she would be sick.

The teamster snapped the reins at the horses and the wagon turned into a tree-lined drive. The deep shade from a double row of sycamores brought Madeleine a reprieve from sun-stroke. Feeling light-headed, off-balance, nauseous, Madeleine tried to compose herself, to regain her focus as the wagon rumbled slowly up the drive. Stopping in front of a large brick building, theteamster dismounted and came around the wagon to help Madeleine down. He tipped his hat to her and without a word drove the wagon around to the rear of the building.

Madeleine stood uncertainly in the shade of the gravel drive looking up at the building and the white cupola that graced its roof. She'd thought that the shade might revive her, but she still felt woozy, as though she'd been startled from a deep sleep. For a few moments, she tried to regain her focus before climbing the stairs to the main entrance.

Inside, the lobby seemed dim after the brightness of the sun, almost cool, sparse, utilitarian, and clean. The dark wood paneling and the banisters were polished to a shine and the smell of wax was heavy on the air. Behind a counter stood a woman shuffling through a stack of papers. She was dressed all in white as was Madeleine herself, but unlike the ivory tint of Madeleine's dress, her attire was snowy white. On her head she wore a starched white cap. Her hair, in striking contrast to her uniform, was a brilliant red. When the woman looked up at Madeleine's approach, Madeleine saw that her hair competed for an observer's attention with her equally dramatic green eyes.

"Yes," queried the woman.

"I've come to see an inma . . ., that is, a patient . . . ." Madeleine felt foolish, fumbling uncertainly for words; she tried again. "I've come to see my cousin, Chester Mallorey." The woman stared at Madeleine as though she did not understand English and Madeleine grew even more uncomfortable. "Ah, . . . Mr. Chester Mallorey," she repeated, enunciating the name slowly and clearly. Still, the woman stared as if measuring her, finally breaking into a smile as though the words had come from a long way off and she'd had to await their arrival.

"Oh," she said, "you must be Miss Halsten. But of course, we've been expecting you. I'm Nurse O'Kelley." The woman's smile seemed genuine, and she extended her hand in greeting. Still Madeleine had the feeling that the woman was appraising her and as a result of that appraisal, found her somehow amusing. There was an intensity and a knowingness in the woman's eyes that caused Madeleine a fleeting sense of *déjà vu*. That look penetrated what remained of Madeleine's sense of self and purpose and somewhere deep inside triggered a nibbling sense of anxiety.

"Your cousin is out on the grounds," she said. "I'll have one of the girls take you to him." She turned and disappeared through a door where Madeleine could hear her call for Christine. Madeleine waited alone in the lobby, the smell of wax and disinfectant heavy on her senses. She looked around for some place to sit down but there were no chairs in sight. Resting against the counter Madeleine thought again of the script she'd so often rehearsed in her mind. She reassured herself that despite her discomfiture she'd be able to convince Chester to sign the papers.

Madeleine had long ago come to feel justified in what she was about to do. There were no longer any moral qualms to distract her or to keep her from her goal. She did not think of herself as an ambitious or acquisitive woman. Still, despite the fact that she already owned the house on Onandaqua Street that she'd inherited from her parents, she wanted also the country property of her aunt and uncle whom she'd seen only once in her life. That and the $5347 that waited patiently in the Broderton State Savings Bank. This did not, however, make her a greedy person. Practical, yes, but greedy - she didn't think so. She could still hear her mother say, as she'd so often said: The lord helps them as looks out for themselves. And that was precisely what Madeleine meant to do.

The will had of course been unequivocal; Chester was the one and only heir to the property and savings. That had bothered Madeleine at first, but she'd pondered, she'd reasoned, she'd rationalized, and in the end, she'd concluded that the property and money rightfully belonged to her. As matters stood Chester would never be able to make use of his inheritance. The house would fall into ruin, the money would lie idle in the bank. And when Chester died intestate, all would go to the state. A perfect waste, utter nonsense. Madeleine mentally stamped her foot.

For heaven's sake, she thought, Chester is a loony. The word was in her mind before she could head it off. She felt immediately guilty for thinking of Chester in that way. A poor unfortunate, she amended, although at some level she did think of him as a loony. Rising rapidly to her own defense, the words forming silently on her lips; Chester is an inmate in this asylum and in all likelihood will remain so his entire life. I'm simply doing the sensible thing; I should have that inheritance. "Of course, you should," said a voice somewhere off in the distance, a suave, convincing, saccharin voice.

Madeleine's thoughts were interrupted by Nurse O'Kelley's return and for an instant, she thought that it had been O'Kelley who had spoken. The nurse had in tow a young girl who wore the pink and white striped attire of a nurse's aide.

"Christine, this is Miss Halsten. She's here to see her cousin, Chester. Show her where our Chester is working today." "Yes'M," said the girl and stared vacantly at Madeleine as though she was a sack of potatoes to be dragged back to the pantry. Madeleine caught the phraseology, "our Chester" and the perplexing reference to work. What an odd way of referring to Chester, she thought. She was also surprised that her cousin was "out on the grounds", although that might mean another building on the grounds. Still, the words boded ill for the scenario she'd worked out.

"You know where Chester is today?" O'Kelley asked Christine. The girl nodded and without a word or gesture to Madeleine started down the stairs toward the front entrance. Madeleine hastened to catch up, following the girl out of the lobby and around to the side of the building. Leaving the shade of the sycamores, they headed down the sloping lawn, the grass already dry in the hot sun. Madeleine did not fancy venturing out into the blazing heat again, nor did she appreciate the ruination of her carefully contrived preconceptions. There would be no little room, it appeared, there would be no carefully scripted interview. Resigning herself, she followed the girl down the slope.

At first Madeleine had trouble adjusting to the brightness and did not notice the lone figure on the grass. It was to this figure that Christine led her. To Madeleine he seemed to materialize out of the glare of the sun, a bearded man who sat on the grass by a flower bed working in the soil. Madeleine looked at the figure before her and for an instant, she thought there must be some mistake; that couldn't be Chester. Kneeling on the grass was a French peasant; a man with a dark beard, wearing baggy pants and a loose jacket of some coarse blue fabric. On his head was a slouch hat that shaded his face from the sun. Madeleine had never seen a French peasant, but there was no doubt in her mind that that was precisely what she was looking at; a French peasant. Momentarily the peasant ceased his grubbing in the dirt and looked up at her. When she saw his eyes, she found herself suddenly back at her aunt and uncle's farm nearly twenty years before.

"Hello, Chester," said Christine, her voice animated with undisguised devotion. The girl's face had come alive with a light that hadn't been there a moment before. "Your cousin is here to see you," she said. As Madeleine stepped forward, she sensed Christine's reluctance to leave, nonetheless the girl stepped away and headed back toward the building.

"Hello, Chester," said Madeleine, stepping closer to the flower bed.

"Hello, Madeleine." he said, "they told me you were coming." His hands continued to work in the soil, but his eyes were on Madeleine. She was surprised to find that he appeared clean, well-groomed, composed, serene even. She'd expected to find a ragged, disheveled man with knotted, ratty hair and a demented look in his eyes. The thought occurred to her that she perceived, despite the dark beard, there was an innocence, a tenderness about him that could even have been vulnerability. Only the striking blue eyes hinted at something else.

Madeleine stood looking down at him as he sat looking up at her. The sun beat down mercilessly and she could feel perspiration beading on her brow, on her upper lip, under her arms, between her breasts. The heat was making her faint, dizzy. She thought distractedly that to anyone observing them, they must appear as a tableau of a lady and her gardener.

Chester made no move to rise, so Madeleine settled down onto the grass across the flower bed from him, her valise on her lap. She drew a delicate handkerchief from the valise and dabbed daintily at her face. Chester sat quietly, watching her, his eyes childlike and inquisitive. They were the same eyes, Madeleine thought, that she'd seen in the face of seven-year-old Chester all those years before. She had the feeling that in those eyes was a request although she had no idea what that might be. It all left her feeling unsettled and off-balance.

With great effort, she opened her valise and pulled out the sheaf of documents the lawyer had prepared for her. Now that she was here, her plans in shambles, she wasn't sure how to proceed. She wasn't sure what she should say, how she should begin, so she held the documents out to Chester, uncertain of what she was doing. Closing her eyes, she took several deep breaths trying to clear her mind. When she opened her eyes, Chester was still looking at her with those inquiring eyes.

"Chester," she said, "I've brought some papers about . . . . " Words failed her. Trying again, she said, "I've come about the house, Chester." He offered no recognition of her words, but continued to stare at her. His eyes were so clear, so intense; she wanted to look away but felt obliged to keep her eyes on her cousin. "The farm," she continued, "Aunt Helen and Uncle Ferd's farm? Well, since your mother . . . . " She'd been about to say died, but the word stuck in her throat. She didn't know whether Chester was aware of his mother's death; she had no idea what he knew or understood.

"Your mother," she said, beginning yet again, "has passed away and . . . . " Madeleine saw the sadness shoot through Chester's eyes, ". . . and you are the owner of the farm." Chester nodded and said quietly, "Yes, Madeleine, I know all that." Madeleine let out a sigh of relief; at least there was some place to start.

"But I don't want to talk about that," said Chester, looking down. It made Madeleine think of a child whose feelings had been hurt. Madeleine was beginning to feel faint; one step forward, two steps back.

"It won't take long to talk about, Chester," said Madeleine, trying to keep to her agenda. Without looking up, he shook his head. Madeleine covered her eyes with her hand and sighed again.

"Oh, Chester, please, let's just talk about it and then it will be over." She knew she was pushing him now, but she'd begun to feel very dizzy.

"You're very pretty, Madeleine," said Chester, looking up at her. The sadness was gone from his eyes and in its place, Madeleine saw a gentle and hopeful glow. Her heart missed a beat and a twinge of guilt tickled along her spine. She continued to look at him and she felt as though she might fall headlong into those limpid eyes.

Reality seemed to slide out from under her as though she was somehow immersed in the person of her cousin. For a second, she closed her eyes, fearful that she might topple over right there on the lawn. When she opened them, however, she found that she was looking out of those blue orbs - at herself.

What a perfectly absurd feeling, she thought, as she took in her perspiration beaded face, her slender young body in its lace-edged dress. Her sun-reddened face flushed a deeper hue as she watched Chester's hands deftly unbutton the bodice and draw apart the fabric, loosening the ties on the chemise. His hands felt cool and dusty as they gently exposed her breasts. Her nipples tingled and an electric shock flickered over her skin.

Madeleine closed her eyes in stupefaction and embarrassment and when she opened them again, Chester was sitting where he'd been, across the flower bed. Putting her hand tentatively up to her bodice, she found that her clothing were buttoned, as secure as when she left home.

I must be suffering from sunstroke, she thought. She looked down at the papers in her hand, the papers the lawyer had prepared, the papers that she must convince Chester to sign. Again, she held the documents out to Chester, but he didn't even look at them. His eyes remained gently fixed on her face.

"Chester, please look at these papers," she tried once more, but her words brought no change in Chester's demeanor. He continued to stare openly, almost in wonder, at her. "Chester," she said, reaching out to touch his hand. Her sense of resolve was beginning to unravel; somewhere out in the summer heat, she could feel frenzy approaching.

"It rained last night, Madeleine," he said, ignoring the papers and her words, his voice child-like. "I heard the rain on my windows in the dark." Madeleine was beginning to grow frantic. She tried to focus on bringing Chester's attention to the issue at hand, but she knew she was losing ground.

Madeleine looked at her cousin and again she had that disconcerting feeling that she was looking at the world through those luminescent eyes. This time, however, it was not her face in the present that she saw. It was the red-haired nurse she'd encountered in the lobby. They were alone in a hallway, pausing for a moment from their errands. Chester looked at the woman with a gentle longing. He wanted to look at her as he had at the younger female inmates and the aides. Some of the other nurses too had let him look. They pitied him, he knew, unaware that his gentleness and vulnerability had already gained him anything he might ask of them. He'd thought about O'Kelley for a long time and now the words burst from his mouth.

"O'Kelley, let me look at you."

"Look at me? You are looking at me," she laughed.

"No," he said, "I mean look at you." She knew precisely what he meant, but she chose to play with him, teasing and bantering. Then, nonchalantly, she gave in. She took him to one of the examining rooms where she slid up onto the table. She lay back, pulled her legs up and let them sag apart as she pulled her skirts up around her waist. Amidst all the frills and petticoats, he was surprised to find she was naked, her crotch covered in a thick reddish-brown fur. He began to reach for her, but hesitated.

"Can I?" he asked. "Can I touch?" She squinted up at him and shrugged.

"Oh, what the hell," she said. "We've come this far - go ahead." Delicately he felt in the fur and found his way into the folds and undulations of her sex.

Heat flickered from Madeleine's reddened face more intensely than ever. She closed her eyes and bit her lip, newly embarrassed and disconcertingly aroused. When she opened her eyes, all was as it had been. The papers lay on the grass at her knees and Chester sat opposite her.

Madeleine took off her boater and attempted to fan herself. The heat made her feel dizzy and weak; she couldn't imagine how she could lead Chester back to the path she wanted them to walk together. In fact, she could barely find that path herself. Before she could gather her wits and attempt a new approach, Chester leaned closer.

"Remember what I did, Madeleine? When we were little?" Of course she remembered; not half an hour ago she'd dreamt that very incident. She looked at Chester, at his mercurial blue eyes. There was a child-like exuberance, an impish delight in those eyes.

"In the beginning," he said, the words drawn slowly, trance-like from his mouth. An eerie feeling came over Madeleine. She looked down at her shoes, at the speckles of mud on the white leather. "In the beginning," Chester said again in a normal voice and his eyes drew Madeleine mesmerizingly into their blue depths. She felt weak, as though she were beginning to fall.

In the beginning, there was the word. But there was no one to hear the word. In the beginning there was the word and the word was - mud. In the beginning there was mud. But for there to be mud, there must be water, there must be rain. In the beginning, was the rain.

The storm had been fierce; it raged for hours in the darkness. The night had grown abysmally black, thunder had rumbled and lightning had cracked; the heavens had opened in a mighty deluge. Then, as quickly as the storm had come, the rain died away, the clouds fled on a crisp wind and the sun came up in a majestically blue sky.

The air was fresh and vibrant, laden with sweet and exotic scents. High above the earth's surface, thick fleecy clouds raced across the radiant sky. The clouds assumed the shapes of plants and animals, of things real and things fanciful, capriciously altering their shapes as they scudded by on the wind.

On the ground, the earth and plants were saturated. The sun was brilliant and hot, and steam rose from the surface of the earth. Everywhere was mud, mud and puddles, and rivers of muddy water. As the wind began to draw off some of the moisture, the mud around a certain puddle began to quiver wondrously. It quivered and shook until it began to flow upward forming a pillar. As if on two legs it rose, and legs manifested from the base of the mound. Arms emerged from the sides and a head of sorts popped from the top of the mud. Crude, very crude was this creature that crept from the living mud. It was as if the mud had dreamt something it had never known.

In the beginning . . . .

A nearly naked brown man knelt by the puddle, staring wonderingly at his reflection. Behind the image of his face, fleecy clouds seemed to tangle in his hair. The man poked his finger into the water and watched his image shatter. It took him a while on this first beautiful day of creation to get used to the idea of being - he existed; how utterly outrageous.

He stared at his reflection wondering at the brown color of his skin, so close in tint to the mud on which he squatted. "I am the Mudboy," he said out loud.

The Mudboy luxuriated in the feel of the sun on his skin, the fecund scent of growth in his nostrils. His mind roamed free over the landscape of his consciousness, poking here, looking there until it came across a concept of exhilarating proportions. I am the Creator, he thought to himself, for indeed he was the only self in all of existence.

I am the Creator; he turned that thought over and over in his mind, looking at it first this way and then that way. He liked the flow of the words and he liked what those words stood for. Looking about at his surroundings, at the lush foliage, the tall trees, and thick jungle growth, the luxuriant flowers and fruits of creation, he claimed them all as his. This was his creation. He looked again into the puddle and watched the clouds at play, creating fantastical shapes.

Suddenly animated, he reached into the puddle and grasped a handful of sticky clay. As the water drained away through his fingers, he began to work the clay, rolling it loosely in his hand.

Thoughts of omnipotence flashed through his mind as the plastic nature of this lump of mud impressed itself upon his equally plastic consciousness. I am the Creator, he thought again, flattening the ball of clay to a ragged disc. I could make a teapot or . . . or . . . a graven image! he thought. Quickly he fashioned those items. But they did not please him and he wrapped his slender brown hand around his last creation and squeezed until the mud gushed out between his fingers.

He squatted by the puddle for a long time, the mud caking his hands beginning to lighten around the edges where the wind began to dry it out. He looked once more at the brown visage that stared back from the muddy surface of the puddle and a decision took shape in his mind. Inspired, he dipped his hand in the puddle and again began to work the lump of clay in his hand.

Slowly he began to fashion a figure, a sort of doll that bore a ragged approximation to himself. To a pudgy body he added a round little head, little arms and legs that stuck straight out. With a sharp piece of stick, he defined fingers, shaped the stumps of the legs to feet and, looking down at his own feet, poked and scratched until there was a full complement of muddy little toes. Leaning once again over the puddle, staring at his face amidst the clouds, he used his stick to make a slit for a mouth, added a little more mud and quickly shaped a nose. He poked two recesses on either side of the nose, and casting about him, found two seeds which he set into the rudimentary sockets.

He held his creation flat in his hand staring at it, inspecting it. He looked down at himself and ran his mud-caked fingers across his midriff. He poked with his fingers at the indentation there at the middle of his belly, wondering what purpose this little depression served. Then he took up his stick and gave his little doll a similar indentation.

He compared the doll to his own image and had to admit that it was a very crude representation. But what now? Obviously, something more was needed, but for the moment he couldn't imagine what that might be.

"In the first place is the breath." The words materialized in his mind. As he'd sat thinking, clouds had covered the sun but now in their haste to be somewhere else, they passed, and the sun emerged again in all its brilliance. The Mudboy brought the doll up to his face and just as the sun's rays touched it, he let his breath flow across his little brown creation. Gently the Mudboy placed the doll on the ground beside the puddle.

As he sat watching, the little doll suddenly sat up and began rubbing its little seed eyes with its little mud fists. It looked around at the damp grass, the mud puddle, the jungle beyond, and finally at the brown man who towered above it. It scratched its little mud head and croaked: "Where am I?"

"How you doin', Adam?" asked the Mudboy, astonished at the name that popped unbidden and unconsidered from his mouth.

"Where am I?" repeated the doll. "Who are you? How did I get here? What's going on?" "You sure are full o' questions, ain't you?" said the Mudboy.

"Well, what is all this? And who are you, anyway?" said the mud doll in a disgruntled tone of voice. The doll stood up.

"All this, as you put it, is creation," said the Mudboy, "an' I'm the Creator." He peered at the mud doll standing by the puddle, wanting to take great joy in his creation. But the doll's demeanor put him off. "An' you're an adam," the Mudboy added by way of explanation.

"An adam? And you're the Creator?" The mud doll's words were tinged with insolence as he stared sullenly at the Mudboy. "You're no creator. You're just a scruffy old black man," snapped the adam.

"Scruffy ol' black man, am I?" snarled the Mudboy, anger rising uncontrollably in him on this first beautiful day of creation. All of his other creations had accepted their creating with equanimity and some, such as the birds and many of the animals, had done so in good spirits. He had no experience with the need to be patient and understanding. Without hesitation, he reached out with his fist and - splat! - squashed his creation flat. The Mudboy mumbled to himself as he squatted beside his once and former creation. He almost resolved to try something else, but the idea of the adam nagged at him.

Seizing another lump of clay, the Mudboy rapidly fashioned another adam upon which he breathed and which he placed on the ground by the puddle. A few minutes under the sun and the adam was standing looking bewilderedly at the Mudboy.

"What happened?" asked the adam, scratching its little mud head. "You made me mad, is what happened," said the Mudboy.

"I thought you were the Creator," said the adam, staring sarcastically at the Mudboy.

"Then how come you got angry? Aren't you supposed to be above that sort of thing?" The Mudboy stared at the adam. Nothing backward about this adam creation, he thought.

Instead of answering, he stared at his likeness in the puddle. He leaned forward over the puddle and, searching for his reflection, saw only clouds and sky. Looking closer, he could just make out a shimmering suggestion of himself. Putting aside his annoyance at the adam for the moment, he concentrated on his own presence and gradually his image took shape on the surface of the water. Standing, he looked down to see his legs stretch up from the edge of the puddle to his crotch. There, under the grass skirt he wore, he thought he saw something. Grasping the skirt, he pulled it high and peered between his legs. Nothing but the unadorned flesh where his legs met his torso. Dropping the skirt, he stared again at his reflection. With his toe he poked in the water and found, there where his crotch had been reflected, a piece of root sticking up out of the ground. He looked at the root, he looked at the adam and a mischievous grin spread across his face.

He grasped the doll and held it up for a closer look. The mud doll immediately began to squirm and shout.

"Hey," shrieked the adam, "what are you doing? Put me down! Let go of me!" The Mudboy ignored the adam's protestations. He reached down and grasped a pinch of clay. Quickly he rolled the clay into a root-like appendage and affixed it to the adam's crotch. The doll shrieked louder, its language growing more abusive.

Holding the screaming doll at arm's length, the Mudboy turned it this way and that, examining the addition protruding from its crotch. Hmm, he thought, that looks dumb. He thought for a moment as the mud doll struggled. Looking around, his gaze fell on the crotch of a tree whose trunk divided into two heavy branches, like the legs on his body.

Two, he thought, looking down at his legs, looking at his arms and hands. With another pinch of clay he made another root which he planted on the doll's crotch next to the first. But the result did not please him; it too looked dumb. He pondered for a moment until the obvious fell into his mind - one, two, three. Of course - three; a holy member . . . er, number. My, my; he had to laugh at himself. Inspired, he snatched up more clay and soon the adam had a trio of tiny roots protruding from its crotch.

The Mudboy looked at his handiwork and burst out laughing. The adam's cries of indignation rose many decibels.

"One looked dumb, two looked dumb, but three is ridiculous," said the Mudboy out loud.

Still, he kind of liked the idea of three; a trinity, such a solid, sturdy number.

"Put me down, put me down!" screamed the mud doll, but the Mudboy paid him no mind. After a bit, he plucked two of the tiny roots from the doll's crotch and proceeded to twirl them between his fingers. Producing two pill-like little eggs, he attached them to the base of the original root. Holding the doll at eye-level, he again examined his craftsmanship, shrugged and put the doll back on the ground.

"You brute," shrieked the adam. The doll looked down at itself, peered intently between its legs and looked up at the Mudboy. "What is all that stuff? Why did you do that?"

"Because I felt like it, is why," snapped the Mudboy.

"Oh yeh, well take this," yelled the mud doll angrily as it stomped over to the Mudboy, and kicked his toe.

The adam looked down at his flattened mud foot. It looked hesitantly up at the Mudboy, just in time to see the brown fist coming. Splat!

"What an insolent creation," said the Mudboy, turning away from the flattened lump of clay. For no particular reason he looked under his grass skirt and was surprised to find there his own version of that triumvirate of anatomical parts he'd so nonchalantly fashioned for the adam. He reached down and cupped his appendages and felt a warm glow begin to flood through him. The little rod began to swell at his touch and brought a delicious tingling to his groin. Amazing, he thought, wondering what would happen next.

For a time, the Mudboy played idly with the equipment at his crotch, watching it swell and throb, giving himself over to the sensations it brought to his body. Soon, however, for some inexplicable reason, he was again thinking of the adam. There was something about the little creature that would not let him rest, and before a millennium had blinked, he was at it again. Another adam rested on the ground, complete with the little trinity of equipment at the crotch. It sat up and immediately began to complain.

"What is all this stuff?"

"I don't know." Said the Mudboy. "It just seemed like a good idea at the time." A coyote grin slipped slyly across his face like a cloud across the sun, but the adam didn't notice. Mumbling to itself the mud doll went back to the edge of the puddle and slumped down on a tuft of grass. It stared at the equipment between its legs and wondered anew what purpose it could serve. Whatever it is, thought the adam, it itches.

The adam looked over at the Mudboy. "My creator," it grumbled in a less than respectful frame of mind. The Creator was again crouching at the edge of the puddle.

"Well, whatcha think? You wanna live here?" he asked. The mud doll looked around at the wild tangle of jungle, the puddle, and the wild exuberant sky.

"Well," it said, "it's kinda . . . ," it hesitated a moment, still surveying its surroundings, ". . . basic, isn't it?"

"Basic? Whatchu mean, basic?" asked the Mudboy, bending over and looking sharply at the adam. "You got everything you need right here. The jungle is filled with fruit and nuts for the pickin', there's grain 'n' berries growin' everywhere, 'n' there's water nearby. Whatchu mean, basic?" The mud doll stared blankly at the Mudboy, its hands busily probing in its crotch.

"Primitive," it said. The Mudboy's eyes flared and he snorted. "I mean," continued the adam, "what good is any of it?"

"What good is it? What good is it?" said the Mudboy in astonishment. "It's paradise. It's a beautiful place to live."

"Beautiful," sneered the adam, "it's just trees and stuff. What good is any of it?" "Hey, you should be thankful," snapped the Mudboy.

"Thankful! What do I have to be thankful for? Here I am by a mudhole in a drippy old jungle." It slouched on its tuft of grass and looked sullenly at the Mudboy.

"An' what might be wrong with the jungle?" demanded the Mudboy, annoyance gritty in his voice.

"It's a lousy place to get started," moaned the adam.

"Get started?" snarled the Mudboy. "You already is started."

"I have no help. You're so much bigger than I am. I need some tools. How can I get started in this dump?" the mud doll complained. With these words the adam became distracted by the aching in its groin. "I need a woman," it said, a quizzical look crossing its face. The adam looked up at the Mudboy, its face bearing the look of a little boy wondering why the sky is blue. "What's a woman?"

In the beginning . . . .

The Mudboy stared at his creation. He squatted by the puddle thinking about what the doll had said. He didn't like it, not any of it, not at all. Deeply disturbed by what he'd heard, he looked into the puddle and noticed that the clouds were once again visible through his reflection. His image wavered and threatened to disappear entirely. Bringing his attention sharply back to his image, it grew again concrete and clearly defined.

"And where's my mate?" demanded the mud doll. "Is that what a woman is? My mate? I'm starting to remember all there is to do and I need some help. I need a mate. You owe me . . ." "I owe you?" snarled the Mudboy, leaning over to stare closely at the adam. "I owe you, do I?" Without another word the Mudboy reached out and with his fist smashed the mud doll into a pathetic lump of clay. "Hmmmph,:" he snorted and stood up, still staring at the remnants of his creation.

The Mudboy sat on the moist earth muttering disconsolately to himself at the insolence of his creation. He stared at the trees at the edge of the forest, the tall, tall trees and the smaller ones, too. Off to the left, his eyes came to rest on the tree he'd noticed before, the one with the divided trunk. His thoughts were still on his unruly creation, and he did not notice the crow alight on one of those branches. For a long time - an age, perhaps - the Mudboy, lost in thought, was oblivious to the crow. Finally, however, the crow's yammering broke through the Mudboy's concentration and brought him back into the moment. To the Mudboy, the crow's cawing sounded like the words of a phrase, a puzzling phrase with no meaning he could determine. "To woman born . . . . ," he thought. "All things are to woman born . . . . To woman born." Again and again, he repeated the phrase until it took on the qualities of a mantra. He sat staring into the woods, the mantra slipping sinuously through his brain.

In his agitation, the Mudboy reached again for a handful of clay. Unable to leave well enough alone, he quickly fashioned another adam, just as he'd made the others. The sun shone on the doll and the Mudboy enveloped it in his breath. The doll blinked and shook its head as the

Mudboy set it down on the ground. The adam looked around in disgust, then stared up at the Mudboy. There was an uncomfortable itch in the doll's crotch and it did not know how to scratch it.

"Where is she?" the doll demanded. "Where's my mate? And why am I still in this drippy jungle?"

"You have a very bad attitude," said the Mudboy. " thought maybe I'd give you another . . . ."

"Attitude! Bad attitude! I'll show you a bad attitude," shrieked the mud doll, reaching for a stick with which to poke the Mudboy. But before it could lay its little mud hands on a suitable stick, it rejoined the mud from which it had come - whump - courtesy of the Mudboy's fist.

"Man, that is one smart-ass little creation." Still, the Mudboy couldn't keep away. He began to doodle with the clay and before he knew what he was about, another little adam stood before him. Every bit as insolent and cantankerous as its predecessors, it started right in with demands and abuse.

"You better be careful what you say, my little friend," warned the Mudboy. "You could be leavin' in a hurry." The mud doll sneered at its creator.

"I have as much right to be here as you do," sniveled the adam like a spoiled-rotten seven-year-old.

"Oh, you do?" said the Mudboy in amazement. "And just how do you figure that?" "Because you're not the creator; you're only the instrument through which creation

occurs." The Mudboy's eyes opened very wide as his mouth fell open. "Is that so? And just who is the creator?"

"I am," said the adam. "I thought you up to perform the physical labor of creation. I'm the creator; I'm the creator." The very first lawyer, thought the Mudboy, not at all certain what that meant.

"You are very insolent," said the Mudboy, his arm rising over the mud doll. Whump - another experiment in creation come to an abrupt end.

Patience, the Mudboy had come to understand, was his long suit. In the beginning . . . . If at first you don't succeed . . . how did that go again? Oh, yes   try, try again. The Mudboy tried again. This time the adam refused to even look at its creator, but stalked off into the high grass and lay down to sleep. This business of being created was proving to be hard work, taking its toll on the adam. It slipped immediately into slumber.

For the moment, the Mudboy lost interest in his creation and sat dejectedly by the puddle watching the clouds stream by. The day had begun so promisingly; what had gone wrong?

Deep in the grass the adam began to dream. It dreamt of the creation into which it had awakened. The forest, the clouds, the flowers, the fragrances; the adam ambled down a forest trail. Poking here and there along the path, it soon lost interest in the sky and the plants. The songs of the birds, their comings and goings, held its attention a bit longer, but soon it tired of them too.

The adam felt edgy, anxious, as though there was some great work it needed to be about, but it didn't know what that might be. It felt as though it was in the wrong place and time was passing and nothing was getting done.

As the doll wandered along through the forest, it found on the path small stones which it picked up to examine. They too held no intrinsic interest, so it began to throw them at the tree trunks. Then, seeking a more challenging target it began throwing them at the birds, hoping to hit one of those elusive, mindlessly cheerful, targets. Searching for stones, the mud creature dug a rock from the soil. It fit easily into its hand, nestling in the palm with a sharp edge protruding beyond its grasping fingers. A tool, thought the adam. A rock that fit so easily into the hand, a rock that could be used to dig the earth or chop a tree, to scrape a hide, or crush the skull of an enemy. All of these images kaleidoscoped through the adam's head and in the way of dreams, made absolute sense even though it had no idea what any of it meant. It felt right though; it felt as though the adam was . . . was   and then the words came: making progress.

The Mudboy squatted at the puddle watching the clouds when a huge dark cloud covered the sun and for a moment the day grew dark and chill. Looking around, he saw the mud doll asleep on the grass, dreaming, and he had the strange feeling that the chill and the dream were somehow connected. Leaning closer, he peered into the adam's dream just in time to see the sharp rock descend in anger and disrespect onto the skull of another living creature.

"It's your creation," the Mudboy thought, his tongue flickering wickedly, like the tongue of a serpent. He sat at the puddle pulling his tail tighter about his legs. "Born in sin . . . ." The thought stopped dead as anger flared in the Mudboy and again the whump of eternity ended another experiment with adam.

The Mudboy was immensely frustrated. No matter what he tried, the adams angered him no end. Still, something compelled him to go on trying. It was a very trying situation; he couldn't leave it alone. Thinking back over the brief history of the adams, the Mudboy recalled the mud doll's demand for a mate. He thought too of his observations of two: two arms, two legs, two hands, and so on. Way off, on the horizon of his mind, an idea glimmered.

Looking up, the Mudboy saw again the tree with the two branches, the one in which the crow had perched. Immediately the mantra slipped again into his consciousness: To woman born. Again and again, he turned the phrase over in his mind. He looked at it from many different angles until another note intruded into the mantra.

Somewhere, off in the distance, the Mudboy could hear a sweet sound. Somewhere, down by the river, voices were singing sweet and low. "Rock of ages cleft for me " His eyes grew dreamy and for an instant he looked far, far into forever and saw Chester sitting by the flower bed, his voice soft and clear, singing that quintessential hymn he'd sung so often as a child.

The Mudboy looked around his garden. He looked at the flowers blooming in frantic profusion, for the first time lingering to examine the petals and their lush layering. His gaze fell once again on the tree where the crow still yammered and, with the long arm of his imagination, he reached out to touch the cleft in the tree trunk.

The Mudboy looked down and again saw his image in the water. A ray of sunshine broke free from its expected trajectory and probed under the Mudboy's skirt to illuminate his crotch. In the brilliant light, he was surprised to see not his unadorned crotch nor even his trinity of appendages but a cleft of his own. Puzzled, intrigued, the Mudboy reached beneath his skirt and let his fingers travel that cleft, finding there a cavity such as he'd found in the tree trunk. At his finger's touch he began to experience a tingling that raced along his skin. Probing further, he found amidst the petalated flesh a spot where the flesh swelled in a tiny mound. And when his fingers touched there, a jolt of pleasure shot through him.

Oooh, he thought, what hath the Creator wrought? The electric tingles caused his image to waver in the puddle, to fade away so that only a memory of his image remained, transparent against the sky. The Mudboy felt his conception of himself shift in some subtle way and as he did, the image in the puddle began to take on texture and definition and when once again the reflection was whole, she saw that her features had softened, grown more delicate.

The Mudboy sat back, a pleasant glow permeating her body. She stared out across the puddle at the forest, her gaze slipping through the trees, the vines, the flowers, flowing unimpeded to the clouds and sky and beyond. In the beyond where time and dimensions had no meaning, where nothing was everything, she found a room where a woman lay naked on a bed, a man beside her. The man hunkered down within himself and looked at his wife. Although he'd seen her naked so many times before, he felt now as if he'd never before laid eyes on her. He found it hard to look at her, the contours of her swollen body, the whiteness of her skin, were like some alien landscape he'd seen in a dream. It was as if she was some strange animal that had suddenly appeared in their bed. Her swollen body, the sweat standing out on her skin, the wild and tormented look on her face. He'd never seen this woman before and the idea of being beside her on the bed and holding her hand frightened him. Her smell too nauseated him, not the musky, womanly smell that he was used to, but a wild, untamed smell that made him feel sick.

The idea of birth fascinated him as a mystical unfolding of something beyond the mere flesh, something divine. At the same time, it repelled him, a base and vulgar thing attendant with blood and bodily fluids. Things he need not experience in his own flesh, pain and ecstasy which he was both forgiven and denied. No wonder the sex act for her was such an all-pervading force, so unlike the localized intensity of his own climax.

Her water had broken nearly an hour before, and the labor pains were coming closer and closer together. He held her hand and wiped her face with the damp cloth and inhaled the smell of her sweat. He wanted very much to leave the room, the whole process beginning to make him sick. He'd begun to think that he regretted his part in bringing his wife to this state.

He looked up as the midwife entered the room. It seemed as though she was far, far away; everything seemed distorted, and he feared that he might faint.

"It won't be long now," said the midwife, "she's fully dilated." He heard the words and he knew what they meant, but it seemed as though they'd gone to the wrong place in his brain. Beside him his wife moaned, her body seeking out the birth rhythm.

Then it was happening. There, between his wife's widespread legs where he'd so often found his pleasure, the crown of a tiny head appeared. He'd thought that the sight, when it finally came, would sicken him, but he forgot all that he'd ever thought. His revulsion gave way to awe as the tiny body emerged. He watched in growing amazement as this tiny, wrinkled being slid from his wife's body. His excitement mounted and when the midwife moved in to receive the newborn, he nearly pushed her away.

His insides, where nausea and fear had twisted and turned, had become a void and from that void, a warmth began to glow and spread through his body. Like the sun rising over the sea on a brutally clear morning, his heart opened to the tiny creature and his love spread diaphanously in every direction.

As he watched the child emerge from his wife's body, he felt the child's emergence as if it were he himself who was being born. He felt the wonder and the confusion of it, felt the terror of giving up absolute security and the intoxicating sense of the adventure upon which the child was embarking.

"It's a girl," said the midwife as she held up the baby for him to see. Tears burst from his eyes and love burst from his heart as feelings he'd never experienced rampaged through him. He was filled with love for this child and for his wife. Who had manifested this magic. His love flowed out to the midwife and to his neighbors who worked in the fields and farmyards all about him, to the people of the village. Tears streamed down his cheeks, and he wanted more than anything to laugh in wonder. His heart beat with love and pride; it beat with such intensity he feared it would burst.

He touched the child, took the squalling, wrinkled infant into his arms and experienced a sense of life he'd never even imagined.

Of woman born . . . .

The Mudboy felt it all, every shimmering aspect of it. She blinked a tear away and looked again at the tree with its cleft crotch.

Yes, she smiled and without further thought, snatched up another lump of clay and fashioned another adam. This time, however, she left off the little trinity of equipment and instead, using her pointed stick, inscribed a cleft in the figure's crotch. Hesitating a moment, she pondered this new creation. Then she pinched the figure's waist, urging the clay downward to fill out the hips and upward to create two soft mounds. After a moment, touching her own bosom, she said, breasts, I think I'll call them breasts. She wasn't altogether certain why she worked these changes on the adam; it just seemed right.

"There now," she said, staring at the curvaceous and minimally adorned doll.

Something, however, did not seem right. It took the Mudboy a further moment of thought to realize that it was the name. This is not an adam, she thought, staring at the doll in her hand. Not an adam, but. . . but an. . . an eve. The name materialized in her mind like the mists of an autumn evening. Yes, that was it; an eve. A much softer name for a softer, rounder creation. Gently she put the mud doll down on the ground.

Peering at the eve, thinking about the adam, of the dissimilar adornments at their crotches, the Mudboy laughed whimsically at the thought that slithered through her mind. Somewhere off in the jungle she heard the bellow of a bull water buffalo and when she looked, she saw him mounting a female. High in the tree above, two squirrels emulated their larger cousins. And somewhere off beyond the blue horizon, a man and a woman, naked, aroused, slipped slowly down to the sand, the man pressing urgently between the woman's eagerly opening legs. The act kaleidoscoped across eternity, generation upon generation joining their flesh in frantic coupling.

The Mudboy thought again of twos and the concept of mates which the adam had demanded as its right. Mates; it seemed like a good idea although the troublesome nature of the adam made the Mudboy hesitate. Finally, however, she reached slowly for another lump of clay. As the cool and plastic mud filled her hand, she forgot her reservations and for the umpteenth time shaped an adam. Without a thought, she added the little tripartite package between the doll's legs and placed the adam on the ground beside the eve.

She sat for a moment contemplating her handiwork and when she looked into the puddle, she saw that her face had changed again. Her complexion had grown ruddy and two pointy protuberances stood out at her temples. Around her legs a long tail coiled, twitching spastically. The reflection smiled sardonically and a forked tongue like a serpent's flickered at the image's lips. She'd seen this all before.

"Are you sure you want to do this?" asked the image, staring tauntingly at the Mudboy. "Do you realize what it is you're about to do?" Taken aback by the image and its questions, the Mudboy kept her composure and said nothing, waiting.

"Maybe you should look over there," said the image. When the Mudboy looked over there, she saw the adam as a man. The man stood tall and majestic, his legs spread, the adam's tiny root grown to an imposing erection. The Mudboy watched the man grow transparent, the future seeming to unravel from his swollen organ. She saw women moaning in joy and rapture, groaning in discomfort, screaming in pain. There were women whose legs opened eagerly to receive the maleness and legs that were forced open; women who writhed in excitement and women who struggled in degradation and fear. Tears of joy and tears of pain flowed freely until the scene became so blurred that the Mudboy could no longer see what transpired.

The image in the puddle contemplated the Mudboy, eyebrows arched, eyes wide. "Well?" said the image. The Mudboy shrugged. It wasn't all pain and misery, she thought; there was pleasure too. There was, after all, free will; the adam and the eve had a choice in the matter.

"There's more to it than just pleasure and pain," said the image. "You're focused on this clever little trick that you're playing with complementary parts. But that isn't the whole story." The words drove deep into the Mudboy's consciousness, and she suddenly recognized the all-consuming reality she was in the process of creating. The Mudboy grew very still as she contemplated the breadth and depth of her creation. The memory of the adams, arrogant and contemptuous, flooded her mind. She could still hear the adam berating her, telling her she had it all wrong, that he, not she was the true creator. She could see the two of them, the adam and the eve, stomping defiantly out of the forest, their tricky and imprecise little mud minds rearranging events to suit themselves. Clear as the air that surrounded her, the Mudboy could see the trail of tears and pain, destruction and disappointment that lay before them, the damage they would do to the garden before even the tiniest glimmer of wisdom manifested in their tiny brains.

The Mudboy thought of the feeling of squeezing those little mud bodies until the mud gushed in blobs from between her fingers. Her hand hovered momentarily over the two dolls and then she withdrew it, smiling enigmatically.

From the puddle the image was smiling at her, its eyes glistening with voluptuous delight. The image began slowly to shake its head and wave its finger in negation. "Don't do it; they're mine too and I say don't do it." The image winked.

The Mudboy thought for a moment more, weighing pros and cons. "Yes," she said resolutely, 'I'll do it." She'd come too far to turn back now, and she let her breath flow across the dolls. The image faded from the puddle and the long unquiet tail uncoiled itself from around the Mudboy's legs and slithered off into the grass. The sun shone on the dolls and within seconds they were sitting up rubbing their little seed eyes. The Mudboy looked lovingly and tolerantly upon her creations and then stared off into the distance. There, at the edge of forever, she found Chester, kneeling over his beautiful cousin, delicately drawing her skirts up to peer between her legs. Chester let the skirts fall back into place and looked up at the Mudboy, his eyes filled with wonder.

The Mudboy laughed and the image fled. She laughed at all she'd seen and all she'd imagined and at all she'd failed to imagine as well. In the puddle, she saw her face once more materialize. The clouds still slipped by in the heavens above, the sun still sparkled on the muddy water. The brown face, however, lost some of its delicacy, shifting on the spectrum of male and female. But the eyes did not change. They were Chester's eyes.

Madeleine sat up and rubbed her eyes. She must have swooned and collapsed on the grass. The sun blazed down on her, and she felt dizzy and unsteady. She blinked and looked around to find Chester where he'd been, quietly humming to himself and digging in the dirt.

Uncertain of what to do, Madeleine tried to collect her thoughts, to bring some focus to the situation. She was no longer certain what it was that she'd intended to do. The sheaf of documents in her hand seemed alien to her; she let them fall to the grass. She found her valise and pulled it to her. She found her boater on the grass, and plopped it haphazardly back on her head.

She should go, she knew; her business here, whatever that might have been, was finished. A reluctance plagued her nonetheless; she didn't really want to leave Chester. The feeling confused her. Aside from the anger and hurt she'd experienced at the age of seven when Chester had soiled her with mud, she'd never had any feelings one way or the other for her cousin.

In the midst of her befuddlement, she realized that it was his eyes. From those eyes flowed a serenity and love that permeated her being, awakening feelings she'd always considered suspect. Her parents had loved her, she knew that. Young men had come courting and some had even said they loved her. But she knew that the love she saw in Chester's eyes was something she'd never seen before. Her parents had loved her because she was their daughter; the young men had loved her because they wanted to possess her. The love that emanated from Chester's eyes was different; it knew no bounds. In her naïve fashion, Madeleine fumbled toward the limits of his love, and she could find nothing that hinted at boundaries. The love seemed to flow seamlessly and ceaselessly from a generosity of his soul that was even more alien to her than the idea of love. Generosity was not an emotion that had ever meant much to Madeleine and now it was sweeping irrepressibly through her. She felt as though her being was crumbling, falling away in dust and ashes.

Madeleine struggled up from the grass to stand unsteadily before her cousin. She felt utterly empty, spent, abandoned, and yet, paradoxically, full and complete. She felt as though she was being born, light and energy coursing up through her body.

She stood there in the sunlight speechless, immobile. She tried to speak, stammering, but no words would come. Chester sat looking up at her, his eyes pinning her to the sky. She felt naked before those eyes but rather than self-consciousness and discomfort, she was at ease, unable to tear her eyes from Chester's.

Chester rose from his flower bed and stood before her. His hands sought hers and he gathered her in his arms and held her, hugging her tight as a child might. Madeleine melted into him, uncertain where she stopped and he began. The sun rose and set, the moon waxed and waned, the seasons changed, the rivers flowed. Madeleine felt her life race by, felt the cycles of life and death, love and fear, meaning and chaos roar through her like the winds of a summer storm. Slowly Chester released her, kissing her gently on the cheeks. When he finally let go of her hands, she felt as though she was falling into nothingness.

"Goodbye, Chester," she said. To disguise her dizziness, she turned away abruptly and made her way slowly up the grassy slope toward the main building. She moved unsteadily, the sun beating down on her, making thought all but impossible.

Inside, in the lobby, it was cool, and Madeleine ascended the stairs holding fast to the banister. The girl Christine stood behind the counter, her face vacant, immobile, as though she was a statue put there merely for the effect.

"I'll be leaving now," said Madeleine. "I've finished my visit with. . . my cousin." Something in her wanted her to say, "our Chester," but she'd restrained herself.

"Yes , Miss," said Christine in a flat voice. "There's a carriage waitin' as brought some other visitors. It'll take you back to town." Madeleine thanked the girl and headed for the stairs. As she started down, she heard the rustle of skirts and looked back. Nurse O'Kelley stood by the banister.

"Oh, Miss Halsten. Did you have a . . . pleasurable visit with your cousin?"

"Oh, yes," replied Madeleine, "quite." She'd stopped unsteadily on the stairs, grasping the railing. Somewhere in her near delirium the thought occurred that the woman had chosen her words strangely. Pleasurable? Didn't she mean pleasant? Madeleine looked at the nurse and saw her on her back, her legs spread, her sex exposed to Chester's view. The woman's green eyes sparkled with a lasciviousness that Madeleine hadn't noticed before. In her uncertain state, she felt as though she'd been caught in some lewd act. She felt, she realized, like a simple two- dollar whore and her face flushed with embarrassment. O'Kelley stared at her, eyes probing with a fiery intensity, appraising Madeleine as she had upon her arrival. Almost instantly the eyes softened, and a smile appeared on O'Kelley's face as though she'd found Madeleine to be somehow acceptable. Inexplicably Madeleine felt a sense of holiness flood through her and in her disorientation, she nearly laughed out loud.

"Well," said the nurse finally, "have a pleasant journey home. I hope we'll see you again." Madeleine's eyes opened wide for she was certain she'd seen the woman's tongue flicker between her lips like the tongue of a serpent.

"Yes . . . yes," she stammered, "goo . . . goodbye." She turned quickly and hurried down the remaining stairs and out the door, down to the waiting carriage. As she stepped again into the sunshine, she felt a calm like a gentle breeze settle over her. She crossed the drive to the carriage, climbed in, and instructed the driver to take her to the station. Settling back in the leather seat, relieved to be able to sit down, she found herself in a very strange state of mind. On the one hand, wanton, lustful, almost whorish; on the other, holy. A holy whore, she thought.

The carriage moved around the circular drive and as it entered the tunnel of trees, Madeleine looked up at the brilliant blue of the sky, the sanctified white of the clouds. It is as if, she thought, the clouds and the sun have distilled themselves in my blood; as if I have champagne in my blood. But no, it was more than that; as if all the cells of her body had begun to disintegrate, the atoms and molecules drifting off into the cosmos to commune with the trees and the rain, the sun and the planets. Madeleine had the oddest feeling that she was not only herself, but the grass upon which she'd walked, the air she breathed, the sun that baked her brain.

In amongst the sycamores, it was cool though Madeleine didn't notice for the coolness was as much a part of her as the searing sun. Madeleine thought of her reaction to Nurse O'Kelley's remark about seeing her again, thinking as she left the building that she'd most certainly never see this place again. As the carriage rattled down the shaded drive, she knew in her heart that that was false. She'd parted from Chester only a few minutes before and already she felt a longing to see him again. She knew succinctly that she would be back, that no amount of rational thought would overcome her need to see Chester.

Madeleine let her head fall back against the seat. She felt light and insubstantial. The carriage seemed like a toy she'd played with as a child. Looking up through the foliage she could see bits of sky, tatters of cloud.

As the carriage approached the end of the lane Madeleine saw above her, blotting out sky and clouds, a brown face peering down at her. A brown hand came down between the trees and gently pushed the carriage along the way out into the main thoroughfare. As Madeleine looked at the brown face, the Mudboy seemed to shimmer before her eyes, now male, now female, eyes glowing like the stars of distant galaxies. Madeleine began to laugh and the Mudboy began to laugh, their laughter twining and intertwining in a celestial melody.

Madeleine closed her eyes and a feeling she'd never known before, a feeling she could think of only as bliss settled over her. She fell into a child-like slumber.

In her dreams, Nurse O'Kelley greeted her with those knowing eyes.

Wide Open

The moon was already well past its zenith when Albert and Webber left the farmhouse. They drove out the lane, the old pickup bouncing and rattling over the stones and holes in the deeply rutted drive. There'd been a full house for the meditation, nearly twenty people, and the session had been rich in imagery and steeped in a profound sense of balance. People had lingered late into the evening, talking, philosophizing, soaking in the serenity of the country setting. Albert and Webber had been the last to leave.

At the end of the lane, Albert punched the gas pedal and the old truck moved off rapidly down the two-lane blacktop. Although it bore a striking resemblance to an old wreck, Albert had invested countless hours in the mechanical essentials, so the truck's appearance was but an illusion. They drove in silence for a while, each lost in his own thoughts, bemused by the wash of silver moonlight across the midnight landscape. The purr of the truck's engine mingled with the hum of the tires, generating a mantra that rolled easily through the men's consciousness.

"You know," Webber said, as Albert pulled up to a stop sign, "sometimes I wish I wasn't so damned evolved." Albert swung out onto the county road, dropped the truck into third, and punched the accelerator. He looked over at Webber, his face illuminated in the vaporous glow of the moonlight.

"What do you mean by that?" asked Albert, running a quick check through his memory banks to see if this was unfinished business. Webber stared straight ahead, his wide brimmed- black hat pushed back on his head. Albert could see from the glow in Webber's eye that he was thinking of something off in the past.

"Well, what I mean is, I wish I could sometimes be just like normal people and let go of the reins of my emotions. Just cut loose instead of always being so aware of the ramifications of every word, every action." Webber said his piece slowly, his conscious mind responding while his vision ranged off somewhere in the red rock canyon area where Jose Abeyo, the soft-spoken curandero with the wicked twist of brujo, had taken them to learn their craft. First, they'd practiced on animals and then, later, they'd traveled into town to work minor conjuring on unsuspecting locals.

"Oh," said Albert, tooling the truck tightly through a hairpin turn, for the moment a genuine cowboy in an exuberant frame of mind. "Yeh, I can see where you'd feel that way from time to time. I do myself, I have to admit." He pushed his long hair back behind his ear and glanced sideways at Webber. He was still out there somewhere. "But what brings this up just now?" Webber didn't immediately answer. He sat in silence for a while as the truck shot down the road, the first cluster of houses appearing along the way. Soon they'd be in Pinedale. A car approached, the headlights bringing Webber back to himself.

"Oh," Webber said finally, "I was just thinking about that little blonde girl in the circle tonight - Laurie," His voice was still a long way. "I just got the itch to take her home and have my evil way with her." He laughed at himself as Albert tskked teasingly. "She was such a vital, juicy little animal," Webber went on, his words flowing on the moonlight, recreating the girl before his eyes. His voice had that floaty quality of meditations. In no time Albert was lost in the vision himself, the truck virtually driving itself.

"So, what's the problem?" asked Albert finally, intruding into Webber's vision of enchanting physical beauty. He glanced over and caught Webber's eye.

"You know damned well what the problem is," he said to Albert, turning on the seat to face him.

"Maybe so," responded Albert, "but I also know you make too much of it. After all you're just a man." Webber chuckled softly.

"Yeh," he said quietly, "just a man. But we know so much more. It's like having an unfair advantage. Like a doctor-patient relationship, or lawyer-client or something like that." He lapsed into thoughtful silence, his memory again ranging over the landscape around Kayenta where they'd worked on their medicine bundles and practiced on the unsuspecting.

"Well, I get the point all right. I've thought of it often myself. And we have talked about it before. But I still don't see it as the same thing. You met her in the circle, you were attracted. What's the big deal? It's not like you'd been in her brain rearranging the connections to make her do something she didn't want to do - is it?" He looked over at Webber his eyes wide in query. "If she were working with you on a regular basis, I'd say: OK, that's different. So, look at it this way, if a doctor or a lawyer went to a professional meeting and met a woman there, what ethical codes would be violated if he jumped in the sack with her? None. So why is this such a big problem? Impure motives, perhaps?" Albert turned to Webber and wiggled his eyebrows Groucho Marx style.

"Yeh, yeh," said Webber, "I always have to accept intellectually that you're right, but still, it seems as though I have an unfair advantage, like I'm somehow using powers on people that I shouldn't be using. At least, not in that way." He looked out the side window and watched the increasingly suburban landscape slip by in the moonlight. Funny, he thought, even this shit looks half-decent in the moonlight.

"I agree wholeheartedly that we shouldn't be using our powers over people just to get our way with them. That does strike me as being unethical. But in the present instance, where it's a man-woman thing, I don't see your point at all. Remember when we started with massage and bodywork? Remember what Fred said to us? What was it - three, four sessions into it and he started telling us how women were always falling in love with him."

"Oh yeh," said Webber, the memory coming back to him, "I'd forgotten all about that. It was almost like a litany after a while."

"Right," said Albert, "He had some kinda real problem there. But my point is this: women are obviously going to be attracted to you. You are visibly a person of power, and people - not just women - want to get to know you. So, if you're attracted to a woman and she's attracted to you, what's the harm?" Webber sat silently on the seat, but Albert could see the beginnings of a contented smile on his face. "Anyway," Albert went on, "women would be attracted to you even if you were a ragamuffin. You've just got the look, so why deny it?" Albert concluded his summation and lapsed into silence as the truck purred contentedly through the moonlit countryside.

They slowed down for the clustered houses of Pinedale, came to a stop at the T at the end of town, and turned right onto state route 7. Albert accelerated a little above the speed limit, but nothing too conspicuous. As they passed the Texaco station at the edge of town, neither noticed the white Chevy with the black and grey stripes down its sides idling alongside the diesel pumps.

Inside the Chevy sat Harley Jenkins. He'd been there for maybe twenty minutes and hadn't seen a single likely prospect. He was thinking of moving on down 7 towards the Blue Gardenia when the old Ford pickup went by. It wasn't moving suspiciously fast, but Harley caught sight of the two men in the cab. He looked at his watch; it was 1:09. In his mind an old pickup with a long-hair and a guy wearing a cowboy hat at this time of morning was definitely suspicious. He slipped the Chevy in gear and pulled out onto 7, following discreetly along behind the Ford.

Harley liked driving the big Chevy squad car with its immense reserve of power, its lights and siren. Whenever he slipped behind the wheel, he thought of it less as a car and more as an extension of his very being. He liked being a cop too, wearing the uniform and keeping the "citizens" alert. And he looked like a cop, an image that sent a warm glow of satisfaction through his body. He was six feet tall, a little on the stocky side, thick dark hair cut short and a thick dark mustache. A real cop mustache, he thought to himself whenever he looked in the mirror. He never thought of himself as a mean cop, just a tough cop. Thorough and efficient when dealing with the "citizen". But there were things about the job that he didn't like. He didn't like the way people looked at him when he stopped them. He didn't like the easy attitudes that people had; they ought to show more respect, he thought. Maybe they ought to show a little fear now and then. That wouldn't hurt at all. Those were just a few of the things that Harley Jenkins didn't like. And he didn't like weirdoes cruisin' around in junky old trucks late at night.

He followed the Ford for a couple of miles, checking the speed. They were out in the open, a 55 zone, but the Ford had settled back to a pretty steady 53. The taillights were all working; nothing for him to jump on there. But he didn't like the feel of those two guys.

He grabbed the microphone, called in and reported he was about to stop two men in a Ford pickup. "Routine check," he said to the dispatcher. The radio squawked and he heard the dispatcher's voice over the crackling of the radio asking if he wanted backup. He hesitated for a moment, thought about Buddy Mason in car 118 who was probably just up the road. "Affirmative," he said and put the mike back on its hook.

Harley tipped his cap at a rakish angle, flipped on his high beams and over-heads and tapped the Chevy's accelerator. He loved the feel of the car as the big police interceptor engine growled out of its purr, and rocketed the car down the road. He closed on the Ford in seconds, coming up right on its rear end, following it onto the shoulder as it slowed and came to a stop.

The lights caught Albert and Webber by surprise. They'd been lost in their ethical discussion that rested gently on a vision of soft skin and blonde hair. Their conversation should have ended in soft reverie, not the harsh intrusion of police flashers.

"Uh oh," said Albert, "we weren't paying attention. What did we do?"

"I don't know," said Webber, "but now we have to deal with the man. I hope it's not one of those redneck saps." They sat in the cab, the glare of the cruiser's headlights unpleasantly illuminating them from behind. Albert looked in the side mirror but could see nothing but headlights. He dug out his wallet, reached across and got the registration out of the glove compartment and rolled down the window. The cop took his time walking up to the window, so that even before he saw the cop, Albert knew what kind of confrontation it was going to be. He sensed the swagger in the man's walk and he could feel that brooding sense of superiority that some cops emanate. Then the cop was standing there, and Albert leaned out the window, his driver's license and registration in hand.

"Good evening, Officer," said Albert affably, his hand relaxed on the windowsill, the cards between his fingers. The cop said nothing, hauled out his big police special flashlight, and shown it full in Albert's face. Albert was blinded, but smiled steadily at the man behind the light.

"Did we do something wrong, Officer?" asked Albert, his voice smooth and neutral.

"I'll ask the questions," said the cop harshly, dropping the beam of light to the cards between Albert's fingers. He grabbed them and shined the light on them, studying them for several moments. Then he flashed the beam back on Albert's face and asked his name and address. Albert answered and the cop had to shift the light back to the cards. He grunted at the correctness of Albert's response.

"Where you coming from?" asked the cop, his voice as uncompromising as the beam of light. Albert looked over at Webber and smiled. The smile tickled the ends of his lip, and he could feel the cop bristle.

"Well, Officer," he said slowly, we were at a little party out by Georgie Meyer's place. You know Georgie Meyer?" The cop didn't answer; he pushed the beam of light across the cab into Webber's face. Albert kept on smiling, but he was beginning to find it very annoying the way the man used that flashlight like a truncheon.

"No," said the cop finally, "I don't know any Georgie Meyer. Where is this place? And what were you doing there?" The cop's tone of voice was edging into the downright nasty category and Albert could sense that Webber was working up to something. He could almost feel the energy begin to crackle around Webber's head.

At that moment, the scene was interrupted by the arrival of another police car, its red and blue lights flashing as it shot by and skidded to a halt on the shoulder just in front of the pickup. The car had barely stopped before the figure of another cop emerged from the dust, adjusting his cap on his head and dragging his big cop flashlight out of its loop on his belt. The whole scene was now bathed in the strobing flashes from the newly arrived car and Albert could see Webber's face turning red and blue and red and blue and red and . . . .

As the second cop approached, the first turned away from the truck, taking his light with him. Albert looked over at them, watching the new arrival, a shorter thicker man, but with the obligatory cop mustache. He stood with legs spread, looking at the truck, his face a mask of contempt. Albert and Webber watched the first cop talking to the second cop. They looked at one another and each could see in the eyes of the other an unpleasant resolution.

Buddy Mason had oozed out of his squad car and sauntered over to meet Harley. As he approached, he looked in the truck cab and watched the two faces turning red and blue and red and blue. A long-hair and some kind of specimen wearing a big black hat it looked like. Buddy didn't care for creeps any more than Harley did and he figured anybody with long hair or weird dress must be a creep. Especially if they were riding around at night in a beat-up old jalopy.

"Hey, boy, whatcha got here?" he said as he came up to Harley. Harley stood about twenty feet from the truck, his back to it. Buddy hitched up his pants and took a stance with his legs spread, a pose he particularly liked because he thought it tough and manly. He watched the two in the cab as Harley held out the two cards and pointed at them with his flash.

"Two creeps," he said, nodding toward the truck for emphasis. "They're right on the edge of gettin' wise," he added.

"Well, ol' boy, let's take 'em down a peg or two," said Buddy, swinging his flashlight around toward the truck. He started toward the truck, Harley falling in at his side. The two shared a feeling of comradeship, a feeling of omnipotence, bolstered by the guns riding on their hips, the nightsticks slapping easily against their thighs. They were men of power, men in uniform.

"Jesus," said Webber, watching from the cab. "Look at this. The new one looks like even a bigger asshole than the first one."

"Yep," replied Albert, watching out of the corner of his eyes, keeping his head front. "These boys sure are looking to make some trouble here."

"Yup," said Webber, pursing his lips and shaking his head. They watched the cops approach, the eternal aggressors descending on their prey, their intent evident in the way they moved.

"OK, you two, out of the truck," snarled Officer Buddy Mason as he came up to the driver's side of the pickup. He swung his flash on Webber, while Officer Harley Jenkins shined his light in Albert's face. "Come on, make it quick. We don't got all night."

The smile on Albert's face never wavered as he opened the truck door and climbed from the cab. Webber wasn't smiling; his lips were set in a hard line and a sharp metallic glint flickered in his eyes as he slipped from the truck and came around to the driver's side.

"Up against the fender," yelled Harley, jabbing Albert in the ribs with the butt of the flashlight. "Turn around, get your hands up. Spread those legs." His voice had the hard edge of a no-nonsense professional; it should have scared these two assholes shitless. But the long-hair - Albert was his name - was still smiling and that made Harley mad. And just a little apprehensive.

Albert was up against the door, spread out, the smile engraved on his face. Just to his left, splayed out against the fender was Webber. Albert looked over and saw that Webber was looking at him.

"Eyes front," snapped Buddy Mason, jabbing Webber in the back. He backed off then and undid the catch on his holster, readying his automatic. Harley moved in and began patting down Albert. He ran his hands up and down his body and then stepped back. "He's clean," he said to Buddy. Then he stepped up to Webber and started to repeat the process.

The hard lines that marked Webber's face relaxed in the strobing red and blue lights from squad car 118. The cops didn't notice the release flow into Webber's face; they didn't see the energy begin to flick along his limbs as his mind reached out to touch Harley Jenkins. Harley felt something like a little electric spark flick in his brain, a flick that had its origins in Webber's mind where he could see the nerves that controlled Harley's bladder. Webber could see the energy snap out like a whip and close the synapse that told Harley's bladder that it was time to let go.

Harley had barely felt the electrical spark in his brain when he felt his bladder release. He felt the piss pour out of him, down his legs, darkening the crotch of his grey uniform pants. The sudden gush of warmth, the sudden release of his bladder made him shudder; a tingle that was almost sexual fluttered through his body. He dropped his flashlight, dumbstruck.

"Hey, you dropped your light," said Buddy, turning his flash on Harley. The light played over Harley standing there, a huge dark stain on his pants, his legs bowed awkwardly. "What the fuck," snapped Buddy, "you pissed yourself."

"Goddammit, shut that light off," croaked Harley. "What the fuck's with you? You pissed your pants."

"Shut the fuck up," yelled Harley. "You don't haveta announce it to everybody in the whole damn county." He turned and waddled away, heading for his squad car.

"Hey," yelled Buddy, "where ya goin'? You're not gonna walk off just because ya pissed yourself, are ya?" He shined his flashlight after Harley and broke out laughing. He chuckled for a few moments, watching Harley Jenkins climb into his squad car. Then he turned back to Albert and Webber who still stood spread against the side of the truck. Harley pissed himself and it only figured that somebody was gonna have to pay for that.

"He pissed himself," Buddy Mason said, "He pissed himself and now he's running away. I can't fuckin' believe it." He paused, shining his flash over Webber. "OK, creep, hold still while I frisk you." He stepped forward to begin his sweep of Webber's body.

But Webber's mind had already sent a thin strand of energy into the mind of Officer Buddy Mason, and somewhere in there, amidst all the links and switches, the controls, the handcuffs, the rules and regulations, and all the other cop-stuff, he found the nerves that controlled Buddy Mason's sphincter. In that selfsame moment Officer Buddy Mason experienced a pleasant feeling of release that spread warmly through his body.

What the fuck, what the fuck, what the fuck, screamed the mind of Officer Buddy Mason as he realized what that warm feeling of release meant. But too late, too late, too fucking late. He'd lost control and shit his pants. His mind panicked, as the smell of his own shit reached his nostrils, he could think of nothing but flight. Stricken, he waddled off toward his squad car. Behind him Officer Harley Jenkins' squad car roared off the shoulder and shot recklessly across the road in a ragged U-turn. The car nearly took out the No Passing sign as it wallowed onto the opposite shoulder. The tires squealed in agony as the car tore off down the road, the red and blue lights still flashing dolefully in the moonlight.

Squad car 118, too, screeched away, gravel and dust spraying back over the Ford and the two men still standing spread against its side. Webber looked over at Albert, his eyes glistening in the silvery light. He wore a sinister grin that nicely balanced the insidious smile that still graced Albert's face.

"Now what do you suppose that was all about?" he said to Albert as they collapsed onto the gravel in gales of laughter. They laughed until the veins pounded in their heads, until their bellies contracted in agony, until their ribs ached. And when they finally gained control of themselves, they were filled with a righteous fervor that glowed nearly as bright as the moon above them.

Albert finally pulled himself up and walked over to the edge of the asphalt where the first cop's flashlight lay, still shining brightly. Nearby he found his driver's license and registration card. He turned and offered the flashlight to Webber who'd risen to stand by the fender.

"Need a flashlight?" he asked innocently. "Somebody seems to have lost a perfectly good flashlight." Webber took it and began laughing again. Albert leaned back against the truck and looked at Webber palely illuminated in the moonlight.

"Well now," he said slowly, "what was it we were talking about? Something about not using our knowledge on the unsuspecting? Eh?" Webber stood in front of him holding the flashlight.

"Yeh, well, what can I say," Webber replied. "I guess I pulled the rug out from under my own arguments."

"You could put it that way," said Albert.

"But those guys were gonna fuck us over royally. You must have seen the auras around those two bozos. I can't remember when I've seen uglier light emanating off two human beings. Assuming, of course, that they were human. I think I'll have to plead extenuating circumstances. It was self-defense." Webber turned on the flashlight and held it under his chin. He looked like the monster in a horror film, "Besides," he continued after a few moments, turning off the light again, "those guys were so wide open you could have driven an eighteen-wheeler through the chinks in their defenses. Don't they teach cops anything about really defending themselves in cop school?"

"They sure as hell were wide open," agreed Albert. "They were so easy it was almost a sin. If they hadn't been such nasty-spirited specimens, I'd be ashamed of us for taking advantage like that. But they did virtually all the work for us. I think we could have done it all by just thinking at them."

"Yeh," said Webber, staring up into the sky where clouds were spinning hues of pink and blue around the moon. He looked back at Albert and flashed the light at him. "Hey, we better get out of here before those jokers change their pants and come racing back here for a rematch."

Albert started laughing again. "In diapers," he said, pulling open the door of the truck and climbing in.

It was about a month later that officer Harley Jenkins was sitting in his squad car out on 7 at the intersection with Wehler Road. He was parked in a blind spot where he could watch for people running the stop sign. He was feeling a lot more relaxed than he'd felt in nearly a month when he saw an old Ford pickup roll up to the stop sign. Sweat broke out on Harley's brow and palms. He wanted to look away, to not see that truck and the two faces he knew would be there in the cab. But he felt helpless, perversely helpless as he stared at the vehicle. As the truck slowed down, didn't exactly stop, and then slid through the intersection onto 7, Harley knew that in a second or so he would no longer be hidden from the two in the truck. At that very moment, the thought still in Harley's brain, the driver looked right into Harley's eyes and waved. Harley felt his bladder relax and a wet warmth spread slowly over his crotch.

In the cab of the pickup, Webber smiled sweetly and said: "Have a nice day, officer."

Milton Keynes UK
Ingram Content Group UK Ltd.
UKHW041136020924
447770UK00007B/584